REASONS TO LEAVE

REASONS PART ONE

LISA J HOBMAN

Lisa J. Hobman
Copyright Lisa J. Hobman 2015

First Published by 5 Prince Publishing 2015
Second Edition Published by Lisa J. Hobman

Front Cover The Graphics Shed

First Edition/First Printing June 2015 Printed U.S.A.
Second Edition/Second Printing February 2018 Lisa J. Hobman, UK

ISBN: 978-0-9956658-4-2

To Rich, my hero and my true love. You keep inspiring me after all these years. You have my heart.

And to my Gee for being beautiful, entertaining and the best hug giver.

PROLOGUE

'*O*h darling, look at you. You look so grown up.' Stevie's mum clasped her hands in front of her face, her eyes welling with tears.

Stevie rolled her eyes. 'Um...Mum I hate to break it to you but I'm *eighteen* which legally means I *am* grown up.'

The sales assistant at the suburban London boutique had come to join the let's-stare-at-Stevie party, and she was beginning to feel a little like a museum exhibit in a prom dress.

'What do you think, darling? Is this *the* dress?' Her mum looked so hopeful.

The dress was ankle length and had a bodice that fit a little like a vice, but she loved the purple iridescent fabric and how it shimmered under the halogen spotlights of the dressing room.

The Leavers' Ball was only a week away and as usual Stevie had left purchasing a suitable dress until right at the last minute. Her mother had been urging her to get organised for weeks, and all of her friends had long ago purchased their outfits and accessories. Carrie, Stevie's closest friend besides Jason, had had hers hanging on the door to her walk-in closet

1

for over a month. Carrie was like that though—uber organised—Stevie wondered why it was *she* who'd been allocated the role of Head Girl and not Carrie.

Baffling really.

Stevie bit her lip. 'Um...yes. I think it's the best one I've tried.'

'I agree...and I'm sure that Jason will think you look stunning too.'

She rolled her eyes again. 'Muuum.'

Her mum was always fishing for information about her relationship with Jason. She had lost count of the number of times her mother had subjected her to *the talk*. And she had also lost count of the number of times she had informed her mum that she and Jason were *not* having sex.

Not even close.

However, this was not through want of trying on her part. She loved her boyfriend and had been with him since they were thirteen, for goodness sake. But Jason insisted that he was just not ready to take that next step. He wanted it to be special, not rushed and fumbled like the first times their friends had experienced.

She had presumed at one time that the real reason was because he didn't want her, but his words and actions—and his body—showed her otherwise. He was just a gentleman. He had told her that they were a permanent fixture in each other's lives, and so there was no rush to lose their virginity. In the end, she surmised that she was just a ball of raging hormones and that she could wait too, if she must. Although she had a sneaky suspicion that after the Leavers' Ball things might take a step in the right direction. After all, her mum would be out with her best friend Jilly, and Jason would be escorting her home. For this reason, the dress had to be perfect.

'I'm just saying, sweetie. You look so beautiful.' A wistful look washed over her mum's features. 'You have a look of your dad now that you're older.'

Dana Watts was a wonderful mother. She did the job of two parents, and she did it to perfection. Stevie's dad, a failed musician and the exciting older man, had been a roadie and sound engineer working for London based bands after he left college. His passion for music, especially Fleetwood Mac, had given Stevie her name. He had apparently doted on Dana, and although at twenty-four years old was initially shocked at discovering his nineteen-year-old girlfriend was pregnant, he was excited about being a father.

Soon after her birth, Stevie's father had been offered the chance of a lifetime to leave London and tour the world with some famous rock star and had grabbed it with both hands, leaving Dana to bring up her daughter alone. After keeping in touch for a while and sending birthday cards and letters, there was a long telephone conversation in which he informed Dana there would be another tour with another band immediately after the current one. He claimed to still love Dana but said that the long distance thing wasn't working, that it was unfair to their daughter to be a dip-in-and-out-of-her-life kind of father and so it would be more beneficial, although not easier, for all concerned if he broke ties.

He chose never to return, and so Stevie had never met him. Thankfully, she was so young when he left that she hadn't been cognisant of the heartbreak her mother went through. Her mother's best friend Jilly had been the one to pick up the pieces and she didn't have many positive things to say about him. All Stevie *did* know as she got older was that her mother was very careful with her heart.

There had been a lovely man in Dana's life, when Stevie was around eight-years-old, who had been special to Dana, and Stevie had adored him. Her mother had broken up with him when he had announced he would be working in Ireland for a period of three years. Dana wouldn't even consider the relationship continuing as she presumed the inevitable would happen; he would figure out that the long distance thing would not work for him and she would be left alone yet again. There had been no one else since. As far as Dana was concerned—and Stevie was reminded regularly—Stevie was her life and it would stay that way.

She knew little of her father, other than what her mother or Jilly had deigned to share. Although from the photos Stevie had seen, it was evident that she took after him in so many ways, physically that is. Her long auburn hair and bright blue eyes were all Jed Marks. And her height for that matter; she was tall just like him. It was moments like this though, standing there in a prom dress and being told by her wonderful mother that she looked like *him*, when anger bubbled up for what that man had put her mum through. But as always she smiled sweetly and said nothing.

Two Days Later

'So...do I get to see what you bought?' Jason rubbed her shoulders and breathed heavily into her hair just above her ear. Shivers travelled down her spine, melting each vertebra in their wake. They were propped on his bedroom floor, Stevie sitting between his thighs as the DVD played to itself and the popcorn lay untouched.

His voice was low and tinged with a kind of sadness. Trying to lighten the mood, she slapped his leg playfully. She glared over her shoulder at him. 'You certainly do *not,* Jason Reynolds.' She smiled and leaned up to nibble his chin.

He pouted and fluttered his eyelashes. 'Pretty please.'

She turned fully in the space between his thighs and kissed him on his protruding bottom lip. She adored him. There was no other way to put it. He was the centre of her universe. And she was his. He was every bit the stunningly gorgeous bad boy with his collar length, scruffy, thick, dark hair and a chiselled jaw. His dark eyes held a kind of mystery that she vowed one day to get beneath. He'd been blessed with the looks of a male model and--from the ridges and striations of his abdomen tangible through his T-shirt—he had the body to match.

He'd been a little quiet and sullen lately, like the weight of the world rested on his shoulders. She put it down to all the pressure of finals and revising. Add to that the stress of college applications and the prospect of several years of university apart from each other, if things didn't go according to plan, and you had a recipe for one unhappy Head Boy. Tonight, however, he was hers again. He was the playful Jason she had always loved and had known for what seemed like forever.

It felt good.

She reached up and ran her fingers through his luscious, messy hair. 'You'll see it next Friday when you pick me up for the Leavers' Ball and not a minute before.' His gaze dropped as he picked at a thread on the hem of his duvet cover. 'What's wrong?'

'Ah, nothing. Just a little sad that it's all going to be over soon.'

She sniggered. 'Jace, we're leaving school. We're not lining up for a firing squad.'

He smirked and rubbed his nose on hers. 'Duh...I know that... It's just...well, it's the end of an era, that's all.'

'Yes and the beginning of a whole new one. And if I get into Brunel, we'll still be close to each other and not too far from home.'

Jason clasped her hand in his. There was an almost pained expression in his eyes. 'Have you ever thought about... oh, I don't know...*not* going to uni?'

She frowned at his question. 'No...never. It's what I've always planned. It's what *you've* always planned too. You've studied so hard. Don't worry. I just know you'll get the grades the Oxford board is looking for.'

He huffed the air from his lungs. 'Yeah...I know...I just...I don't know...I wonder what it would've been like if I'd been an average Joe. You know...*average* intelligence. There would've been a lot less pressure on me.'

She kissed his nose. 'You've just got pre-results blues, that's all. One day, you'll be a doctor without a doubt.' She leaned her forehead on his. 'Your mum and dad must be so proud of you. I know I am. And you're the best role model for Dillon.'

Jason nodded but his eyes were filled with sadness. 'Thanks. I just get a bit tired of having to be the *best* at everything. There's no room for error. Failure is not an option.' He spoke as if quoting someone. 'It wears me down, Stevie.' His jaw clenched.

'Well, you shouldn't be so bloody talented then, eh?' she teased.

He dropped his gaze again. 'That's just it though...the more I do well, the more people *expect* from me. It's getting ridiculous.'

Worried about his current train of thought, she crawled into his lap and looked into his eyes. 'What's brought all this on?' She stroked his cheek lovingly.

He gazed up at her, tenderly tucking her hair behind her

ears. 'Oh nothing...just ignore me. You're probably right about the pre-result nerves.' He pulled her down and kissed her until she melted into him once again and forgot what they had been discussing. And then he whispered her favourite words, his mantra. 'Hmm, Stevie...*my soulmate*.'

She smoothed her hands down his chest to his tight stomach and his muscles flinched beneath her touch. 'I could always...help you take your mind off things...if you'd let me try.'

He lifted her and placed her beside him. His eyes were pleading a message, but she couldn't quite read it. 'Stevie...not here...not yet. It's not that I don't want you...and I do love you...but...can we wait? Please?'

Once again, he had rebuffed her advances and she felt foolish. But she smiled and nodded, tucking herself into his side as she turned her attention back to the DVD on the screen.

~

Leavers' Ball Night

Stevie smoothed the dress down over her curves and added a little more gloss to her lips. It was ten minutes past the time Jason was supposed to pick her up. He was *never* late. She paced the hallway, getting more and more annoyed as the minutes ticked by.

'Have you tried his mobile?' Dana asked as Stevie became increasingly upset.

She narrowed her eyes and put her hands on her hips. 'Oooh, do you know I never thought of that!' she snapped, immediately regretting her harsh tone. She sighed heavily.

'Sorry, Mum...there was no need for that... It's just *so* not like him. I don't get it.'

Thankfully, Dana didn't get upset easily. 'Well, what did his mum say?'

'Nothing. She wasn't in. No one was in. Dillon has no idea either. Jason wasn't home when he got back from school.' She chewed on a painted nail. Her other hand clung to the silver coloured heart shaped pendant around her neck that Jason had made for her in his metal work class. He had engraved her favourite words on the reverse. *My soulmate* .

Dana stopped her daughter in her tracks and pulled her hand away from her mouth. 'Keep doing that and we'll have to redo your nails, sweetie. He'll *be* here. Please try to stop worrying.'

An hour later—and after several phone calls aiming to discover the whereabouts of her boyfriend—the mystery was no nearer to being solved. Dana was doing her best to comfort her daughter, who was distraught with worry.

The house phone rang and Stevie leapt to grab it. 'Jason?' she gasped into the phone, desperately hoping she was right.

'Stevie? No love... It's Shirley.' Jason's mother sounded like she was crying. Stevie lowered herself to the sofa, dreading what she was about to hear.

'Shirley, what's going on? Where's Jason? I'm really worried.' Her words came out in a rush.

'Sweetheart...he's...he's *gone*...Jason's gone.'

Her heart plummeted like a stone in a deep pond and her skin became cold and clammy as dread washed over her. 'What? What do you mean he's gone? Gone where?' Suddenly Shirley's words hit her and something resembling a sob and a scream left her body. '*No!*'

Dana flung an arm around her daughter as the phone slipped out of her hands.

With a rapid movement Dana caught the falling handset and fumbling a little with her daughter encircled in one arm, she manoeuvred the phone to her ear. 'Shirley? Oh my God, Shirley, what's happened?'

Stevie was light headed and faint. The room spun and echoed. She felt as though she was disappearing, receding down a long tunnel as the room retreated from view. Her mum shouted her name before everything went black.

The light hurt Stevie's eyes as she slowly fluttered her eyelids open to find Dana hovering over her. 'She's coming round, Shirley.'

'Oh, Stevie, sweetheart, you gave us a fright,' Shirley said as she stroked her hand. Stevie pulled herself upright and couldn't quite understand why Jason's mother was

a) in her living room and

b) not hysterical at the news that her son was somehow...*dead*.

Thinking the thought again made her lip quiver, her heart ache, and her stomach roll.

'I'm going to throw up,' she informed the two wide-eyed women before she retched. Luckily, her stomach was empty thanks to her lack of appetite that evening and the dry heaves turned to sobs once again.

'Stevie...don't cry, darling. Listen to what Shirley has to say, okay?' She nodded, looking from one woman to the other and feeling very confused.

Shirley inhaled and squeezed her hand. 'You've misunderstood me, darling. I'm pretty sure Jason is fine. I'm so sorry for scaring you. It wasn't my intention. I was just shocked. I mean, I'm sure he's alive...he...he just...*left*.'

Stevie took a moment for the words to sink in. Something wasn't quite right. *This* wasn't right. 'What do you mean he left? He can't have just left. Where would he go? *Why* would he go?'

Shirley squeezed her hand again. 'We have no idea. He just cleared his closet out and took his savings. But he left his mobile phone behind. Wherever he's gone, he doesn't want to be contacted.'

Stevie shook her head in disbelief. 'There must be some mistake. He wouldn't do that... It was the Leavers' Ball... He was supposed to take me... He loves me...and there's Oxford... He loves me... I don't...'

Shirley put an arm around her shoulder. 'I think perhaps he just needed to get away for a while. He's been under lots of pressure with the exams and his application to Oxford. I'm sure he'll come home when he's had a few days away. Let's try not to worry, eh?'

Flooded with relief Stevie nodded and inhaled a deep, shaking breath through pursed lips. 'Yes...yes you're probably right. He'll be back... He *has* been stressed, I do know that... and a little quiet...but I know him and he wouldn't just leave like that...not for good... He loves me. I *know* he really loves me...'

The two women hugged her and held her hand as her eyes darted back and forth between them. 'He loves me. I know he does. He'll come back.'

CHAPTER ONE

Ten Years Later

Stevie sighed down the line on hearing her friend's bad news. 'You can't possibly be serious about this, Mollie? You're due to leave on that stupid Outward Bounds trip next bloody week! *How* can you have broken your ankle?'

'Honestly? I don't even know. One minute I was upright and the next I was sprawled out, face down on the brushy things with my leg facing one way and my ankle at a weird, jaunty angle.'

She shivered. 'Eugh! Mollie I don't need to *know* the details. I can do without the mental image, thanks. I can't believe you're not going to be able to go. It's all you've bloody talked about for months. You and David from P.E...alone together.'

Mollie huffed. 'We'd hardly have been *alone*. A coach load of teenagers isn't what you could, in any way, call conducive to a blossoming romance.'

'Ha! *Blossoming romance?* I'd say it's still at the *seed in the packet on the shelf at the garden centre* stage at the moment. Let's not get delusional, Moll.'

'Hey, now that's just mean. And I can't help it if he only has eyes for a certain Science teacher with long, auburn hair.'

'David. Does. Not. Fancy. *Me.*'

Mollie laughed out loud. 'No, you're right. He *never* sits there staring all dreamy eyed at you in the staff room. And he *never* makes a beeline for the Science department's table on training days. *Never.*'

'Oh, shut up. And anyway, the feeling is *not* mutual. You can have him.'

'Well, that *was* my intention when we went up north, but I won't get the opportunity now.'

'Hmmm, you're right. It's clearly not happening now. So... who's going in your place?'

There was a pregnant pause from the other end of the line. 'Ah, well...that's just the thing, you see...the Head teacher asked me who I thought would be a good replacement and—'

'Oh my God, you didn't? You wouldn't *do* that to me.' Silence. 'You did, didn't you? You told Anthony I'd do it, didn't you?'

'Weeeell...I may have suggested—'

'Mollie Sumner! You cow! I can't *believe* you'd do this to me. I'm your *best friend*. You know me better than anyone, and you know I hate *anything* to do with the outdoors! How could you?'

'Don't be mad, babe. Please! He put me under pressure. I couldn't think of anyone else.'

'He put you under pressure? You're terrified of the man. That's all. He only has to look at you and you volunteer for anything. And now he's going to approach me to go on this bloody trip with David and a bus load of spotty snot bags!'

'That's what I love about you, your love for the kids you teach.'

'I *love* them when I can go home at the end of the day! When I can drink a bottle of red wine on a weekend and forget them for a while. How would I manage a *whole week* with the blighters? Seriously, Moll, I'm so bloody upset with you right now.'

~

One Week Later

Day One of Hell

A ten-hour journey north from London with a coach load of fifteen-year-olds was *not* the way Stevie had intended spending the beginning of her week. Or *any* part of *any* week, for that matter. She cursed Mollie Sumner for her broken ankle. *Honestly, what kind of teacher goes dry slope skiing for the first time a week before an Outward Bounds trip that she had agreed to assist on? Doing such a thing was asking for trouble, tempting fate in the worst possible way.*

Mollie, the Biology teacher, had *always* been clumsy and accident prone—outdoorsy, but clumsy all the same. This latest accident just proved what everyone else already knew—she was a walking disaster. After trying to find reasons to *not* go on the trip, she had drawn a complete blank. A female chaperone was necessary and Anthony, the Head teacher, was *very* persuasive. Although *legally* he wasn't allowed to say so in *actual words,* she got the distinct impression that it was going to go in her favour when the Head of Science position became free in the autumn, and so she had agreed, albeit very reluctantly.

Her case was crammed with just-in-case items. She had thermals, just in case it was freezing—well Scotland wasn't known for its tropical temperatures. Insect repellent, just in case there were lots of midges—the rest of the Science department had been teasing her about being feasted upon. A small bottle of Vodka, just in case the stress got too much—although she realised there was little chance of having a sneaky drink, and she was also very much aware that she could lose her job if it was spotted. And so it went on. She thought she had covered pretty much every eventuality, but it didn't make going any more palatable.

Since leaving the sprawling metropolis of Glasgow with its high rise blocks, shopping malls, and map flailing tourists in the latest leg of the journey; and after the toilet stop necessitated by some girls who had drunk far too much cola, the passing scenery was a pleasant distraction from the noise of the argumentative teenagers surrounding her in this new version of hell.

The roads were long and surrounded on both sides by bracken-covered rocks and little streams. Every so often there was a small lake reflecting the mountains and bright blue sky like a mirror. It was peaceful, so very tranquil, the complete antithesis of her normal, everyday life.

She loved her job. Passionately. But the beauty of it was that she usually got to leave the kids behind on an evening and weekend. But there she was on a Saturday, her favourite day of the week, travelling up to the middle of goodness knows where with a coach load of *them* and facing the prospect of being unable to leave them at all for the coming seven days.

Her travel companion and colleague of four years, David Harris, Head of P.E., returned from the back of the coach where he'd been mediating a dispute over an *allegedly* stolen iPod. David was a nice guy. Conventionally handsome.

Stocky but not fat with neat, blonde hair and green eyes. He had a friendly smile and had been very chatty ever since she started work at the school. She had a good working relationship with him. She reckoned he was around six years her senior, putting him at around thirty-four years old. His job clearly kept him fit.

He slumped into the seat beside her and she glanced up at him. 'Kids...who'd have them?' He rolled his eyes. When she didn't respond, he leaned towards her. 'Penny for your thoughts, Mrs. Norton?'

Her attention was pulled away from the mountainous vista with its azure blue backdrop. 'Sorry, what?'

'You looked deep in thought. Is everything okay?'

She smiled. 'Yeah...yeah I'm fine. I was just thinking that there are...oooh...about a million things I could be, and would *rather* be doing, than spending a week in Scotland with a group of hormonal adolescents.'

David nodded and laughed. 'Ah, the joys of teaching in high school, eh?'

'Hmm. *Joy* is not a word I would necessarily apply to this *current* predicament we find ourselves in, Mr. Harris.'

'Oh, come on. It'll probably be fun. Things usually are when you don't expect them to be.'

She shook her head in disbelief and snorted derisively. 'Where the hell did you hear that load of crap?' She smiled despite her tone.

David cringed. 'Hmm...okay... I admit it. I made it up. Total lie. Things are usually pretty crap if you expect them to be.' He nudged her shoulder with his own. 'Brought your insect repellent?'

She rolled her eyes, reminded of her recent ribbing by her friends over the week. Clearly news had travelled. 'Oh yes. I intend to *bathe* in it hourly.'

After graduating from Brunel University, Stevie had accepted a job as a newly qualified teacher in the Science department at Wilmersden High School. Wilmersden, a leafy suburb of London, was comfortable and familiar because it was close to where she grew up. The four years since she started at the school had been fun. The other Science teachers were a rather crazy bunch—a necessary qualification for teaching Science, so she'd been informed. Her life revolved around school. Even outside of working hours, she socialised with her colleagues, especially her best friend Mollie. That had been part of the problem for her and Miles.

She had met Miles at uni during her first year. They had been in several classes together and had a common interest in all things scientific. Whilst she was intending to one day be a teacher, Miles was hoping to go into the field of chemical research. At first they had just been friends, but it had been clear right from the start that Miles was attracted to her. He was a good-looking guy with copper coloured wavy hair and green eyes. He was no male model but he *was* attractive in that kind of boy-next-door way. He'd flirted with her for months before finally plucking up the courage to ask her out. She'd known it was coming. But she had still said no.

The reason for her initial negative response was due to the fact that she had been seeing a guy she met in the student cafeteria. Sid had been very demanding, and she'd struggled to keep her virginity intact. Eventually, he had become aggressive, and she had been reminded yet again that men were not to be trusted. When she hadn't given in to him, he dumped her quite spectacularly in front of his friends, embarrassing her and calling her frigid. The only saving grace was that she hadn't loved him.

And so even though many years had passed since Jason's disappearance, her broken heart, with its misplaced pieces, just wasn't ready to be glued back together and handed over to *another* man.

Men left.

It was a fact of life.

Well, a fact of *Stevie's* life anyway. First her father and then her first love. Both never to be seen again. And then there had been the Sid debacle. She'd decided, very early on in adulthood, that she would never trust another man enough to give her heart away again. She would keep it firmly under lock and key. She considered herself broken beyond repair. A fact that she had grown to accept since she was eighteen.

There were so many conversations with her mother over the matter. They always took the same format.

'Why don't you just give Miles a chance sweetie? He clearly adores you. It's been years since Jason left and you really need to start living again.'

'But Mum, I can't move on when I'm still in love with him. What if he comes back?'

'Darling, I think we both know that's not going to happen.'

'Shirley thinks it will. She thinks he'll come back any day now.'

'Stevie, I don't mean to be cruel but she's his mother. She's clinging on to false hope. Please don't do the same. If he was going to come back he would have done so by now. Darling, you're an adult and I can't tell you what to do or what to think. All I can tell you is that Shirley is living in a dream world. Something happened to make that boy so unhappy that he couldn't stay here. He's not coming back and you need to accept it and move on. Miles is a good man. I know he'd treat you right, unlike that Sid character. He was vile and I have no clue what you saw in him. But Miles...Miles is sweet and

caring and clearly adores you. All I want is your happiness, sweetie. Please, give him a chance.'

The conversation would be followed by angry tears, shouting, and words spoken in the heat of the moment that would have her sobbing her apologies to her long-suffering mother later.

It was always the same.

Eventually, after much convincing by her mother, she agreed to go on a date with Miles. He took her to a nice restaurant and treated her like a princess. From that first date, their relationship developed further and their friendship deepened. The only problem was the tiny not-so-insignificant fact that she never gave Miles her heart. She cared for him. Of course she did. He was dear to her. But she had never fallen *in love*.

After dating for almost a year, she had finally given him her virginity and soon discovered a deep enjoyment of sex and the abandonment she could achieve in the throes of passion. She was happy to share her body with Miles whilst they were in a relationship. But she had decided that love would never enter into things. Not if she could help it. And that was the one thing *she* controlled. He was comfortable to be around though, and the sex, although she had nothing else to compare it to, was in her humble opinion, good. Not mind blowing. But good. He was such a good person. Kind hearted and thoughtful and she managed to convince herself for a while that he was what she needed.

The marriage lasted several years before Miles finally admitted defeat. It was his persistent talk of having babies that eventually drove her into admitting that she could never be who he wanted her to be.

They had made love and were lying in bed, both sated from their orgasms, and Miles was drawing gentle circles on her tummy.

Laying his palm flat against her skin he whispered, 'I'll still love you when this gets bigger, you know.'

Dread washed over her as it did every time he tried to have this conversation. 'I'm sorry, what?'

'When you're pregnant with my baby and your belly gets all big and bulbous. I think you'll still look sexy as hell.' He dragged his fingers lazily through the soft, dark curls covering her sex.

She pulled herself to a sitting position and looked down at him. 'Miles...I...I don't want kids. You know this. We discussed it before we got married and many times since.'

He narrowed his eyes. 'Oh, that? Yeah, but you'll change your mind. All women do.' He smiled up at her, his green eyes adoringly piercing hers.

She turned to fully face him. 'No...no, Miles you're wrong. I *won't* change my mind. And you're being very presumptuous and arrogant if you think that I will. I told you my feelings on this, and you said it didn't matter. You said that as long as you had *me*... I'm sorry...I just...I don't want kids.'

He sat up and took her face in his hands. 'You will. One day. I *know* you will. There's no rush though.'

She pulled his hands away as anger rose within her. 'Will you *listen* to me?' She raised her voice. 'This is *me* telling *you* that I won't! I. Do. Not. Want. Children.' She spoke slowly and punctuated each word to try and get it through to him.

'Look, sweetie. We're good together. We're a team. We'd be good parents, fantastic parents in fact. Not every relationship ends in disaster you know.'

She scrunched her brow. 'Meaning what?'

'Meaning that your dad left your mum when you were tiny. I won't do that. I won't leave. I'm not your dad and I won't just disappear without trace. I'm sticking around for the long haul, Stevie. I'm not J—'

With haste she clambered up from the bed as she seethed and clenched her fists. 'Don't you *dare* mention his name to me! And I can't believe you just brought my parents' relationship into this!'

Miles frowned and he rubbed at his brow. 'Well, that's what this is about, isn't it?'

'No!' She ran her hands through her hair, exhaling loudly and then inhaling the strength to speak her next words. 'Miles, I don't want children. Not with *you.*'

His face crumpled with hurt. 'What's that supposed to mean? *Not with you?*' He mocked her voice as his face reddened. It was evident that her words had cut him and he was getting angry.

Her voice became a sad whisper. 'It means exactly what it sounds like. I care for you deeply. I really do.' She closed her eyes. 'But...but I should *never* have married you.' She opened her eyes and looked directly at him.

He gaped at her and blinked rapidly. His mouth started to move, opening and closing but no sound came out. This went on for what seemed like five minutes—him just staring and doing a good impression of a fish out of water. Eventually, he made eye contact with her again and his were now glassy. 'But the sex...' His words trailed.

'Yes, the sex is good. We have *good sex*. And we're such good friends, but that's all. And you and I both know that sex isn't love. We're like...like friends with benefits. But that's it. I'm not...*in love* with you. I never have been. I think deep down you knew that.' She was well aware that her harsh words were stabbing him in the heart, and she felt terrible at her own admission, but it needed to be said. Especially now that babies had been mentioned *again*. Last time she had let it slide but now...now it needed dealing with once and for all.

He silently stood, wiped at his eyes and went to the

wardrobe. He pulled down a large duffel bag and began to calmly fold his clothes. He paused momentarily and looked at her. A tear escaped from one eye and trailed down his smooth cheek. 'Thank you for being so brutally honest. Thank you for stabbing me in the heart. At least I know where I stand. I'll go and stay at my mum's until we decide what to do next.' He clenched his jaw and spoke through gritted teeth. 'What *he* did to you... I hate him for it. I've treated you right...always. I would *never* hurt you like he did, but even after all these years he's still there, isn't he? And you...you really are an ice queen, aren't you?'

She gasped at his observation, feeling her own stab of pain in the heart. But she didn't cry. Once he had finished packing, she silently allowed him to leave. After that night, he didn't return to live with her.

There were several conversations during the first week where he tried his best to convince her she was wrong, but there were no raised voices. In fact, all in all, it wasn't a particularly acrimonious break up. It was fairly emotionless on her part. The one thing that had hurt more than anything was that, despite knowing her history, Miles had cruelly called her an ice queen.

She wasn't an ice queen.

She was broken hearted and there was a vast difference. None of what she had done was intentional or premeditated. None of it had been malicious. She had *tried* to love Miles. He left her alone for a while, but after things had settled down, he had made contact again and asked to take her out for a drink as friends. She wanted to be friends desperately and so she agreed.

They had a nice evening, but she couldn't help thinking that this was his way of giving her space without actually *giving* her space. There were several evenings like this until she finally admitted to herself that this was a ploy to win her back and it wasn't going to work. It was his way of reminding her *why* they had been together, how good she'd had it with him. It was a bid at reconciliation on his part but she wanted none of it. Seeing him socially was not a good idea. The main issue being that Miles eventually admitted he was still in love with her and would do anything to get her back.

Back to present day and a year on, nothing had changed. Miles would regularly turn up on her doorstep, begging her to take him back. It was quite ridiculous considering he wasn't really in the wrong. But she calmly kept telling him that it was over.

Back in the real world and the coach pulled under a large wooden sign, which looked like it had been bitten and scratched by some large wild creature or other. Stevie hoped and prayed that this was simply for effect only. It read *Wild Front Here*. She rolled her eyes at the play on words as their vehicle began to travel up a long dirt track road surrounded by yet more trees.

The place was miles from anywhere. Miles from a supermarket, miles from a chemist, miles from a Starbucks, miles from...*Miles*. In fact, miles from any civilisation at all. Who'd have thought you could be so remote in the UK?

The crammed bus finally stopped in a clearing and the driver announced their arrival. The teenagers on board erupted into whoops and cheers, and David did his best to get their attention so he could calm them down. She climbed down from the bus and made her way over to the petite blonde woman in khaki shorts, who was waiting with a clipboard.

'Hi! Welcome to *Wild Front Here*.' She gestured her arms around them with a flourish. Her green eyes smiled.

Stevie wasn't in the mood for the over-enthusiastically jovial greeting. 'Erm...yeah. Thanks. Can you tell me where the toilets are, please?'

The greeter deflated a little. 'Oh right...yes...over in that direction, through the trees. Watch your footing though. Lots of branches and things.'

'Thanks.' Stevie headed off in the direction that the woman had gestured. As she walked, her phone rang in her pocket. Checking the screen, she realised it was her mum doing her usual have-you-arrived-safe check. She truly believed the woman still thought she was a child. But she humoured her regularly without too much complaint. Ever since she was eighteen, things had changed. It was as if Dana constantly expected her to go off the rails or have a meltdown. It was infrequent that she snapped, but today—after the seemingly endless journey she had just endured—could well be one of those days depending on the tone of the call.

Stevie sighed. 'Hey, Mum.'

'Hi, sweetie. Did you arrive safe?'

She was about to bite back with, 'Do I sound like I'm dead in a ditch to you?' Instead she took a deep breath before replying. 'Yes...I'm fine. Can't talk long though as we've only just arrived.'

'Yes, no worries honey. Just checking you're okay. Speak soon, love you.'

'Love you too, Mum. Bye.' She ended the call feeling somewhat relieved that it had been brief and relatively calm and painless for once.

The cabin housing the toilets was built from rustic looking logs, and she half expected to see holes in the floor to pee in. Thankfully, she was pleasantly surprised at the modern and clean facilities that greeted her. They even smelled fresh. *Bonus.*

After using the conveniences, she exited the log cabin and stretched out her back. Sitting on a coach for so long played havoc with her muscles, and she hadn't been able to get to the gym this week thanks to preparing for this wretched trip. Science club and parent consultations had taken up two further evenings. She inhaled the fresh Scottish air into her lungs enjoying the lack of exhaust fumes and traffic noise.

Movement in her peripheral vision and a grunting noise caught her attention through the trees to her left. Being inherently inquisitive—okay, extremely nosey—she made her way over to have a sneaky look at what was causing the commotion.

A stunning sight greeted her, and she gasped quietly, appreciating the view before her.

He was naked from the waist up, and his tanned skin was glistening with sweat as the sun's rays beat down on him. The muscles in his back rippled and flexed when he lifted an axe above his head and brought it down with great force on the huge chunk of tree trunk. He grunted fiercely, a raw and almost carnal noise, as the axe made contact with the wood, splitting it right down the middle. An involuntarily twinge tugged between her thighs.

The man had a large tribal tattoo beginning on his left shoulder that reached part way down his back, and another that she couldn't properly make out but looked like some kind of script, that stretched down the right side of his torso. His hair was around collar length and almost black due to its dampness. The top part was scraped back and secured with a band, no doubt to keep errant strands from his eyes whilst he wielded the sharp weapon in his grip.

He wore khaki cargo pants that hung low on his hips so

that the dimples in his lower back were just visible. His biceps bulged as he lifted the axe aloft once more. Interspersed with the muscles and tattoos was the dirt that clung to his sweaty, masculine body.

Her mouth watered and her heart rate increased. She dragged the back of her hand across her damp forehead, suddenly feeling rather feverish; a strong reaction to quite a magnificent specimen of male.

No doubt he must have the face of a bulldog chewing a wasp or at least the personality of an ogre, she surmised. *He couldn't be that perfect, really. Could he?* After looking behind her to ensure she wasn't being observed in all her voyeuristic glory, she leaned in the direction of the hunk to get a closer look, squinting to try to make out the tattoo on his right side or at least get a glimpse of his face to prove her point.

She tried to step forward slightly, but her foot caught on a low branch causing her to lurch in the direction of the man and land on her hands and knees with a squeal. The sharp stony ground beneath her knees dug into her flesh as her eyes began to water. Biting down on her lip she tried to fight the urge to yelp even more and draw attention to her faux pas.

Her heart pounded in her chest, hammering at her ribs as if to make its own escape from the embarrassing situation she now found herself in, and she clamped her eyes shut. She quaked inwardly when she heard heavy footsteps rapidly coming towards her. She opened her eyes and stared down at a pair of dirty work boots.

A deep husky voice with a slight Scottish accent asked from overhead, 'You okay down there?'

Feeling the heat rise in her cheeks, she wished that the ground would break apart beneath her feet and swallow her whole into its yawning chasm. 'Oh...yes...sorry... I'm fine...I um...got a little lost.' She rambled and stammered her flustered words.

'Here, let me help you up.' A large calloused, dirty hand appeared in front of her face. She gulped down her shame and reluctantly grasped it, allowing herself to be pulled up to her feet. 'You should be careful out here. Lots of things to...you know...trip over.'

She slowly lifted her gaze up from his toned stomach where his ridged abdominal muscles were clearly defined and a V disappeared into his waistband. Up...up to his pecs...hard as rock. She could now see that the tribal tattoo on his back continued over his shoulder and part way down his chest. His body was, of course, just as delicious from the front as from the rear. The smell of pure male was pulled into her nostrils as she inhaled a deep shaking breath. As her eyes raked upwards she noticed the line of stubble that graced his strong, chiselled jaw, and his full lips were pulled into a hard line. He was clearly not amused. Her eyes continued their journey northward as if in slow motion until she was gazing into the eyes of the man she had been ogling from her hiding place, deep chocolate brown eyes that she could happily melt into. *Familiar* eyes. *Wait a minute...* She gasped a sharp involuntary breath. Her eyes widened and her heart almost stuttered to a halt.

'*Jason?*'

CHAPTER TWO

*T*he puzzled look on the man's face told Stevie he wasn't quite sure *who* he was looking at. But his expression suddenly changed. Darkened somehow as apparent realisation dawned on his stunning features. A cold shiver travelled her spine, her stomach knotted and dizziness struck as she stepped back, almost falling again.

He grabbed her around the waist and pulled her against his hard body. 'You need to be careful. You're going to get hurt.' His voice was a low, husky rumble that filtered through his gritted teeth.

She snorted. 'Yeah? Well, you'd know all about that, wouldn't you?' Placing her hands flat on his bare, damp, tattooed chest, she pushed him, struggling in vain to free herself from his vice-like grip. 'Get your hands...*off*...me!' Her voice was a strangled sob.

'Not until you stop struggling. If I let you go now and you fall, you'll be poleaxed by the huge, sharp branch sticking up behind you.'

She noted the difference in his accent and wondered why

that was. She stopped struggling and looked directly into his now cold eyes. 'Like you'd care if that happened.'

He grimaced at her and a line appeared in the middle of his forehead. 'Of course I'd care.' He cleared his throat. 'This is my livelihood after all, and I could do without the law suit, thank you very much.'

She gasped in horror at his harsh, emotionless comment. 'Well, we wouldn't want *that*, now would we? Who knows the trouble you'd get into? You'd have to *disappear* to avoid all the hassle... Oh wait...you did that ten fucking years ago!'

He moved his face so that it was an inch from hers. Her breath caught again and her heart continued to pound relentlessly, almost painfully at her ribs. He glanced down at her mouth and then back into her eyes as he spoke through his clenched jaw. 'You need to watch your mouth, there are kids around.'

He pulled her away from the protruding branch and let go of her. She stepped back carefully, straightening her clothing and smoothing down her hair. 'I...I need to get back.' She turned to go back in the direction that she had emerged from.

Jason grabbed her arm and swung her around again. 'Wait —why are you here? And how the *hell* did you find me?'

'Don't *flatter* yourself. I'm here under duress...as a teaching chaperone with my school. I hadn't got a *clue* you worked here. If I'd known that you did, I can assure you I wouldn't have set foot in the place.'

Jason's grin was one of disbelief. 'Of course you hadn't... and I don't *work* here, sweetheart. I *own* the place. But of course you'd know that, wouldn't you?'

Arrogant arse! 'How the hell would *I* know *that*?'

He huffed incredulously. 'Oh, come off it. It's my guess that you've been looking for me. I guess you've been playing detective for some reason after all these years.'

'Yeah? Well I don't *care* what you've *guessed*. Because the *fact* is you're wrong. Now let me go. I need to get back. Goodbye, Jason.' She tried to free herself from his vice-like hold again but instead it tightened further.

'So you were just ogling me then? Through the trees? You were ogling someone who was, to all intents and purposes, a complete stranger, and on work's time too. Tut tut. Is that common practise for teaching staff these days?' He chuckled but the laugh was laced with something dark and menacing.

She gritted her teeth. 'Get over yourself, you *arrogant pig*. I heard a grunting noise and came to investigate. I'm with a coach load of teenagers and it's *my* responsibility to ensure their welfare. That's *all*.'

He laughed humourlessly. 'Whatever, sweetheart.' He leaned into her ear. 'We both know the truth.'

She shivered and scrunched her face in disgust. 'My God, Jason, what the hell *happened* to you?'

He let go of her and scowled. 'I had a big dose of life and reality, darlin'. That's what.'

'Yeah? Now there's something to be proud of, eh? I'm sure that all those people whom you left behind would be *so* delighted to hear about that. And I'm *not* your sweetheart *or* your darling.'

He grabbed her by the arms again, this time with both hands, pulled her against his hard chest and bent so that his nose almost touched hers. '*They* will be hearing *nothing* of the sort because *you* are going to keep your mouth firmly *shut*. Do you hear me?'

Her chest heaved against his. He had changed beyond all recognition and not for the better. The smell of body wash mixed with sweat infiltrated her senses and clouded her mind. It was a heady cocktail that fuelled the lustful feelings she'd had when she had been oblivious to whom he was. Angry with her body for betraying her mind, she closed her eyes for a moment, and when she opened them again her resolve was restored. 'Or else *what*? You'll run away again? Or do you *threaten* and *hit* women now to keep them quiet and get them to do your bidding?'

He recoiled, letting her go and staggering backwards as though she had struck him. His brow furrowed and he looked pained by her words.

She smiled sardonically. 'You should be careful, Jason. Lots of things here to...you know...fall over.' She growled as she used his own words against him before turning and walking as fast as she could back to where the coach had parked.

The coach was nowhere to be seen, and suddenly she was overcome with emotion as realisation and the reality of her discovery began to sink in. Her rush to get away had left her winded and she bent double, resting her hands on her knees as tears stung behind her eyes. She gulped the fresh air deeply into her lungs trying her best to rein herself in.

Ten years he'd been gone, and of all the places she should bump into him, it had to be when she was *completely* out of her comfort zone, in more ways than one. The shock knotted her stomach, and her heart was forming a brand new erratic rhythm all of its own.

The last thing she needed was to have to fabricate something on the spot if she was discovered in her current distraught state. Once she had gathered herself, she wiped her clammy hands down her jeans and made her way in the direction of the log cabins.

'There you are! I've been worried sick! I thought you'd been dragged off by a mountain lion or something.' David looked relieved.

'David, we're in the Cairngorms, not the Yukon,' she snapped.

Her colleague raised his eyebrows. 'Sorry...I...I was just worried.'

She softened her face. 'I'm sorry. I got a bit...lost...but don't tell the kids, okay? I'd never live that down.'

He smiled. 'My lips are sealed. Hang on... Did you fall or something? Your knees are all scuffed and dirty.'

She bent and tried in vain to brush the dirt from her jeans. 'Yes. I tripped over a stupid branch. I'm fine though.'

'Okay...if you're sure... Look, I hope you don't mind but rather than leaving it outside I took your bag into your cabin. Come on, I'll show you the way.'

She followed him to a row of log cabin dorm rooms where their charges were happily unpacking their belongings. They were surprisingly quiet, probably exhausted from their long journey. David kept his hand at the bottom of her back, a gesture that seemed a little too familiar and intimate for work colleagues, but she let it ride for now, seeing as she was devoid of the energy to protest. He gestured to a small cabin at the end of the row, which sat opposite a cabin of the same size. 'This is you, and I'm opposite.'

'Thanks, David.'

'No worries. Your bag's on your bed. I drew the line at unpacking for you. Didn't think you'd like me going through your smalls.' He grinned and blushed.

She shook her head without smiling. 'No. I wouldn't. I'll just get unpacked. What are the arrangements for dinner?'

'Dorcas says there'll be a barbecue in about an hour. She'll come and collect us before that though, as there's a briefing first.'

She scrunched her face. '*Dorcas*? What kind of name is *Dorcas*?'

'A biblical one,' David replied, looking rather proud for knowing that little snippet of useless trivia. 'She was the little blonde girl who greeted us. She's very sweet, and I think a couple of the boys already have the hots for her, so we'll have to watch them. Anyway, I'll leave you to it.'

He turned on his heels and made his way over to a group of kids who were messing around with cups of water and squealing like banshees. Turning her back on the ridiculous scene, she climbed the steps into her small cabin and closed the door. She walked over to the bed and sat, glancing around at her new surroundings. The cabin was simply furnished but comfortable with a single bed, bedside table, dressing table, and chair. There was a small en-suite shower room at the end too, which she was relieved to discover.

Inhaling a deep breath, her mind wandered back to the startling encounter that took place only minutes before. Hindsight is a wonderful thing, and she would *not* have boarded the bus if she'd known that *he* would be here.

Or *would* she?

Ten years was a long time to nurse the wounds left after being abandoned by the man you thought you were going to spend your life with. Ten years and not a word. Not knowing if he was alive or dead. Not knowing if he was happy or if he had met someone else. Ten years without his touch, his kiss, his voice. Ten years that had left her a shell of her former self, unable to trust *anyone*.

The whole damned situation had caused her to lose her friends, her heart, her self-esteem, and her confidence, along with her faith in men; or the tiny shred that she'd had left. All gone. And here he was. Large as life.

Her immediate thought was that she wanted to leave, to get away rather than face this thing head on. It was one of those fight or flight scenarios she'd heard about. The trouble is, the more she played it over in her mind, the more she wanted to go with *both*. To slap him and demand answers, *and* to phone for a cab to take her back down to London. But duty wouldn't allow that. She was trapped here.

Trapped.

For. A. Whole. Week.

And shit, he *owned* the damn place. There was no escaping him. At all. There was a knock on her cabin door, and she turned to face it, staring, as if by doing so it would reveal who was on the other side. Was it him? *Oh shitty shit! Calm, Stevie. Calm.* After a few moments, she stood and slowly, reluctantly made her way over to open it, fearing who stood beyond.

It was David. Relief washed over her and she smiled widely.

He responded with a wide grin. 'Dorcas has asked that we make our way over to the clubhouse hut now. Apparently, the safety briefing is happening very soon.'

Almost breezily she answered, 'Oh...right, yes. Give me a minute to change my jeans.'

'Oh, I wouldn't bother.' He looked her up and down. 'You look fine. You look the part, all...you know...rugged and... wilderness.' His cheeks coloured. *Poor guy, he must be getting whiplash from my change in mood.*

'Okay, well, I'll just brush my hair. Two minutes.' She closed the door before he could drool over her further and rifled through her bag for her hairbrush. Releasing the clip, she allowed her long, auburn tresses to fall loosely in waves around her shoulders. She brushed out the knots, dropped the brush onto the bed, and checked her appearance in the full-length wall mirror before making her way out to join David.

He looked a little put out, standing there with his arms

folded over his chest. 'Come on...the kids have already gone over.' She rolled her eyes and followed.

They walked to the largest of the log cabins where the kids were filing in remarkably quietly again. It seemed as if she had wandered into the Twilight Zone. She and David followed behind and waited until all the teens were seated before she glanced to the front where a now showered and changed Jason stood.

His hair was damp and was no longer tied back at the top. It hung loosely around his face, and it was now evident why he'd needed to scrape it back earlier. His stubble remained and he was wearing clean jeans and a fitted T-Shirt with the *Wild Front Here* logo on his left pec. It clung to the muscles she had felt, and seen, at first hand earlier today. Her heart skipped, and inwardly she cursed herself as her body reacted against her will once again.

She had to admit that he looked every bit as stunning as she remembered, although more rugged, mature, and masculine. Definitely broader. He glanced up and caught her looking at him. She froze. Should she look away? Should she smile? Should she make a face? All too soon, his smouldering gaze was torn away as Dorcas placed her hand on his arm and leaned in to whisper something. He smiled widely at her, placing his hand on her shoulder as he nodded.

Bitch.

The word popped unwelcomed into her mind. *Whoa, Stevie, what was that?* She shook her head to eradicate the thought. She had no right, nor any *desire* for that matter, to be possessive over the man. Well, at least her *right* mind hadn't. Her subconscious appeared to think differently.

Great.

Once the chatter had died down, Jason glanced around the room. 'Good evening, everyone. My name is Jason

Reynolds, and I'm the owner of *Wild Front Here*. I just want to run through a few rules and introduce you to the rest of the staff. That way you all stay safe and your teachers stay almost sane.' A rumble of laughter traversed the room. He continued on, informing the kids of the no go areas on camp, where the fire assembly points and first aid rooms were, and what to do in the event of any emergency.

'Remember guys, we *never* ask you to do anything we don't think you're *all* capable of. You have to believe in *yourselves* like *we* all believe in you. Some of the things we'll do will be scary and some of them will be physically tough. But know that we—my staff, myself, and your teachers—have the utmost faith in your abilities. Not many kids get this opportunity so please make the most of being here. Take the opportunity to conquer your fears. Face them with your head held high. And don't forget, we're all here to support you. So all that remains to be said now is that you should be very grateful to your teachers for taking time out of their busy lives to be here with you. Make sure you say thank you. Have fun. Don't do anything stupid and above all, be safe.'

Jason's deep voice resonated throughout the room, and she found herself staring at his mouth. She had always loved his mouth. He had such plump, kissable lips, and she had often wondered what it would feel like to have his mouth trailing kisses down her naked body. But things had just never got that far between them. He left on the very day she was hoping they would take that next step together.

His words were touching, and her throat tightened at hearing his passion and belief in the group of disaffected kids that she was accompanying. She was impressed with his air of authority and secretly very proud of the man he was, standing in front of the group, rousing them up and instilling his confidence in them. It was just a shame that he was such an arrogant arse outside of the situation.

She was snatched from her reverie when the room of teens erupted into applause. Her head snapped up, and she found herself peering straight into the dark eyes of her former boyfriend and first love, whose gaze was also fixed on her. The heat rose in her cheeks as she nervously tucked a strand of hair behind her ear.

Dorcas with the sweet Scottish accent and over-excited, breezy manner addressed the crowd, 'Okay, gang! The barbecue should be just about ready, so if you'd like to make your way out of the main door and down to the left, you'll see where the tables are set up.' Her blonde hair bounced as she spoke enthusiastically. She reminded Stevie of an eager-to-please puppy dog. The teens began to file out of the room with David heading up the line. Several of the boys stared dreamily at Dorcas, taking the journey slowly in order to try and walk along with her. She hung back to ensure that everyone knew where they were going, and Dorcas smiled at her as she passed.

Suddenly, a masculine scent penetrated her nostrils and heat seeped into her skin. 'I think we need to talk.' Jason leaned in so close that his breath caressed her ear as he spoke just above a whisper.

She shuddered.

Damn him.

Spinning around to face him, her anger rose once again. 'I have *nothing* to say to you.' She stormed out of the room letting the door slam shut behind her.

CHAPTER THREE

The door to the large cabin creaked open behind her as she walked away. She didn't turn around but she heard him jogging towards her, and so she picked up her pace. He grabbed her elbow and spun her around to face him.

He growled. 'You can't avoid me forever.'

The smile she plastered on her face was by no means friendly. 'Oh yes, I can. I'm taking my cue from the master of avoidance tactics,' she spat.

His face took on that pained expression again. 'You don't think that maybe *I* have things to say? To explain?' His sexy, Scottish-tinged accent intrigued her, almost sucking her under his spell yet again.

Setting her jaw, she looked directly into his eyes, hoping to portray inner strength even though she felt anything *but* strong. 'I'm afraid it's a little late for that, Jason. Ten years ago would've been the appropriate time for you to explain. There is nothing...let me repeat that...*nothing* that you could say to me that would make what you did acceptable or forgivable.'

Jason's nostrils flared. 'I beg to differ. Look, I had my reasons for leaving, okay?'

'No, it's not okay. Like I've already said, it's *too late* to explain them now.' Her heart was pounding against her ribs again, and her eyes stung with unshed tears. 'Do you have *any* idea how scared I was? Do you know how many hours I cried? How many days? Do you know how long I waited for *one word* from you so that I knew you were safe?' Jason let go of her arm. His gaze dropped to the floor and she could see his jaw working under his skin. 'No, I thought not. You never thought about *anyone* but yourself. For all I knew you were dead.' Tears escaped her eyes and cascaded down her face and she pointed her finger into his hard chest. 'You *broke* me Jason. I can't *love* anyone. I can't *trust* anyone. So yes, that's what you did...you *broke* me.' A sob escaped her throat and she turned to walk away.

Much to her relief he didn't follow this time, and so she made a detour to the toilet block, where she dabbed at her eyes and splashed her face with cold water. Glancing up into the mirror, her reflection was startling. Her face was pale but her eyes were red. *Great, now everyone will know I've been bloody crying.* She splashed more cold water on her face and took a deep steadying breath. She knew that she had a million and one questions buzzing around her head, but *here* was not the place and *now* was not the time to address them.

Perhaps there never would be a good time.

I was broken too, Stevie.

Without speaking, Jason watched her walk away. This was not going well. The fact that she'd turned up *here* out of the blue was shocking enough, but the fact that she looked just as beautiful as he remembered, no forget that...*even more* beautiful, was just damned painful. Although, it wouldn't matter what she looked like. She was beautiful in every single way. He knew what they'd had was special and intense, but he'd hoped to forget her. How the hell could he do that now she was here? He gritted his teeth. *Who the fuck am I trying to kid? I've never forgotten her. How the hell could I do that? I was in love with her.*

The way she used to look at him returned in flashbacks when he closed his eyes, like images being played on a screen. Her big blue eyes would gaze into his, filled with love. Her hair would flutter across her face in the breeze, and she'd tuck it behind her ear with a warm smile that made his heart skip. Why the fuck was she here? How the hell had she found him? *Had* she found him or had this whole thing been some unhappy coincidence?

He had to know.

After walking quickly over to his office, he rifled through the pile of papers on his desk. When he eventually came across the booking forms for Wilmersden High School, he scanned the section for chaperones, and the names of the teaching staff didn't include Stevie's. *Mollie Sumner and David Harris. Not Stevie Watts. Shit...is she even still called Stevie Watts? Maybe she's married now.* That was an unwelcomed thought.

Guilt washed over him. She'd *genuinely* had no clue. When he'd confronted her about looking for him, she *had* told him the truth. His accusations had made her out to be some lying stalker.

He pinched the bridge of his nose and closed his eyes. She didn't deserve the arrogant reception at all, the poor woman. He had no one to blame but himself for her low opinion of him. How the hell could he make amends for speaking to her like that? For handling her so roughly. If he had witnessed a woman being treated in such a way he'd have kicked the culprits arse from here to next year.

He blew out a long breath and resolved to try and make up for his transgressions in some way. If he could just get her to agree to listen to him, he could explain his disappearance. She had a warm heart. Surely when she knew the truth, she'd understand, wouldn't she? Armed with the knowledge that this was all as big a shock to her as it was to him, he made his way over to the barbecue.

There was no sign of her.

Shit. He glanced around, panicking. Maybe she'd somehow gone home. *But how could she? She's here for the kids. Good, that means she's a captive audience...of sorts.* He needed to talk to her. There were so many things she had to know. She had to know that he couldn't have stayed in London, but that it *wasn't* because of her. But he couldn't lose focus. He couldn't fall for her.

Not again.

When Stevie arrived at the barbecue area, everyone seemed to be chatting merrily whilst they ate their burgers and enjoyed the warm summer's evening.

David made a beeline for her. 'Hey, hi. Oh no...tree pollen?' He cringed sympathetically.

She was puzzled by his bizarre remark and pulled her brow into a frown. 'Sorry?'

He gestured to her eyes. 'Tree pollen getting to you? Your eyes are all red. It's a common thing to suffer with in these parts.'

Realising what he meant, she nodded. 'Oh...yes...tree pollen. Forgot my medication,' she lied.

'You should ask Jason. He's probably got a stock of antihistamine. Or he can point you in the direction of the pharmacy. Or the doctor maybe.' He just went on and on...

'Yes...yes...I'll ask later. I'm fine at the moment,' she answered dismissively.

David nodded, but his face told her he wasn't buying it. 'Um...okay. Shall I get you a burger?'

'No thanks, David. If I want one I'll get one,' she snapped. *God he's relentless!* 'I'm not that hungry. I brought some snacks, so I can eat later if I feel like it.'

He smiled and nodded again. 'Okay...well I'll go and do the rounds...make sure everyone's all right and that the boys aren't bothering Dorcas too much.' He hesitated but then walked away, leaving her to stand alone.

'Come and sit with us, Mrs. Norton. There's a space,' Jess, one of the pupils, called over.

'*Mrs.?*' came a husky voice from over her shoulder, making her jump. 'So you got married, then?'

She turned to face Jason as he stood close behind her. There was something in his eyes that told her he was disappointed about his discovery. 'You need to stop sneaking up on me.'

'Miiiss?' Jess called again in a whiny voice.

'Thanks Jess, but I'm okay standing. I can keep a better watch over you all this way.' She smiled. Jess rolled her eyes and turned back to her friends, who were all making eyes at Jason. He was oblivious to the hormonal teenagers.

'Come to my cabin after lights out. We can talk.' He insisted in an almost whisper.

'I've already told you I have *nothing* to say to you.'

He smirked. 'Forgive me if I don't believe you.'

She gave an exasperated sigh. 'Please, Jason. Just leave me alone. It's bad enough that I can't leave, so please can we just stay out of each other's way?'

'No, we can't. Look, just give me an hour of your time. That's all I ask. I just want to explain. After that, if you choose to ignore me then...well...there's nothing I can do about that, but I'm sure I'll survive.'

Why did he have to sound so concerned in one breath, and then jab her heart in the next? 'Sorry, it's not going to happen, okay?' She plastered a smile on her face to keep up appearances. The last thing she needed was to raise the suspicions of the pupils that there was more to her relationship with their host.

His mouth formed a hard line, and he breathed out noisily through his nose. 'My cabin is adjacent to the place we had our little...*brief encounter* when you arrived earlier. If you walk along a little further than the gap in the trees, you'll find a walkway. I usually stay up late. If you decide to come, that's where you'll find me. If not...well...maybe another time, eh? But know this...what I did was for a very good reason. It wasn't a decision I made lightly. I loved you.' And with that he walked away over to where the camp's chef was preparing the food and slapped the man on the back in a friendly manner. He glanced at her one last time, boring into her, pleading with her with his pained, dark eyes. A shiver traversed her spine, and she broke eye contact.

Later that evening, back in his cabin again, Jason changed in to his tatty, old, long board shorts but didn't bother with a shirt. There didn't seem to be any point. After all, it was a warm night, and whilst he'd hoped that Stevie would turn up, he wasn't holding his breath. She seemed determined to avoid the issues that *he* knew needed addressing. She had him pegged as some cruel, selfish bastard. It just wasn't true. Okay, so it *appeared* to be true and that didn't help matters. But once she knew the truth...

Why did she have to turn up and spoil things? He was doing just fucking fine without her. Well, he'd managed for ten years to not think about her beautiful face. Not *every* day anyway. And those eyes. So blue you could just fall right in and drown. Not that he wanted to of course. He wanted to explain why he left. He owed her that much. Then he wanted her to go back down to the hell that was London and fucking stay there. Let him get back to life as it *should* be. As it had been up until today.

He couldn't allow himself to get close to her again. That would be a *huge* mistake. He had made a life for himself here, and he didn't want that to change in *any* way. Maybe the arrogance thing was a good idea after all. At least she seemed to be put off by his attitude. And that *was* a good thing, right? Okay, so she liked how he'd filled out. That much was obvious from her expression and the way her pupils dilated when they made eye contact.

He couldn't deny that *she* looked incredible. Those curves, dammit. She was almost straight up and down when he saw her last, but now... He wondered what her skin would feel like under his fingertips. Would she be all soft and yielding? He'd noted the way her breasts were fuller and wondered what they would feel like in his hands. God he'd love to find out. Her hips were wider too—her smaller waist had been accentuated by that fact. And her sexy rounded arse. God he'd love to squeeze it whilst she straddled him. Her hair was still as beautiful as ever, and he longed to nuzzle and smell it. She was definitely *all* woman.

Gone was the awkward eighteen-year-old he'd left behind. His manhood awakened and twitched at his train of thought. But lust and love were two completely different things and as long as it stayed that way everything would be fine. This was going to be a temporary situation. She would be gone in a week.

Thank fuck.

He paced up and down again, becoming more and more agitated. Checking the clock for the hundredth time, he realised it was eleven thirty.

She wasn't coming.

Surely, she wouldn't come to see him now? He checked out of the window but there was no sign of her. *Fuck it!* She would *have* to listen to him. This week would be his only chance to explain. Now that the past had come back to haunt him in female form, the only *other* option would be going back down *there* to talk to her when she had left. And that wasn't happening. There was no way he would be setting foot in that hellhole. No, he would just have to force the issue whilst she was here. *Make* her listen.

He switched on his iPod in its docking station and paced up and down a little. The soothing voice of Soundgarden's Chris Cornell sang 'Black Hole Sun'.

Why am I so fucking restless? The last time he remembered feeling like this was out in the war zone before going out on patrol. It was his fight or flight mentality kicking in, and this was definitely one time he *wanted* to fight. Not literally of course. But he wanted the chance to explain everything. Although it would depend on whether or not she gave him a chance to do that, and her lack of presence at his cabin wasn't helping the situation. The hairs on the back of his neck stood to attention and he walked over to the kitchen window to look out one last time.

Trying to get twenty fifteen-year-olds to go to bed at eleven o'clock was no mean feat, especially when most of them came from households where a specific bedtime routine didn't exist. By the time the last teen was safely tucked in bed, David and Stevie were exhausted. They said their goodnights and headed off to their respective cabins.

Closing the door on the night, she showered and slipped into her pyjamas. Thankfully, she had remembered to pack her favourite Stewart tartan bottoms and red tank top. At least, she had *something* comforting and familiar. It was quite a balmy night, and she was sure that sleep would evade her, thanks to the days rather perplexing events.

Before flopping onto her bed, she fumbled around in her bag for her iPod, plugged in its mini speaker, selected the random song mode, and hit play. So what if it was almost eleven thirty. Music usually helped her to get to sleep. Unfortunately, her iPod seemed to have other ideas. In fact it seemed to be totally conspiring against her. The first track was 'Head Over Feet' by Alanis Morissette. It was a track that reminded her of Jason. *Typical*. They had first heard it on a music channel that was having a nineties day. She had thought it was one of the most honest songs she had ever heard. She had told Jason that she could have written the words especially for him. He had kissed her and held her close as the song had played.

When tears began to sting her eyes, she reached over and hit the forward button. Next, 'It's Been Awhile' by Staind took over her senses, another track that reminded her of Jason.

Aaargh! He had learned the song especially and had played it to her on his guitar in her room. She had cried silently as she had absorbed the words. There had been such a look of anguish on his face as he sang with his eyes closed. It was as if there was some hidden meaning behind the lyrics that he was trying to express. But whatever it was she couldn't decipher it at the time, and so she had just listened to his soothing voice and watched him play, his fingers caressing the fret board in a way that made her stomach twist. She always loved to hear him play, and in the ten years since he disappeared, her heart ached every time she heard acoustic guitar.

Heaving a deep sigh and feeling very frustrated and far too melancholy, she hit forward again. The next song didn't help at all. 'White Flag' by Dido. This song had been released not long after Jason's disappearance. The lyrics had tugged at her broken heart, and she had spent hours listening to the song, curled into a ball on her bed, sobbing at her memories. She had played it over and over, somehow hoping that wherever he was he would hear it or feel it at least. The words told the Jason that she couldn't see or touch that her heart would be his no matter what. They told him that she would *never* give up. She would *never* love anyone like she loved him. It was the song that sealed her fate. And she had held true to her promise. It was the song that stayed with her.

Of all the hundreds of songs on her iPod, why were *these* the three that played? Why did it seem that an inanimate object was out to get her? To break her heart all over again and bring the hardest memories back to the forefront of her mind? She questioned herself internally as to why the hell she hadn't deleted the songs long ago. But secretly she knew the answer.

She had never let go of him.

She gave up on the idea of music and turned the player off, choosing to lay there in silence with tears streaming from her eyes, trickling past her ears, and soaking into her hair. She wiped them away, but the more she wiped, the more they appeared. The relentless tears taunting her and adding to her heartache at seeing Jason, alive and well and only a few hundred yards away right at that very minute.

CHAPTER FOUR

Day Two of Hell

*S*tevie awoke on the top of her bed covers.
Thankfully, she had fallen asleep before giving in to
the powerful urge to go to Jason's cabin. She wondered if he
had waited for her, telling herself that she didn't care if he'd
sat up all night.

She quickly showered and towel dried her hair before
dressing in cargo pants and a T-shirt. Mountain biking was
the delight she had to face today, and she had as much enthusiasm for that as she would for running naked down
Wilmersden High Street.

From the direction of the main hut, the smell of bacon
infiltrated her nostrils and made her tummy growl. As she
walked, the sound of giggling and conversation floated
through the air as the kids chatted excitedly about the day
ahead whilst they ate their hearty Scottish breakfasts. They
were being collected by coach and taken to a cycle hire place
in the Rothiemurchus Forest. This was a first for her.

The most she had ever done on a bike was when she and

Jason went for a ride by the river, stopping off at their favourite spot for a picnic. She had always loved their trips down by the river. There was a little meadow that led to their favourite spot. They would sit chatting and kissing for hours, relishing each other's company. They never had much time for other friends. Every available minute was spent together, the fact that made Jason's disappearance all the more painful. It was like she'd lost half of herself when he'd gone.

David tapped her shoulder and smiled widely. 'Morning, Mrs. Norton. Sleep well?'

'Yes. I just crashed and didn't move,' she told him truthfully.

'Yeah. Comfy beds, eh?'

'Very. Are you eating?' She backed away and gestured to the hot buffet.

He patted his belly with a smile. 'Already had my fill. I reckon we'll need the energy! I hope you're feeling fit today.'

'Fit to bloody drop,' she muttered.

He frowned. 'Sorry? I didn't catch that.'

'I said, yes, I hope the temperature drops.'

'Ah, yeah, it's a warm one. But drink plenty of water and you'll be fine.'

He walked over to a group of kids who had finished eating and were chatting to Dorcas. He joined their conversation, which had the boys rolling their eyes and the girls simply choosing to walk away.

Smiling and shaking her head at the kids' negative reactions, she grabbed a plate and spooned on some of the fluffy scrambled egg, realising she was starving after the emotional exhaustion of the bizarre events the day before. She placed two slices of wholemeal toast on her plate and made her way to an empty table. Looking around her, she checked for unwanted company and breathed a sigh of relief as she sat down.

'You decided not to come then.' She jumped as the heat of Jason's breath at her ear made her shudder. *Where the hell did he spring from? And for goodness sake, why can't he just let me be?*

She snapped her narrowed eyes up to his. 'I fell asleep.'

'Whatever.' He snorted derisively. 'It's maybe just as well.' He sat down beside her, as the rest of the room seemed to clear. *Great bloody timing again.* He looked stunning. Long shorts and a tight black T-shirt. His dark hair scraped back off his face in that half ponytail thing again. The stubble along his jaw line made her fingers ache to touch it.

She bit her lip and rolled her eyes, wishing he would just leave. 'And why would you say that, Jason?' She sighed.

'Because I'm not sure you could handle being in my presence...*alone*.' He widened his eyes infinitesimally for a split second as he gave her a lascivious grin.

Oh God, he was off with the arrogance again. Clearly, something he resorted to when not getting his own way. She turned to face him. 'You seem to think you're some kind of stunning gift to women all of a sudden. And how *wrong* you are.' She shook her head as if to emphasise her point.

He chuckled, and after checking around conspiratorially, he leaned in to whisper again. 'Really? Is that why your nipples were poking through your top when you were ogling me yesterday?' His eyes drifted down to her breasts.

She rolled her eyes and folded her arms to cover them. 'Oh, for goodness sake. Really? Please *get over* yourself.' Her voice was just above a whisper in case little ears were close by. She snorted incredulously.

He smiled before standing to leave. Relief washed over her. But just when she was beginning to feel safe, he bent so that his mouth was next to her ear again. 'You and I both know how turned on you were yesterday when you were watching me. Don't bother trying to deny it. You liked the view. And *I* had an effect on you. You wanted me to touch you, to run my fingers down your stomach and into your panties. I *know* you did.'

A shiver travelled from the point where his hot breath singed her skin, down her body, and spiked at the junction of her thighs. She clamped her knees together and closed her eyes. Her body's betrayal again made anger well up inside her.

With flared nostrils and clenched teeth, she bit out, 'Fuck off, Jason.'

'Tut tut...and you a teacher too.' He chuckled darkly and walked away.

What the hell was *wrong* with the man? One minute he was desperately trying to get her listen to him and the next he was talking dirty and being an arrogant, self-absorbed arse-hole. Clearly, she didn't know him at all.

Once all the teens were on the coach, David and Stevie climbed aboard. David went straight to the back to settle the usual suspects down from their raucous state whilst she took her seat. Dorcas stepped on the bus next and sat at the opposite side giving her a wide grin.

Stevie forced a smile. 'Oh, I didn't realise you were joining us on the coach, Dorcas.'

'Yes, it makes more sense for me and Jason to tag along with yous lot. Saves taking the Landy or the bike.'

Her eyes widened. 'J-Jason's coming on here too?' She swallowed hard just as David returned.

'Oh hi, Dorcas. Mind if I sit with you?' he asked enthusiastically with a friendly smile.

She patted the seat beside her. 'Not at all. We can continue our chat from earlier.'

Panic rose in Stevie's gut. 'But, David, shouldn't you sit with me?'

'What's up? Scared I'll bite?'

She snapped her head up and was met with the dark chocolate eyes of the mercurial man she was hoping to avoid. 'Of course not...I just...I thought...'

Jason sat down beside her with a bounce and a wide teasing grin, his thigh rubbing up against hers. 'Well, stop thinking. It's not good for you.' He winked. Oh great, and now he was in a playful mood. She was seriously struggling to keep up.

Turning her face away, she gazed out of the window, hoping that he'd take the hint and leave her alone. But his cologne invaded her nostrils. There was no denying the fact that he smelled delicious, masculine, and earthy. And although it was very different to what she remembered from the Jason she'd known before, there was something strangely familiar about it. Maybe it was the underlying smell of just *him*. Whatever it was, it evoked unwelcome feelings from deep within her that she very much wanted to stamp on.

She was *not* going there again.

Leaning in closer to her, he whispered, 'You're going to have to talk to me at some point, Stevie. You can't avoid me all week.'

Hearing him say her name again made her chest ache. Why couldn't he just sod off and leave her alone? She turned to face him, but he hadn't moved back, and so his face was a little too close for comfort. 'I don't *have* to do anything,' she said flatly in a low voice, feeling relief in the knowledge that the coach was large and most of the kids had chosen to sit as far away from the staff as possible.

He smiled sadly. 'Have it your way...for now. But you *will* listen to me.' He dropped his voice to a barely audible whisper. 'Even if I have to tie you down to make sure you do.' He grinned and widened his eyes for a split second. She swallowed hard. *Shit.* He sniggered. 'Don't look so scared. I'm messing with you.' He shook his head as his shoulders juddered. He was clearly taking great delight in her shock.

Flaring her nostrils, she turned away from him again.

Shit head.

They arrived at the cycle hire place and everyone left the bus. Jason stormed to the front to take charge. Each student was issued a bike suitable for his or her height, along with a helmet. Matt, the owner of the bike hire company, came over to chat with Stevie. He was a handsome man, very tall and lean, with cropped black hair shaved at the sides in a kind flat Mohawk and more tattoos than anyone she'd ever met.

'So, you're the one who has the delights of escorting this lovely lot, are you? I'm Matt.' The man spoke in a strong Scottish accent and held out his hand to her. His warm smile revealed a line of crooked teeth. Oddly enough, they were still very white and just seemed to add to his charm.

After shaking his offered hand, she held up her palms. 'Guilty as charged, I'm Stevie.' Her cheeks warmed.

'How long are you up here for?' His delightful accent suited him and increased his appeal.

'Only for the week. Then I get to go back to only seeing them through the day time.'

His laugh was deep and quite sexy. 'So, do you get any

time off whilst you're here?' he asked with a glint in his eyes. She glanced over at Jason who was watching intently, a stern expression on his face.

She cast her gaze back in Matt's direction. 'Oh, I don't know...maybe. But I think we're on a pretty tight schedule.'

'Awww, that's a shame. I was going to ask if I could take you for a wee spot of lunch maybe. Or a drink?' He raised his eyebrows hopefully.

Suddenly, Jason came breezing in. 'All right, Matt? How you doing buddy?' He slapped the man on the back a little too hard.

'Hi, Reynolds. Just chatting to Stevie here. Asking her out but it seems you're holding the reins pretty tight on this trip, eh? No freedom day this time?'

Jason cleared his throat. 'Ah, not sure we have time for that this week. Lots to cram in, mate. You know how it is.'

'Okay, well, if you change your mind, give this gorgeous woman my number, eh?'

'Yeah, I doubt she'll be free.' Jason turned to glance at her through narrowed eyes.

Annoyed at his obvious, misplaced possessiveness, Stevie smiled widely at Matt. 'You can rest assured, Matt, that if I get the time, I'll be sure to get your number from Mr. Reynolds.' She turned to see Jason's nostrils flare. Feeling sure that she was beet red by now, she smiled and stepped away to check on the students.

Jason waited until Stevie had walked back to the kids and turned to Matt.

'Don't push it with her, okay? She's off limits.'

Matt smirked. 'And why would that be, my friend? Got yourself a wee crush, have we?'

Feeling his frustration rising he replied, 'It's not like that. It's...it's complicated. She's...she's just off limits, okay?'

Matt cocked his head inquisitively. 'Just to me? Or to you too?'

Running his hand over his hair, Jason shrugged. 'Like I said, it's not like that. She's from London, and I get the feeling she's the type to get hurt easily, that's all.'

Matt scrunched his face in disbelief. 'That's incredibly observant for someone you've only known for twenty four hours or less. What's going on, Jace?'

Jason spoke through clenched teeth. 'Nothing. Nothing is *going on*. Just leave it.'

Matt held his hands up. 'Okay, okay. But I think you're being unfair to the poor woman. She should be allowed to make the decision for herself. I could show her a good time. Know what I mean?' His look was lascivious.

Jason moved his face closer. 'That's exactly my problem, *mate*. She's too fucking good for you. You can't keep your dick in your pants, and she deserves more. She's not the type you can use for a quick fuck, all right? Trust me. I know.'

Matt gave him a knowing smile. 'Right, right. Been there already, have you?'

'You are walking a seriously fucking fine line. Now you're my mate, but I swear if you disrespect her like that again, I'll come back to see you, and you'll be eating your fucking meals through a straw.'

Matt laughed heartily. Clearly not taking Jason's threat seriously. 'Fuck me, Jace. You've got it bad, mate.' He patted him on the shoulder.

'I said it wasn't like that.'

'Whatever, mate. Don't sweat it. Off limits. Message

received loud and clear.' He saluted and walked away chuckling to himself.

Stevie was the last to be given her bike for the day, and Jason took it upon himself to deliver it personally.

He winked. 'Here you go. This should bring back fond memories.'

'Really? Why's that?' She knew that pleading ignorance was cruel, but she couldn't help herself. Maybe he needed knocking down a peg or two and perhaps she was the one to do it.

He held his chest as if she had shot him. 'Oooh harsh, Mrs. Norton. Harsh.' He smiled, showing those perfect teeth of his, but didn't say anything further on the matter.

'So...freedom day? I get a day off, do I? Maybe I could go for a drink with Matt.' She was testing Jason's reaction. Cruel again.

'Nah. He's a womaniser, that one.' He held his hands up. 'I mean, it's nothing to do with me, but I wouldn't let my sister go out with him if I had one.'

'Well, it's a good thing I'm not your *sister*, and that as you quite rightly stated it's *nothing* to do with you.' She turned and walked away. She hadn't quite received the jealous reaction she had hoped for deep down. He *had* looked pretty pissed off a few moments ago, but he seemed able to switch his emotions on and off like a light switch these days.

Once they had their helmets fixed in place, the kids set off enthusiastically. Stevie not so much. Luckily, the route had taken into account everyone's level of fitness—or lack thereof —and was mostly flat. The road they cycled was laid especially for bikes and weaved its way through the trees. The smell of fresh pine wafted through the warm summer air, and the sun cast dancing white lights and contrasting dark shadows before them as they rode. Rothiemurchus was such a stunning place. She had never experienced such tranquillity and beauty before. Nature was pretty bloody amazing.

Jason pulled up to cycle alongside her. 'This is the life, eh?'

His smile was infectious, and she couldn't help her own taking over her face. 'It's stunning.'

The kids and other staff cycled ahead leaving Jason and Stevie to lag behind. She tried to cycle faster to gain some much-needed distance but of course he caught up to her. She had no chance of being rid of him out here. He was much fitter than she was.

'Will you come to my cabin tonight?'

She turned her head towards him and a serious expression settled in place on his handsome features once again. He was pedalling with one hand on the handlebars and one hand resting on his toned thigh.

She shook her head. 'No, I can't. I'm working. I have responsibilities. I can't just come over like that.'

'Come over after the kids are settled. After lights out. We need to talk. You must have questions.'

Of course she had bloody questions. But she also had *feelings*. She wasn't sure she could stand to hear whatever he had to say, especially if he informed her there had been someone else. Although looking the way he did, there had to have been myriad *someone else's*. She remained silent, inwardly begging him to drop the subject.

But no, he continued pushing her. 'Please, just an hour of your time. That's all I need.'

She concentrated on the road ahead and chewed on her lip. She could see him in her peripheral vision, watching her, waiting for her decision. She sighed. 'I'll think about it, okay? But I'm promising nothing.'

'Okay. That'll do for now... I'll even go shirtless just for you. You know, give you something to drool over,' he teased.

'Eff off, Reynolds.' She hissed as loudly as she could without being overheard.

He laughed heartily. 'Remember...walk along past the gap in the trees to the walkway.'

She didn't answer. Instead, she found a burst of energy from somewhere and took off at a speed to catch up with the rest of the group.

CHAPTER FIVE

*T*he ride was a hell of a lot more enjoyable than Stevie had expected. And although she knew that cycling wasn't her thing, she could almost be convinced that it *could* be if she lived somewhere as beautiful as this.

Jason had left her alone for the rest of the ride. Whenever they stopped for a drink, she had watched him with awe as he took his time talking to the students about the flora and fauna around them. How the plants lived in competition for the sunlight and how there was a vast array of wildlife species all living in harmony under the canopy of the lofty trees. He talked about the circle of life and everyone had laughed when one of the kids had begun to sing a rendition of the well-known Elton John track.

Jason answered questions with enthusiasm and even the ones that the kids had thought a bit silly to ask had been met with positivity and praise for their braveness. He was amazing. And she hated him for it. How could he be so arrogant and lascivious in one breath and then be so nurturing and encouraging in his next? He was a true enigma, this man whom she thought she knew. Clearly he had changed beyond any recognition, and it was disconcerting in so many ways. None more so than the way he turned her on simply by a raise of his eyebrows or lick of his full lips. *Damn him for affecting me so much.*

Back at the campsite, the kids were all buzzing from their cycle ride. The camp's chef had prepared a hearty meal of beef stew and dumplings, which the kids seemed to devour at a rate of knots. After the meal there was a Jim Carrey movie shown in the main hut, and laughter rang out through the thick log walls and echoed around in the still night air outside. She had seen the movie several times, so she sat on the steps outside with her book. Concentrating was pretty impossible thanks to the noise and her inability to get her mind off Jason.

At eleven, the kids were ushered back to their dorms without protest. The fresh air and cycle ride had clearly taken its toll. She checked on the girls, who were all gushing over something when she walked in. As soon as they saw her, they all clamped their mouths shut, exchanged awkward glances, and sniggered.

'He's a bit fit that Mr. Reynolds, isn't he, Mrs. Norton?' Jess blurted as Stevie headed to the door.

She stopped and turned around. 'Well, he managed the bike ride without much effort, so yes. I suppose he is.'

The girls erupted in fits of giggles. 'No Miss, I mean *fit*... you know fit as in phwooooar! *That* kind of fit. Hunky...hot... you know? It's a...erm...what do you call it?' She waved her hands at her friends who stared blankly at her. 'You know... a...euphonium!'

Heat rose in her cheeks, embarrassed for both herself *and* for Jess. 'I think you mean *euphemism*, Jess. And to be honest, I hadn't noticed. But really, girls, I think it's a little inappropriate to speak in such a way about a member of the staff. Now come on, it's lights out!'

She slammed the door behind her as more giggles followed. She rolled her eyes and made her way back to her own cabin.

Once inside, she showered and changed into her pyjamas. She towel dried her hair, letting it fall around her shoulders in damp waves and slumped onto her bed, feeling far too wired considering the amount of exercise she had done. Standing again, she paced the room for a few minutes before she made the same mistake as the night before. Flicking her iPod onto random, she was initially relieved when a more recent track began to play. But after a few minutes of listening to the shiver inducing lyrics of 'Decode' by Paramore, she was in tears again and vowing angrily to completely change her track list.

Suddenly, the urge to go to Jason and get some answers was overwhelming. She wanted to slap his face. Scream at him. Ask him *why*. Hold him and pinch herself so that she knew this was not a cruel dream. Fate, if there was such a thing, had brought her here. Or was it divine intervention? Was this all part of God's mysterious plan?

Whatever it was, she couldn't eradicate the deep-seated feeling that this was *meant* to happen. It was time. Time to face the demons that had haunted her since she was eighteen years old and suffering a broken heart at the hands of the man she loved and trusted more than anything in the world. The only thing she had to ensure was that, no matter what he said, she would be guarded. She wouldn't let him in.

Not this time.

Not again.

Grabbing her fleece, she checked her appearance. Her

eyes were red and her face a little puffy from crying. She scooped her hair up into a scruffy bun on the top of her head, realising she looked a little bedraggled. But she decided it didn't matter, seeing as she wasn't out to seduce the man. She just wanted answers, nothing more. Despite his physical appeal, he had changed and she didn't know him anymore.

Before she could give both sides of her psyche the chance to argue the point and make her change her mind, she walked out of her door, grabbing the little torch that hung on the hook by the window as she passed. She closed the door softly behind her and walked as quietly as possible along the pathway to look for the break in the trees that Jason had mentioned.

Gravel and twigs crunched under her feet as she made her way through the eerie quiet of the night. A few moments later, the gap leading to the walkway stood before her. The cabin was homey looking. Appearances suggested that he actually *lived* here on site. There were solar lanterns hanging all around and some skirted the property on spikes in the ground. There was an orange glow coming from the window. She stood silently contemplating whether she was about to make a stupid, catastrophic mistake. Going down this road could be the answer to all her questions, but it could also shatter the fragile pieces of her heart that remained.

As she stood looking at his home, she saw him. He walked over to the window as if he sensed her presence. She ducked behind a tree so that she could still observe him without being seen. He was bare-chested just like he'd said he would be. His hair was loose once again, and as he looked out, his shoulders slumped and his head dropped.

He'd been looking for her.

Her breath caught in her throat and her heart ached. She waited for him to walk away from the window, and deciding she couldn't go through with it after all, she closed her eyes for a few moments, willing her heart rate to calm, and then she turned to walk away.

'Don't go.' His voice cracked as he spoke and she jumped.

It appeared that he had softened a little since she'd arrived. She wondered what had changed. Perhaps his arrogance was dissipating. He had seemed angry to see her when she had arrived at the camp. Accusatory even. Today, he'd been hell bent on embarrassing her with his dirty talk, but now it seemed he'd changed again. She couldn't keep up with his moods. Mercurial didn't even cover it.

She wasn't ready for a confrontation and this could easily turn into one. She had *no clue* what to expect.

Turning around she came face to face in the dim light with the man she had once loved. 'I can't do this, Jason. Not now...maybe not *ever*. I shouldn't have come.' She turned away once again.

He made a grab for her. 'Please...please. An hour of your time. I know I don't deserve it, but just hear me out? Please?'

She closed her eyes once again as the tears came. The familiarity of his voice made her chest ache. She turned to gaze up at him again. 'Ten minutes...that's all I can give you. And after tonight it's over...for good.'

Chewing on his lip, he nodded reluctantly, released her arm, and turned to walk towards his cabin. She followed.

Once inside he closed the door. 'Can I offer you a drink? I have wine...or beer...or I can make—'

'Wine would be good. I think I need something strong.'

He smiled. 'I have a nice single malt?'

'Wine, Jason, thanks.' His name falling from her lips seemed strange. It wasn't a word she had uttered often in the last ten years, although she had thought of him daily at first.

The thoughts became less frequent, but the dreams were relentless.

She was often haunted by dreams—or nightmares—where he slipped away from her as she tried desperately to grab for him. Or where he told her he didn't love or want her anymore, breaking her heart into a million tiny fragments. Sometimes she had dreams where he made love to her. Those were the most torturous dreams for a young woman to experience. At the age of age eighteen, he was the *only* man she had ever considered giving her virginity to, but it never happened. He left before she could give him that most precious gift.

Clearly an unwanted gift at that.

She watched as he poured two glasses of Pinot Noir from an expensive looking bottle and handed one to her. 'Please... sit.' He gestured to a leather sofa, and she did as he had asked.

Smiling, she glanced around what she could see of his home. 'It's very cosy...your cabin.'

He returned the smile warmly. 'Yes, small but perfectly formed as they say.'

They remained in silence for a few minutes. He came to sit beside her in all his shirtless glory and took her hand. She flinched and he let go.

'I want to start by saying how sorry I am—'

She scrunched her face. 'You're *sorry*? Oh well, that's it then. It's all fixed. I'll be going now.' She cringed at the bitter sound of sarcasm falling from her own tongue, but she still put her glass on the side table and stood to leave, affronted by his audacity.

He stood too, slamming his glass down angrily, slopping some of the contents over his hand. 'No!' He walked to block the doorway. 'I won't let you leave...not yet...not until you've heard me out.'

She closed her eyes and clenched her fists in front of her

body. 'Jason...I *can't* do this. How many times do I need to say that to you? All I want to do right now is to get on a train and go back to London and forget I ever came here.'

'I know and I understand that. Believe me, I do. This isn't exactly easy for me either. But I think you were meant to come here. I thought... Well, at first I thought you'd come here because you'd *found* me, but I know now that can't be true. Your name wasn't on the booking form. I'm guessing you're here to replace someone?'

'Yes, the original teacher, Mollie, broke her ankle. I was drafted in at the end of last week. I didn't even *want* to come.'

'I thought as much.' He chuckled. 'You were never one for the great outdoors. Well, unless it included a picnic down by the river in our favourite spot. Remember when we used to do that?'

She closed her eyes and nodded, determined to stop the flood of memories trying to invade her mind. 'Of course I do.'

His voice softened. 'I used to love spending time with you. I really *did* love you. I hope you believe that.'

She snapped her eyes open. 'No, no you didn't. If you'd loved me enough, you would've stayed. You would've kept your promise to me. We said we would *never* leave each other. Do *you* remember *that*?'

He pulled his lips into a line and inhaled deeply through his nose before speaking again. 'Please...please sit down.'

Reluctantly, she sat once again on the leather sofa. Silence engulfed them for minutes that dragged on like hours. He looked like he was calculating his next words, but it was eventually Stevie who broke the silence. 'How long have you been here, in Scotland I mean?' She picked up her glass and took a large gulp of wine before placing it back down with shaking hands.

He frowned. 'Oh...ahhh...around three years now.'

'Three years? Gosh, what made you decide to do this? You know, run a place like this?'

He ran a hand over his face. 'Lots of reasons. I wanted to do something outdoors. And I wanted to help underprivileged kids.'

'That's very noble of you,' she replied sardonically and immediately regretted it.

He shook his head slowly. 'No...not noble. I didn't do it to be noble. I did it because I realised how shitty some kids have it, and I saw...' He took a deep breath and his words trailed off.

Her interest piqued. 'What did you see?'

He let out a long breath. 'I saw things that I wish I could *un*-see. But the images are etched on my brain forever.' He closed his eyes for a few seconds as if pained by some memory that had popped into his head.

She gasped. 'What? When?'

'It's a long story, and I've only got you here for ten minutes, remember?' He smiled.

'Wasn't that the whole point? Getting me here so you could explain everything?'

'Yes...no...I don't really know. I just...I just wanted to be near you again.'

She smiled a cold smile and shook her head. 'It didn't bother you so much ten years ago.'

He clenched his jaw. 'No, you're wrong. It did. I should've...' His words trailed off again.

'Look, Jason.' She stood again. 'If you can't even finish a sentence, I may as well just go. This is a waste of time. And I need some sleep.'

He crossed the room and grabbed her arms. 'I should've made love to you. I should have given you that much.'

She stared at him wide eyed. 'What? So you could take

my virginity and *then* desert me?' Her acerbic tone left a bitter taste in her mouth.

He let go of her and stepped back, as if she'd slapped him. A line appeared between brows. 'No, no it's not like that. It was *never* like that... I mean, because it was what I wanted more than *anything*, to show you what you really meant to me.'

She clenched her teeth and fought back angry tears as she fronted up to the man who had caused her so much pain. 'Hmmm, let me refresh your memory of just what I *really* meant to you. I gave you my time and my friendship for years, Jason. I loved you with my *whole heart*. My mum—who was not the wealthiest of parents I hasten to add—spent God knows how much money on a *beautiful* dress so that you could take me to the Leavers' Ball, but instead of having the best night of my life I was abandoned, Jason. Abandoned by the *one man* in my life who I *thought* I could trust.' Her voice became louder as her anger grew.

'I gave you my heart and would've given you my body too...*willingly*. I thought you were worthy of my trust but I was *so wrong* about that, silly me. Because just like my arse-hole of a father, you *left*.' She prodded his hard chest with her finger as her voice broke. 'So, thank you for showing me just how much I *meant* to you. And I want you to know that I'm *glad* we didn't add sex into the toxic mix that you dished up to me, you selfish bastard. You didn't deserve my fucking virgin-ity! Now, I think I'll go if you don't mind.' She tried to pass him.

He grabbed her by the arms again. His voice was calm but his teeth were clenched. 'Okay...okay...all very fair points. I deserved to hear that. I get it. I *really* do, but you *don't* under-stand. I *had* to leave.'

'Really? Well, now it's *my* turn to leave. I've learned from the expert. Let go of my fucking arms. I don't want to spend another minute in your presence.' Her lip quivered and the threatening tears that she had been fighting betrayed her by spilling down her cheeks, leaving scorching trails in their wake.

Before she could protest further, he pulled her into his chest and cradled her in his arms. He held her tight as she let out the pain and anguish of ten long years without him.

'*Why*, Jason? *Why* did you leave me? What did I do wrong? I loved you so much.' She pulled away and pounded her fists into his chest. 'You *didn't* love *me*! You *can't* have loved me enough!' He let her hit him until she began to crumple. He caught her and lowered himself to the floor with her in his arms until he was leaning against the sofa with her on his lap. She continued to sob, pouring all her pent up anguish and heartache onto his bare flesh.

Once she had calmed and her sobs had subsided into whimpers, he tilted her chin up so that she met his gaze, their noses only an inch apart. His eyes trailed from hers down to her lips where they hesitated for a moment before locking onto her eyes again.

'I know you don't believe me. And I don't blame you, but you *were* the most important thing in my life. In fact, you *were* my life.'

Her heart fluttered at his closeness. 'Then please tell me why you left me.'

CHAPTER SIX

Stevie straddled Jason's lap, just like she would have done in his room all those years ago. Oddly enough, it didn't feel strange to be sitting this way. Jason tucked a strand of hair behind her ear and caught the last of her tears with his thumbs.

He closed his eyes and took a deep, slow, shaking breath. When he opened them again, he had a hard, distant look about him.

'It started at primary school. I was doing so well in every subject. I was getting really good reports. I was...what...ten?' He shrugged. 'Everything was going great. That is until I got chicken pox from Danny Milton. Remember?'

She vaguely remembered him being off school for a while, but at age ten she and Jason weren't such good friends. He was always teasing her. She nodded anyway.

'It made me really ill. I had such a bad case that I ended up in hospital for a few days and I was off school for weeks. Anyway, when I went back I struggled to catch up. I tried hard, but apparently I didn't try hard enough.' He clenched his jaw and she could feel the tension radiating through his body.

He closed his eyes again.

'Jason?'

He snapped his eyes open as if remembering she was there with him. 'Sorry...yeah. So my dad was...erm...not too happy that I'd fallen behind. He was so used to being able to brag to his friends that his eldest son was the brightest kid in school. Me lagging behind suddenly meant that he had to make excuses for me.'

She frowned. 'What do you mean he had to *make excuses* for you? He's your dad. Why would he have to tell anyone *anything*? You'd been ill, for goodness sake.'

'Yep, most parents would see it that way too. Mum did. But not *him*...no...*he* was pissed off that I got seven out of ten in my spelling test that week instead of my usual ten.'

She swallowed hard. 'So what's this got to do with anything between you and I?'

'He started by just slapping me around the head and insulting me. It hurt, but I was a tough kid.'

'Again, what has this got—'

'Stevie, I'm trying to start at the beginning...please.'

She cringed. 'Sorry...okay...go on.'

'He'd warn me to try harder. I *would* try really hard, but no matter what happened... If I didn't get full marks, he'd slap me around the head and back a few times and call me thick. Tell me I would amount to nothing... I was *ten*.'

She gasped. 'That's so cruel.'

His laugh was humourless. 'You think?'

'Did things get worse?'

'Oh, hell yeah. I didn't dare get poor grades for anything. I even tried lying. But I'm human...humans make mistakes, although *he* wouldn't accept that. No kid of his was going to make him a laughing stock. That's what I was reminded of regularly.'

An unwelcomed picture began to build in her mind. She bit her lips to stop herself from speaking as he continued.

'The older I got, the harsher the punishments were if I didn't quite meet his expectations. He had a piece of garden cane that he kept in his shed. If I got less than the expected full marks, he'd remind me with the cane across my back just how badly I'd done. Not that I needed reminding. I felt humiliated enough simply by hearing him belittle me, telling me how stupid I was. Telling me how he wished I'd never been born and that I was an embarrassment. That I'd ruined his life. I'd ruined his life.' He shook his head as if disbelieving his own words. 'But he was clever...he never left permanent marks. The hits were hard enough to hurt like hell, but not enough to scar me, initially. I was told that if I tried to complain things would get worse and that no one would take me seriously anyway.'

As tears welled up in her eyes once again, she had the overwhelming urge to comfort him. To hold him and try to erase the horrid memories he'd harboured for all this time. But instead, she sat silently, allowing the tears to spill over as she listened.

'The further on in school I was the stakes got higher and higher. It became less about my grades and more about him just hating me. He'd use any excuse.' He snorted a dry mirthless laugh. 'By the time I was eighteen, we'd gone beyond the garden cane and moved on to the leather belt.' Suddenly, he made direct eye contact with her and held her face gently in his hands. 'Stevie, what I wanted...what I desired more than anything in my life at that time was to make love to you. To lose myself in you. To just forget everything. I wanted to love you and be loved by you...but...I couldn't. The marks that were being left on my body then were...ugly... I didn't want you to see. I didn't want you to be repulsed. And I didn't want you to know what a coward I was by letting it happen.' His lip trembled as he spoke.

She watched the man before her begin to crumble. His glassy eyes held so much pain and regret. He had tortured himself more than she could ever hurt him. Not that she wanted to do that. Not *now*.

Her tears were relentless. 'How could you think that? How could you think I wouldn't still love you? What we had went way beyond looks, Jason. How could you think that I would have let that continue? I could've done something to help.' Her voice was just above a whisper.

He smiled sadly. 'You couldn't have done anything. You were such a beautiful girl...inside and out. I didn't want you to be tainted by knowing all this shit back then. It was *my* problem to deal with.'

'But why didn't you report it? Get someone to make him stop?'

'I didn't know who to tell back then. And I didn't want him to get into trouble, as stupid as that sounds. He was still my dad, and he would still tell me he loved me when Mum and Dillon were around. I'd believe him, and then it'd be back to the beatings when I'd not done the right thing. I still...still have faint scars, but the worst marks weren't the physical ones. He made me feel worthless...like I didn't deserve happiness. He took a wrecking ball to my self-esteem. I hated myself as well as him. I was so sure that I deserved the treatment. I was so sure that I'd done something terrible to have been punished in such a brutal way.'

A sob left her throat as she imagined him being so terrified that he couldn't tell anyone and that he'd felt the need to stay covered up in front of her, the girl he loved. She had always thought he was waiting. He had always told her that's what he was doing, and she'd had no reason to disbelieve him. He had told her he wanted their first time to be perfect, but in the end, she thought he hadn't wanted her at all. Clearly, now she realised she was so very wrong,

'I'm so sorry, Jason. I should've known.'

He gripped her arms. 'No, don't you *dare* blame yourself. This is *not* your fault. I won't have you feeling guilty for me. There was *nothing* you could've done.'

She placed her hands on his chest. His heart was racing under her touch. 'But it wasn't *your* fault either. You didn't deserve any of that.' She reached up to touch his cheek.

'I didn't know that at the time. I felt...I felt like such a disappointment...like I could do nothing right. You were the only light in my dark tunnel of a life. I just wanted... no...*needed* to get away from *him*...from my life.' His bottom lip quivered and a tear balanced on his lower eyelid, teetered for a spilt second and then fell. 'I knew I hadn't done as well in my finals as he'd want. I *knew* I wasn't going to get the required four A's.' His voice broke again.

'That was going to be another reason for him to hit me and make me feel like shit. *He* wanted me to be a doctor. *I* never wanted that. It meant more to him to be able to brag to his friends and live vicariously through me than it did to have me happy. And if I'm honest, I have no idea what would've happened if he laid another finger on me...or belt...or whatever the hell implement of torture awaited me. But I'd turned eighteen, and I couldn't wait around to find out. I would've killed him. I'd been on the verge of retaliation so often, but I didn't want to *be* like him. And I couldn't tell you. I couldn't tell Dillon. I couldn't tell *anyone*. When I left I didn't *want* to be found. If I'd have been found, I would've ended up coming back to more of the same or...or worse. I would've ended up in prison...or dead.'

She nodded and lifted her hands to gently wipe his tears away. She wished at that moment that she could go back. She would've done anything she could to stop it all from happening.

'I hope you understand why I couldn't tell you. I know how much you loved me, and I know you would've tried to intervene. So I couldn't risk you getting involved...not in *any* way.'

'Did...did your mum know?'

Jason huffed out a held breath. 'I honestly don't know. It was all so well hidden. But she can't have been totally oblivious to the fact that our relationship was strained. How can you live in the same house as someone who's capable of that level of cruelty and not know? But I didn't blame her. She was probably scared too.'

'Did he do the same to Dillon? Or your mum?'

'No, I kept an eye on Dillon. I think I maybe *would* have killed him if he'd started on my little brother...and my mum was always just so...positive all the time. They never argued. Well I never saw or heard them. She was maybe in some kind of denial, self-preservation and all that. I'm guessing if she did know she believed if she ignored it long enough it would stop...or go away maybe. I really don't know. I know how much she loved me though. My heart tells me she had no idea.'

Placing her hands on either side of his face, she rested her forehead on his. 'I...I hate him. I hate him so much for ruining your life...and in turn, ruining my life too.'

Jason clenched his jaw and closed his eyes for a few moments. 'No one hates him more than I do. *No one.*'

'Have you seen him since?' She wondered how much he actually knew about life back home.

'Nope. I never made contact with anyone. Once I left, that was it. I drew a line under everything. I couldn't look back. I joined the army and tried to forget.'

She raised her brow. 'The army?'

He smiled at her reaction. 'Yes, I needed some way of getting my anger and aggression out in a controlled way. The army taught me how to channel my feelings into something positive. I needed the discipline. Fighting for my country was...well...if anything good could come from all this shit, then *that* was it.'

'When you talked about wanting to un-see things, was that connected to your time in the army?'

He nodded. 'I saw terrible things. I saw my friends killed. I saw innocent people killed. It was horrific. I still have nightmares about the things I experienced.'

She closed her eyes, dreading delivering the next piece of information. 'Oh God, Jason, you don't know.'

'Know what? What's wrong?'

'Oh Jason, I'm so, so sorry. Your mum...she passed away... two years ago.'

A pained sob left his body, and he crumpled into her chest

CHAPTER SEVEN

*S*tevie held onto Jason as he convulsed with agonising sobs. She could tell that the news of his mother's death had been like a blow to the solar plexus. The painful heart rending cries racking his body were almost too much for her to bear. But bear them she did. She stroked his hair as he rested his head on her shoulder, his tears soaking through her fleece and tank top. Her own tears fell silently as she clung to him.

She had visited Shirley in hospital on several occasions and had been support for her through the years that Jason was missing. Shirley had always said Stevie was like a daughter to her. Her illness had simply gotten worse and worse until it finally took her. Stevie now knew that guilt could have played a huge part in her not fighting the heart disease. It was as if Shirley felt it was somehow a befitting and just punishment. Looking back now, things made a lot more sense.

Jason cried for what felt like an age. When he finally stopped, he gazed up at her with a look of deep regret. 'I should've been there.' He paused for a moment, deep in thought. 'I think I always presumed they'd go on forever...you know...somehow frozen in time. Don't get me wrong, I know people change and life goes on, but naïvely I just thought Mum would be fine.' His voice broke again and her heart lurched.

'A lot can happen in ten years,' she whispered sadly.

'I'm realising that now. It doesn't feel like ten years. God, I was so selfish.' He covered his face with his hands.

She gripped his hands and pulled them away. 'No, Jason. You did what you had to do. I know that now. I had no idea any of those things were happening. And I'm so angry with your dad. I—'

'He's not my dad. He stopped being my dad the minute he laid a hand on me. I have no father. I have some wanker who donated sperm...that's it.'

'Sorry, I didn't mean—'

'No, don't be sorry. I'm the one who's sorry. I went about everything the wrong way.'

She shook her head vehemently. 'No, you were still a kid. We'd had only just turned eighteen. You took yourself out of a very difficult situation. That was the only thing you could do.'

He glanced at the clock and shook his head. 'Look, it's gone one. I'm exhausted. Why don't I walk you back to your cabin and we'll talk tomorrow... Well, later today.'

'It's fine. I can make my own way back. You should get some sleep. It's not far to walk. Unless I'm going to be eaten by mountain lions or something.' She giggled.

He frowned. 'Stevie, this is the Cairngorms not the Yukon.'

She smiled at his answer. 'Funny, I had the same conversation with someone the day we arrived.'

He smirked. 'Eh? What are you on about?'

'Oh nothing. Right... I'll be off.' She stood to leave.

He stood too and enveloped her in his arms. 'Thank you.'

She pulled her brow in. 'For what? Making you cry?'

'For letting me explain.'

'It's fine. It fills in the missing pieces...mostly. But I'm sure you have more to tell me.'

'Why don't you come again after lights out and we'll talk more? I have more wine.'

'It's a date.' She clamped her hand over her mouth as soon as the words had fallen out. 'Sorry, I didn't mean—'

'That's okay. I know what you meant.' He kissed her head. 'Are you sure you don't want me to walk you back?'

'No, some of the little blighters might see if they're up, which I wouldn't put past them. I don't want to be giving them the wrong impression. Goodnight, Jason.'

'G'night.'

She switched on her little torch and made her way down the narrow path, which led to the main clearing. The night was spookily quiet apart from the odd hoot of an owl and the rustling of the gentle breeze through the trees. The moon cast a pale glow over the site and the mountains in the distance, highlighting everything in an ethereal silver glow as she walked wearily back to her cabin, feeling emotionally drained. Once inside, she collapsed into her bed and fell into a fitful sleep plagued by nightmares of a frightened adolescent being hurt with canes, belts, and horrid words.

Day Three of Hell

Stevie awoke with a start at seven and sat bolt upright. A faint knocking rattled her door. *Ugh, that must be what woke me.* She stretched as she walked over and opened the door.

David stood there smiling. 'Morning, sleepyhead,' he all but whispered. 'Breakfast is being served down in the main hut in about half an hour, so you need to get a move on.'

'David, why are you speaking to me in that rather bizarre, theatrical whisper?'

He cleared his throat. 'Oh, sorry, I'm not sure. Are...are you coming for breakfast?'

The sun had already made an appearance and the weather looked bright and warm, but all she wanted to do was to crawl back into bed and go back to sleep. 'Yeah, can you give me ten minutes or so? I didn't sleep too well, and I need a shower to wake me up.'

He nodded. 'Oh yeah...sure... I'll go and make sure the kids are all getting ready. Although, *you* may need to chivvy the girls along a bit. They're all too busy applying full make up in the hope that Jason will ask one of them to marry him, or something.' He rolled his eyes.

She couldn't help but snigger at that. She could see the appeal though. Jason was certainly an attractive man. His dark hair and dark eyes, along with his stubble and outdoorsy ruggedness, made him incredibly sexy. And that was before you considered his defined, sculpted physique. A shiver ran down her spine, making her physically shake.

'Oooh, I hope you're not coming down with something, Mrs. Norton.' David wagged a finger at her accusingly.

She rolled her eyes—which was becoming a regular occurrence around this guy. 'What? No! I'm just waking up, David. I'll see you in ten.' *Good grief.* She slammed her door in his face, and heard him chuntering as he walked away. *He can be such an irritating arse.* She grabbed her towel and toiletries, went into her small en-suite, turned the water on, and allowed it to heat to piping hot before stepping under the cascade where she let the water relax her tense shoulders.

Ten minutes later, she was dressed in black shorts and tank top with a pale blue shirt over the top. She laced up her walking boots and pulled her hair into a scruffy bun atop her head. She applied sunscreen to her face and went without makeup; apart from a little concealer to hide the dark circles that were there as a result of a lack of sleep and crying the night before.

When she entered the main hut, there was a buzz of conversation, which meant she could enter almost unnoticed. She got in line for food and glanced around the room almost immediately, making eye contact with a rather tired looking Jason. His hair was scraped back into a half ponytail again and he wore a black fitted T-shirt with the WFH logo. The shirt showed the definition in his chest and biceps that she hadn't had an opportunity to appreciate the night before thanks to the drama that had ensued. He smiled warmly and nodded at her. He gestured to the seat beside him, and she nodded her acquiescence.

Once her plate was loaded up with bacon, scrambled egg, haggis, and a tattie scone, she made her way across the room to where Jason sat surrounded by girls. Once she had placed her tray down and sat beside him, he leaned in and whispered, 'Thanks for saving me from my fan club.'

She sniggered as the girls looked daggers in her direction. 'Girls, if you're all finished up, can you go and find out which groups you're in for the day please?'

The girls whined and moaned but left the table and made their way over to where Dorcas stood with a clipboard, smiling broadly as always. She glanced over and her smile faded as her gaze flitted between Stevie and Jason. Her brow crumpled in what could only be interpreted as confusion.

'What's the story with you and Dorcas, then?' Stevie enquired, looking down at her food.

Jason's fork stopped mid-air, en-route to his mouth. 'Story? There isn't one. She works for me...full stop.'

She tried to sound nonchalant. 'So you're not...you know...*together*?'

He chuckled. 'Absolutely not. Whatever gave you that impression?'

She looked up into smiling eyes. 'Oh, just the way she looks at you. Like you're her hero or something.'

He laughed heartily. 'The way she *looks* at me? I don't know what you're talking about.' He shook his head incredulously.

'Oh come on. She positively swoons every time she speaks to you.'

'Well, I can assure you that she and I are nothing but colleagues.' He popped a mouthful of food in and chewed with a wide grin on his face. 'Not that it's any of your business if we were *more*.'

The heat rose in her cheeks, and she stared down at her plate again. 'I wasn't asking because I'm *interested*,' she muttered.

'Oh, but you are.'

She snapped her head up to look him in the eye. *Oh we're back there again are we? Arrogant shit.* He was staring intently at her, which made her heart rate increase. 'Oh for goodness sake, I've said it before, but here I go again...get over yourself, Jason. Not every woman drools over a muscular man with come-to-bed eyes,' she snapped in a loud whisper rather like the one David had been using earlier.

A smile spread across his face. 'Oh really? So ogling a shirtless man through the trees is just something that one does to while away the hours, is it?'

She stood. 'Suddenly, I appear to have lost my appetite,' she snarled. Hastily, she left the table and went to empty her food into the garbage. When she glanced over, Jason was laughing to himself. *Idiot*. She chuntered under her breath. *How dare he presume that I'm still attracted to him? Arrogant, self-centred pig.*

CHAPTER EIGHT

*S*tevie stood frozen to the spot, staring towards the ground eighty metres below her position at the top of the rock face. She was expected to abseil down it.

Hmmm.

'Come on, Mrs. Norton! You can do it!'

'Yeah, Miss! Go on! We've all done it!'

'It's not that scary, Miss. The only bad thing that could happen is that the rope could break and you could fall to your death, but...well that *hardly ever* happens.'

The words of encouragement from her students were doing little to spur her on, or to make her believe that jumping off a cliff with a thin harness around her crotch was a good plan.

Jason stood by waiting for her to pluck up the courage to do the activity that everyone else, including David, had already done...*twice*. Heights were never something she had worried about, but then she had never walked off any attached to a rope before. She had always maintained a safe distance from the edge of such lofty summits. And unlike *some* people, she had never had the desire to bungee jump, paraglide, or go up in a hot air balloon. No, Stevie and heights had a mutual respect—she would keep away from them if they would keep well away from her. Terra firma was King.

Much to her chagrin, David appeared beside her. 'Not going over, Mrs. Norton? It's fine...really it is, if you're too scared. Perhaps you should look after the lunches and things when we go kayaking tomorrow, eh?' She narrowed her eyes and turned to stare at the grinning imbecile who insisted on patronising her.

'I'm not *scared,* David. I'm just...a little...*nervous.* There's a vast difference between trepidation and fear.' She turned to see Jason sniggering. *Oh great! So no one thinks I can do this. Right. I'll bloody show the lot of them.* She stomped over to where Jason stood and placed her hands on her hips. 'Okay, Mr. Reynolds...strap me up.'

'Now you're talking,' he whispered, as he leaned in to check and secure her harness, and in her opinion, he spent a little too much time doing so. Her cheeks flushed at the suggestive way in which he addressed her. *Whatever is that supposed to mean? Oh God, he's turned into some kind of pervert in the last ten years, hasn't he? All this talk of tying me down and strapping me up with that glint in his eye. Just great.*

Once everything was secured and double-checked, Jason placed his hands on her shoulders and squeezed. 'Come on, you can do this. Just remember the instructions I gave you, and you'll be absolutely fine.'

Taking a very deep breath, which did nothing to calm her jangling nerves, she got into position. Teetering on the edge, she began to feed the rope through her gloved hands as she had been instructed. Her heart hammered, as if trying to escape through her sternum, and a sheen of sweat broke out on her upper lip.

'Okay, Stevie, push off with your feet and feed the rope through like I showed you,' Jason called over the edge to her.

Following the instructions, she pushed off the rock face and plummeted a few feet with a loud squeal. The pupils both on the ground beneath her and looking over the cliff face cheered and clapped. She glanced up and caught a look of obvious pride on Jason's face as he stood applauding along with the others.

Before she knew it, she touched down on good old terra firma again, and once she was uncoupled from the ropes, the waiting group drew her into a hug. She felt exhilarated and relieved all at the same time. A sense of achievement washed over her, and she couldn't help jumping around and applauding herself too. *What a buzz!*

After completing the abseil several more times, the staff and students hiked towards their next activity. Rock climbing. The outdoor climbing wall was something that many of the kids were excited about. Once again, she was dreading it. She'd spent the morning conquering her fear of descending from a great height and now she would have to climb one. And even though the direction of the journey was different, the prospect of plummeting to her death still preyed on her mind as a distinct possibility. And at least this morning had involved little effort as the ropes did most of the work. This time there would be muscles involved that she hadn't used in a very long time.

Jason caught up with her. 'So, you did it.' His wide, gorgeous grin almost had her swooning on the spot.

'Did you doubt that I would, Mr. Reynolds?' she asked defiantly.

'Not at all, Mrs. Norton. But I'm still proud of you.'

Her heart swelled in her chest, and she couldn't help the smile that became fixed in place. Remembering the events of the night before, she glanced up at him. 'Are you okay today? You know...after our...after what I told you...and what you told me?'

He pursed his lips. 'I'm not sure if I would say I'm *okay*, but I'm feeling a little better about things...you know, after what you said about my decision.' He stopped and grabbed her arm so that the rest of the group passed them by.

'Oooh go on, sir, give her a kiss!' One of the students jeered as others wolf-whistled, earning themselves a glare.

She held her hand up and cupped her ear. 'What's that? Are you asking for a month's detention when we get back, Mr. Carter...Mr. Hanks?' She scowled in the teenagers' direction.

The boys cringed. 'Erm...no, Mrs. Norton...sorry, Mrs. Norton.' They walked on.

'What is it, Jason?' She frowned when the students were out of earshot.

He looked hesitant. 'I just...wanted to say that...well, it meant a lot to finally be able to explain things last night. I still feel guilty, but you helped such a lot. Thank you.'

'It's fine. I think maybe I can move on now. You know, getting closure on this is a huge thing for me. I was angry at you for so long.'

He nodded. 'I totally understand. Are you still coming to talk again tonight?'

'Oh...I...I don't really think—'

'Please, come round. I'd like you to. I still feel like we have unfinished business.'

Taking no convincing at all, she nodded. 'Okay. I'll come around again.'

The huge wall with its colourful hand and foot holds loomed

over them. Stevie gulped as her eyes trailed up, up, up. There were indentions and protrusions mimicking those of a real rock face. The kids stood in awed silence, craning their necks up to the top of the face. Some exchanged worried glances.

'Okay gang. Now listen up.' Jason's voice boomed out around the clearing where the fake rock face stood. 'This is a little more effort than this morning. And that's why we do it this way around. You'll need your wits about you, and you'll need to believe in yourselves. You *can* do this. I know it may look daunting, but you will be very safe, so there is nothing to worry about. Listen to the instructions you're given, and pay attention to any further instructions whilst you are on the ascent. But most of all...have fun!'

The students whooped and cheered their appreciation and set about collecting their helmets and harnesses from the wall's staff members.

She watched as he instructed his group of kids on how to carry out the activity safely. She couldn't help admiring once again how he dealt with the over eager teens. He was calm and authoritative whilst remaining approachable and friendly at the same time. He was so good at his job. She could see why he loved it so much too. Seeing the faces of these usually disinterested and often angry children light up was such a privilege.

An hour or so into the activity, she was chatting to Suzie, one of the wall's staff, when a boy cried out. She ran over to see one of the students frozen half way up the wall. Corey Carter was usually the class joker and was known as a tough kid. Not now though. Now he looked terrified and so young. Her heart ached as she longed to help him. She watched as Jason attached his karabiner to the safety line and began to make his way with ease up the hundred-foot wall.

All the time he was climbing, he was calling out to Corey

to keep his attention. He managed to make him laugh, which had all the other frightened-looking kids joining in. Stevie's heart swelled with pride. Her eyes were drawn to Jason's muscles as he climbed with little effort. His calf muscles tensed and relaxed as his feet flexed and moved from one hold to another. His biceps bulged, expanding and contracting with each grip. Finally, he reached Corey and patted his shoulder, talking to him and eliciting a series of nods from the boy who had visibly begun to relax. She couldn't hear what was being said, but it was evident that whatever it was Corey was gaining confidence. His whole demeanour changed. It was truly remarkable.

With assistance and support from Jason, Corey began to make his ascent again and was rewarded with cheers from both the ground and the top of the face, his peers encouraging him and willing him on. Tears stung her eyes in response to the immense sense of togetherness she was witnessing. Not *once* had anyone laughed *at* him for being afraid. Surely, this was down to the way Jason had encouraged them to work as a team from day one at the camp.

Escorted all the remaining distance to the summit, Corey eventually made it to the top and was immediately pulled into a group hug. Applause and cheers rang out, and she joined in, awash with an overwhelming sense of pride for both Corey and Jason, who had very quickly become her hero.

On the way back to the coach, she caught up to Jason. 'You were amazing today. Thank you so much for what you did for Corey. I'm sure he'll never forget you.'

Jason shrugged. 'Yeah? Well, now you can see why I love my job so much.'

It was true. He was every bit in his element here. He was in the right place for him. And that both saddened and thrilled her. The contradiction of her feelings was becoming familiar to her.

When the coach arrived back at the camp, Jason went straight to his cabin. Before entering, he had decided to gather a few flowers from his wild garden. The blues, yellows, and pinks of the wild blooms were so pretty they would surely impress Stevie. This train of thought suddenly concerned him. *Although...why do I want to impress her?* He shook his head. There was no point trying to analyse the garbled emotions racing around his psyche at the moment. He'd been on a rollercoaster ride for the last twenty-four or so hours, and she was only here for a few days. Nothing could happen, even if he wanted it to. This was a fateful meeting meant to bring closure to them both. The sooner he accepted that the better.

He checked around the cabin and tidied away the sheet music he'd been going through. He placed his guitar back in its stand and cleared the dirty laundry from his bedroom floor into the hamper. Not that he was expecting her to spend any time in *there*. Of course not. He was merely thinking there was always the possibility he would show her around. That's all. Nothing else.

Not. A. Thing.

When stepping out of his cabin again, he caught the aroma of chef's chilli wafting on the slight breeze from the main cabin. His stomach growled, protesting its emptiness and he set off. When he arrived at the main hut, she was once again nowhere to be seen. He grabbed a quick bite to eat and then went back to collect his guitar and make his way to the log circle near the clearing, ready for the evening's camp fire sing along.

Harry, one of the other camp staff, had already collected the logs and set the fire going. The huge bags of marshmallows and toasting forks were on the small wooden table. Everything was set. Jason smiled as he took his seat and began to tune his guitar.

He hadn't sung in a long while. Under normal circumstances, Dorcas did all the singing. She'd studied music at university and had a beautiful voice, apart from when she was listening to her iPod and singing along. It amazed Jason that someone so musical could sound like a strangled cat. Tonight, he needed to change things around. The trouble was there were only so many songs that he was confident singing and playing. One in particular was a song that brought back painful memories. Should he do it? Should he take the plunge? He wasn't sure.

'So, are you going to sing tonight, Jason?' Dorcas must have read his mind. She sat beside him on a large tree stump in front of the fire.

He shook his head. He still hadn't quite made his mind up. 'Oh...I don't know about that.'

She smiled. 'You forget that I've heard you singing in the shower.'

Oh God, not that again. She makes it sound like she was in there with me. 'Yeah, well...less said about that the better, I think.'

She bit her lip. 'Oh, I don't know. I liked it.'

Oh great and now she's flirting with me again. 'Well, be thankful you only heard me through the wall, eh? Up close and personal may not be the same.'

'I think I could handle it.' She gave him a look that contained both lust and sadness. *Poor wee girl.* It was never going to happen, and deep down she must have known that. He didn't answer her right away. What could he say?

When the right words evaded him, he said, 'Yeah...well... can you give me a hand to get some more wood for the fire? There's a pile over there.' He gestured behind them in a desperate bid to change the subject. Placing his guitar down, he went off towards the trees, pulling extra logs to the fire in readiness for the evening's festivities.

Dorcas followed close behind. 'You seem to be getting on well with that teacher. What's her name? Stevie? Strange name for a girl.'

'Oh, yeah. She seems...erm...nice. And...*you've* got the cheek to say *her* name's strange.'

'Okay, fair comment. Any special requests for me to sing tonight?'

'Nope. Just sing what you like. I tend to know stuff that the kids won't. I show my age.' He laughed.

'I'm only five years younger than you, you know.'

'Yes, exactly. You're five years closer to the kids' age than I am.'

Dorcas didn't seem impressed with his answer. She mumbled something about going to grab her fleece and stomped away. Jason scrunched his brow in confusion, shook his head, and picked up his guitar once again.

To Stevie, the chilli was a welcomed delight after such a physically exhausting and gruelling day. After dinner, the students were all invited to join the staff for a good old fashioned sing along by the campfire. She took the opportunity to return to her cabin, shower, and apply some after sun lotion. She changed into black linen trousers and a white long sleeved T-shirt. The evening air was thick and humid, and the fire would mean she was plenty warm enough. Combing through her hair in front of the mirror, she decided to leave it to dry naturally, meaning that it fell in dark auburn waves around her shoulders. She applied a little lip-gloss and went to join the students as they sat around waiting for the marshmallows to be handed out. It wouldn't be a proper campfire sing along without marshmallows after all.

The atmosphere around the fire was buzzing with anticipation. From what she had gathered, she knew that none of the kids had ever been camping, nor had they been involved in a sing along like this one. Her heart filled with happiness at seeing their young faces glowing in the amber light of the fire as it crackled away before them. Jason wasn't around, but Dorcas was chatting to Harry at the opposite side of the group.

A hand appeared on her shoulder and she turned smiling, only to be disappointed when it was David. 'Oh hi,' was all she could manage with little to no enthusiasm.

He crouched beside her and whispered, 'Hi, Stevie... listen...I was wondering...I brought a nice bottle of single malt with me and wondered if you might fancy a nightcap after the sing along? You know...once the kids are all tucked up in bed.'

She cringed at his encouraging smile. 'Oh thanks, David, but I'll pass. I'm not a whiskey drinker if the truth be told, and I really am shattered. I think I'll just go back to my cabin and read.'

His smile faded, and he looked very disappointed, rather like a chastised puppy dog. 'Oh yes...of course. No worries. I just thought I'd ask.'

'Well that was very thoughtful, thank you.' She suffered a little stab of guilt for lying. He stood and made his way to the other side of the fire to sit down.

Dorcas and Harry disappeared through the trees but soon returned, and this time Harry was carrying a set of bongos.

They all sat down once again and continued chatting with the students. Dorcas handed out some percussion instruments much to the delight of the eager kids.

Jason arrived soon after and picked up the guitar that was propped up against the large log at the opposite side of the huddle. *Oh my word, he's going to play.* A surge of nervous excitement shot through her at the prospect of seeing him strum his guitar again. He looked so right holding it. Like some kind of rock god with his long hair and muscular arms. And she was eager to hear him sing again. But after he had greeted the group, he nodded to Dorcas as he began to strum the opening chords of something she didn't recognise. Suddenly, Dorcas began to sing. Her sweet voice carrying through the air and making the teenage boys swoon. Disappointment washed over her as Dorcas sang of wanting what she couldn't have, and she wondered if Dorcas had chosen the song for Jason. Some of the kids sang along with big smiles on their faces.

She had a nice voice. But it wasn't *her* voice that Stevie wanted to hear, although it was wonderful to see and hear Jason play his guitar again. His sleeves were rolled up, and the tendons in his arms flexed as he played. *Why the hell does that do something to me?* He was such a talented guitarist, and she had often wondered why he never joined a band when they were younger like many of their school mates had. But then again, he spent most of his time with *her* so that would explain it.

A few more well-known songs followed and had the kids clapping and singing along enthusiastically. She turned to find David joining in and singing completely out of tune with a huge grin on his face. She couldn't help laughing.

Dorcas then sang a solo again, accompanied by Jason. She smiled longingly at him as she sang the words to 'Love Story'

97

by Taylor Swift. Oblivious to the message she was trying to send out, Jason strummed with his eyes closed as the group of teenagers joined in at the chorus. It was a song that she had loved ever since one of the more challenging girls from her year five Chemistry class had wowed the whole school with her rendition at the Christmas concert last year.

Watching him play made her heart ache. He looked so wonderful immersed in the music with his mouth forming the words silently. She wanted to climb into his lap and kiss that mouth, but she knew that she couldn't.

When she had finally given up hope of hearing him sing, he cleared his throat and her heart lurched into her mouth. He looked kind of shy and a little embarrassed as he glanced around the crowd but avoided any eye contact with her.

He cleared his throat for the second time. 'Okay you lot... you've heard the talented singer amongst us, but now it's my turn.' The girls' eyes lit up and they exchanged wide smiles and excited nudges. 'Now judging by the ages of most of you, I'm guessing you've probably never heard this song before but bear with me. It's one of the only ones that I *can* sing, and I think Dorcas here could do with a rest.' He glanced at her as she touched his arm, smiling warmly.

Stevie suddenly felt very possessive, and her nostrils flared involuntarily at seeing the intimate exchange.

'Anyway, this song is from a band who were quite well known back when I was around eighteen. And that's...oh...ten years ago. I...I learned to play it to impress a girl...' Her heart lurched as the group wolf whistled and giggled at his admission. 'Anyway, the original has got a couple of swears in it, so I'm going to perform the toned down version.' The group booed, making Jason chuckle. 'So...it's a song by a band called Staind. This is 'It's Been Awhile'. I hope I don't ruin it too much and that you enjoy my little contribution.'

Stevie pulled her lips between her teeth, and her eyes began to sting as he began to strum the opening chords.

She closed her eyes and was transported back in time ten years, to his bedroom floor where she sat as Jason played the song and sang the words to her. In her mind's eye, she could see the pain etched on his face as his hair flopped over his closed eyes. Now that she knew the hidden meaning behind the lyrics, her heart ached, and she chewed at the inside of her cheek, trying to get hold of her emotions and fend off the threatening tears.

No one would understand if she got emotional here and now. But the words evoked so much pain that she was sure her eyes would overflow with the salt water desperate for release, regardless of how much she tried to stop it from happening. *Why did he choose to sing this tonight?* She opened her eyes and was met with the dark gaze of the man she had once loved. She listened and every single word he communicated to her touched her soul. Certain lyrics sent shivers down her spine, and she swallowed hard as she watched his lips form the heart breaking words. As the song ended, he smiled at her but only briefly before closing his eyes and dropping his head. The group erupted with applause and cheers, thankfully oblivious to their exchanged glances.

After the campfire sing-along, Jason made his way back to his cabin to mentally prepare himself for Stevie's visit. Would she come after what he'd done at the campfire? If she did, what would he tell her today? Would he tell her about the warzones in which he'd seen active service? Would he tell her about the dead bodies, the bloodshed, and the screams and cries of the innocent people that plagued his nightmares? He doubted that he could even bring himself to talk about that. Would he tell her about the wealthy businessmen he'd acted as security for after the army? He really didn't know.

Should he tell her that he hadn't loved anyone since her? That all he'd had was loveless sex to release tension and to help him remember what it was like to be held by someone? He doubted that she'd want to hear any of that, even though he was compelled to tell her. And that almost every time he'd fucked a woman, he'd pictured *her* beneath him in his mind with her hair spread around her on his pillow as she bit on her lip and moaned his name. The times he hadn't pictured her had been because he was drunk or angry about some shit or other. And he refused to picture fucking her when he was angry. Even the memory of her didn't deserve that.

Maybe he should ask more about *her*? Yes...that made more sense. He knew so little about what she had gone through since he disappeared from her life, without a trace, ten years before. She was married, that much he knew. But were there children? For some reason, the thought of her carrying another man's child made his insides churn and his heart ache simultaneously. What would he say if she told him she was happy with someone else? Could he bear it?

He decided that his scratty old lounging pyjama bottoms were the least sexy thing he owned and so he slipped them on with a T-shirt. The last thing he wanted was to give her the wrong impression. Especially since he knew so little about her life right now.

Once the students were all settled in their cabins, Stevie sat on her bed contemplating going to go see Jason again. A flutter of excitement danced around her stomach and her heart began to skip. She would ask why he sang that song tonight. She would ask more about his relationship with Dorcas, because in spite of his denial about the matter there certainly looked to be more to it than he was letting on. Certainly on *her* part. Although Stevie was baffled as to why this bothered her so much.

When she checked her watch and discovered that it was almost midnight, she slipped on her fleece, grabbed the little torch, and set out for Jason's cabin. On arrival, she tapped on the door and waited.

He opened the door with a warm smile. He was dressed in blue, checked pyjama bottoms and a plain blue T-shirt, and she had never seen a more sexy sight. She clenched between her thighs. *Dammit.*

'Oh...were you about to go to bed?'

'No...not at all. Just relaxing. I've been waiting for you, but I wasn't sure you'd show up. Come on in. The wine's chilling.'

She stepped past him to walk into the spacious lounge area. She caught the smell of body wash and cologne as she breezed in. He smelled delicious.

Calm yourself, Stevie.

Once inside, he took her fleece and hung it on the coat hooks by a door that she presumed led to the bedroom and bathroom. Sitting on the sofa, she watched him as he stood fidgeting as if unable to settle.

She hadn't taken much notice of the cabin on her previous visit, and so she glanced around the space with interest. The interior was whitewashed and there was a large rug in the middle of the lounge area. The kitchen was at the other end in front of the window she had seen him through the night before. A dining table was set in the middle of the floor in front of the kitchen cabinets, and a vase filled with wild flowers was placed in the middle. This little detail made her smile.

'What's so funny?' Jason enquired as he eventually handed her a chilled glass of white wine.

'Nothing. I was just smiling at the fact that you have flowers on your table.'

'I'm a man who can appreciate the beauty in all things.' He spoke quietly, but didn't take his eyes off her. She shivered, which seemed to make him frown. 'Are you cold? I can light the wood burner if you like.'

'No, no. I'm fine. This is nice.' She gestured towards her glass.

'Yes, it's a Chilean wine. I've had it before a couple of times.'

'When you were entertaining ladies?' She smirked.

He seemed displeased, almost offended with her question. He pulled his lips into a hard line. 'Erm...no. I haven't had anyone back here in ages, actually. I don't tend to bring women here. It wouldn't feel right.'

'Not even Dorcas?' She tried to smile nonchalantly but had no clue if she was pulling it off.

His eyes narrowed. '*Especially* not Dorcas. And I don't know why you keep pushing that issue when I've told you that she's just my employee. We have a *work based* relationship and that's it.' It was clear that the subject was closed.

She felt a little awkward at the stern tone of voice. He'd thoroughly chastised her, and her cheeks heated as a result. She gazed down at her glass uncomfortably.

'Why did you play 'It's Been Awhile' tonight, Jason?' She was determined not to show him that he'd affected her in any way with how he'd spoken to her.

He cleared his throat, just as he had before singing it.

'Because it's the only one I can play well enough to sing along.'

Oh. That's disappointing. Silence fell between them until she could stand it no longer.

She inhaled deeply, beginning to feel impatient. 'So what did you want to talk about?'

'You,' he stated plainly, sitting beside her.

'Oh. There's nothing much to tell.' She shrugged.

'I find that hard to believe.'

'It's true. After you disappeared, I spent a long time mourning you. Or rather, mourning the loss of you from my life. I had no clue whether you were alive or dead...so *mourning* is the only way I can describe what I went through.'

He nodded and cast his eyes downward. 'And when you went to university? Did you meet your husband there?'

'Yes. It took a while for Miles to convince me to go out with him. Well...Miles and my mum. He wasn't my type. He wasn't *you*...and *you* were really my only type. You were all I'd known.' The heat rose in her cheeks again, and she was thankful for the subdued lighting.

He smiled at her words. 'Tell me about him.'

She sighed. 'He was a very kind...very intelligent man.'

He frowned. 'Was?'

'Well, he still *is* as far as I know, but we split a while ago so...'

'Oh, I'm sorry to hear that. Anyway, please go on.'

'Okay, so he was studying Science too and we ended up in a few classes together. Eventually, I kind of...*gravitated* towards him I suppose. We went out for a while, and I felt...I don't know...*comfortable*. So when university was over, he asked me to marry him, and I said yes.'

He scratched at the stubble on his chin. 'But it doesn't sound like you were *in love* with him.'

She shook her head. 'No, I wasn't. I cared for him. But after you left, I decided I wasn't going to give my heart so readily again.'

Jason ran his hand through his shaggy hair and huffed the air from his lungs as if shocked by her words. 'I see....so...no children?'

'Oh, God no!' She cringed.

He raised his eyebrows and dropped his head. 'Right.'

'The sex was good.' She smiled absentmindedly.

He snapped his head up. His sad eyes penetrated her soul. 'Was he the one? Did he...did *he* take your virginity?'

She pulled her brows in. 'Not that it's any of your business, but...yes...he did.'

His expression changed to one of sadness. 'Was he gentle?'

She nodded.

'Did he...did he *satisfy* you?'

Her nostrils flared now as anger bubbled up at his intrusive questions. 'If you mean did he make me *come*, Jason, then yes. *Always*. He was a very attentive lover, and he learned my body very well. Satisfied with that answer?' She snorted derisively. She knew her words were cruel, but she had no idea why he needed to get so personal.

He clenched his jaw and closed his eyes. 'It should've been me.'

'Yes, but you weren't *here* Jason, and after I waited years for you to come back, I wasn't about to hang on any longer in case you decided to show up, was I? I had a life to start living.' A sudden pang of regret stabbed her. 'But I wanted it to be you too...so much.'

Jason placed his glass on the table and took hers, doing same. He moved closer to her on the sofa and lifted his hand to cup her face tenderly. 'I wanted it to be me, too.'

The look of deep sadness in his eyes made her swallow past the lump in her throat and chew the inside of her cheek, doing her best to fend off the tears that were threatening.

He traced her bottom lip with his thumb. 'Let me...now I mean...let me make up for it.'

CHAPTER NINE

Stevie pulled away and scrunched her face angrily. 'What? You want *sex*? Is that why you invited me here? So you could find out what you've been missing all these years?'

He closed his eyes momentarily, but when he opened them again, his eyes were darker. 'No, Stevie, it's not like that. I want to make up for what I spoiled. I want to give that to you, to both of us, that's all.'

'So you think you can fuck me and everything will suddenly and miraculously heal inside of me?'

'No...not at all. You've got me all wrong. Please calm down.' He held his hands up in surrender. 'Forget I said anything, okay?' A pained expression washed over his handsome features. She'd hurt him. His jaw clenched and unclenched as he turned away from her. He ran both hands through his hair and leaned so that his elbows rested on his knees. His head dropped forward.

'So...why did you split up? You and...erm...Miles?'

'He was in love with me. He wanted us to have a family but I didn't feel the same. And he deserved to be with someone who loved him back. I couldn't give him what he wanted.' Her lips began to quiver as she thought back to the day when she told Miles it was over. They had just made love, and he'd been talking about babies. He had been so sure she'd change her mind. She had felt so cruel, and he'd called her an ice queen. He accused her of stabbing him in the heart with her words. Thinking back, she realised he wasn't far off the mark.

Jason looked up and leaned towards her again. 'Hey, I'm sorry. Please don't get upset. I didn't mean to pry.'

'No, it's fine. I just hate myself for what I put him through. He didn't deserve that. Looking back now, I see that I should never have married him.'

'Hindsight is the bomb, eh?'

She sniggered through her tears. '*The bomb*? What are you, fifteen all of a sudden?'

Jason smiled broadly and slapped his forehead with his palm. 'Occupational hazard, working with teenagers.' He smiled widely, and her heart skipped whilst butterflies choreographed a dance routine in her belly. He was always *incredibly* good looking, and age had just made him more so.

She plucked up the courage to ask him the burning question. 'So what about you? Have you got any serious relationships under your belt?'

'I've had...hmmm...what should I call them that won't offend you? Encounters? Conquests? Hook ups? I think you get the general picture. Relationships have never been my *thing*...well...since you that is.'

She formed her mouth into an O but made no sound to accompany it. She pondered his words for a few seconds. 'So, you've never been engaged? Married? Anywhere close?'

He laughed. 'Not anywhere *remotely* close. Close and I weren't even on the same planet.'

She joined in his mirth. 'That bad, eh?'

'Oh yeah...*that bad*.'

Okay, now I'm intrigued. 'How come?'

He shrugged. 'Oh, I don't know. It may sound stupid, but I think maybe I felt like I would have been unfaithful to you in some bizarre way.'

She frowned at his admission. 'But you had plenty of sex.'

'Stevie, you said yourself that you slept with Miles but didn't love him.'

She folded her arms across her chest. 'No, I said I wasn't *in love* with him. I cared for him deeply.'

'Okay...sorry. I didn't mean to offend you. I don't explain things very well, do I?'

She softened a little. She had no reason to be offended. 'So you haven't *loved* anyone since me?'

'No, I haven't.'

They sat silently for a while, sipping their wine. Every so often they glanced at each other but neither spoke. Eventually, she decided to break the next piece of news.

'So you never knew how you'd done in your finals? You never checked?'

'No. Once I left, I separated myself from my previous life entirely.'

She nodded, but bitterness washed over her on hearing his words. 'You got four A's, Jason.'

His eyes widened and he opened his mouth, but no sound came out. Standing, he shook his head and paced the floor for a few minutes before walking over to lean on the kitchen counter top.

Eventually, he snorted. 'Well fuck me sideways.' He shook his head again. 'In your fucking face, *father dear*.' He clasped his hands atop his head, puffing out his cheeks and closing his eyes briefly. Then he glanced over at her, grimacing. 'The fucker would have been so *very* proud.' His voice dripped with sarcasm as he wiped both hands over his face and dropped his arms by his side.

She walked over to stand beside him and then bit her lip. 'I'm so sorry. I seem to be dishing up lots of things that maybe you'd rather not know, don't I?'

He shrugged his shoulders and huffed out a long breath. 'It's okay. I'm just a little...*shocked* by everything. This time last week, I was still a total failure with only one decent parent. Now I'm a grade A student with *no* parents.' Sadness washed over his features, and a line appeared between his brows.

She reached up and squeezed his arm. 'Hey, you're in *no way* a failure. Okay, so you no longer have the...you know... clean-cut-head-boy look going on.' She gestured up and down his body. 'I mean...now you're all ripped muscles, long hair, and tats, but I'm not complaining.'

He laughed at her words and rolled his eyes. The heat rose in her cheeks once again when she realised she'd just said the whole sentence out loud and had admitted she actually *did* find him attractive.

Oh shitty shit. Ground, swallow me up now!

When her embarrassment had subsided a little, she stroked his arm up and down in a weak effort to comfort him. He responded with a warm smile. Turning to face her, he ran his fingertips down her flushed cheek. '*You* haven't changed at all. You're still very beautiful.' His voice was soft, and her heart ached at his words. 'I used to feel like the luckiest boy at school, you know? I'd sit there, in the biology lab, looking over at you when I was supposed to be answering textbook questions, but I just couldn't concentrate. It was the class where I had the best view of you. And that's why I used to love biology.'

He took her face in his hands, caressing her cheeks tenderly with his thumbs, and she shivered at the contact, closing her eyes.

'I couldn't concentrate because all I could do was stare at you. You'd be laughing at something Carrie had said...or you'd be chewing on your pen looking all intense and studious. It was such a turn on, you know? And all I could do was think about taking you in my arms and kissing you. I used to dream of undressing you and touching your bare skin...kissing you all over. To just...*be* with you...have you naked in my arms...skin on skin...sharing my body with you...and us taking that next, intimate step together. To feel you around me as I moved inside you. God, Stevie, it was *all* I wanted.'

Her heart began to race. A deep ache throbbed between her thighs, and she suddenly became a little light headed. 'It was all I wanted too. But I thought you didn't want me. Because I didn't know what was going on, I was left thinking that I somehow wasn't who you really wanted.'

He closed his eyes and shook his head slowly. When he opened them again, he bent to rest his forehead on hers. 'No, don't *ever* think that. You *were* all I wanted. You've always been the one I wanted...even now... I can't give my heart away because you still have it in your hands.'

She gasped just before Jason's lips crushed hers. His hands slipped roughly into her hair, and he cradled her head. His lips were firm and the kiss demanding. The trace of stubble on his jaw grazed against her skin, sending shivers down her entire body. He tasted of wine, and she just couldn't get enough. His tongue thrust into her mouth, and she met it with her own as she found herself gripping his T-shirt in case her legs gave way beneath her. Her heart hammered as she pulled herself into his hard chest while his lips moved urgently over hers.

He deepened the intense kiss as one of his hands slid from her hair and trailed down her back, leaving tingles as it travelled. When his hand reached her lower back, he pulled her closer so that their bodies were completely aligned and his prominent arousal pressed into her. His tongue explored her mouth, and his breath hissed in and out of his nose. The noise that emanated from within his body sounded almost pained. He pulled away, his chest rising and falling rapidly. She was panting as she gazed dreamily into his eyes that were now dark with desire.

He caressed her face as he spoke. 'I'm going to take your hand and lead you to my bedroom...then I'm going to undress us both...and if you don't stop me, I'm going to sink myself inside you...like I wanted to all those years ago...because now I have no barriers and that means I can't think of a single reason why I shouldn't.'

His intense gaze caused her muscles to clench again with the need to feel his touch. She wanted this. She wanted him. *Desperately*. She nodded her acquiescence and he took her hand, pulling her behind him through the door leading away from the lounge.

Once inside his bedroom, he stood before her, still breathing heavily. She glanced around the cosy space and smiled. It was just how she pictured it, whitewashed walls and white bed linens. Simple but beautiful. Soon her eyes were locked on his again as he almost devoured her with his chocolate brown gaze.

He pushed her hair away from her shoulders and ran his index finger around the collar of her T-shirt. Goose bumps rose on her skin, and she closed her eyes anticipating his next move. Reaching for the hem, he grasped it and dragged it up and off her body in one swift move. He paused and she opened her eyes to look deeply into his.

He slid his palms along the curve of her waist and inhaled sharply, biting his bottom lip as his thumbs caressed the underside of her lace-covered breasts. In a split second his mouth was on hers again, tasting and teasing. She was overwhelmed with desire and something that felt a little bit like fear. She didn't want to think too much about what she was allowing to happen, lest she stop him and regret it forever.

He pulled away again, and his eyes stared intently into hers, his hands moved up and fisted in her hair. Regarding her with a look of intense hunger, his voice came out in a husky whisper. 'I've dreamed of this moment for the last ten years. But I never imagined it would *actually* happen. To have you here...now...and to know that I can touch you.' He inhaled deeply through his nose and shook his head. 'I'm almost afraid to do it in case you turn out to be a figment of my imagination.'

She held his face in her palms. 'I'm here. I'm real, and I want you so bad right now...touch me...please?'

Her words seemed to fuel his already evident arousal, and he reached out and slipped both of her white lace bra straps from her shoulders.

With a confidence she didn't realise she had, she bent her arms around and unhooked her bra letting it fall to the floor but keeping her eyes firmly fixed on his to gauge his reaction. He was mesmerised. He stepped closer again and smoothed his hands slowly from her collarbone, down over her breasts. He cupped them reverently and ran his thumbs in circles over her nipples, which peaked as he moved. She couldn't help the whimper that escaped as she closed her eyes relishing his touch.

Stopping his ministrations briefly, he removed his own T-shirt, which he tossed onto a chair in the corner of the white, wood panelled room. She reached up and smoothed her hands over the taut, tattooed skin of his chest until her hands were tangled in his hair.

He pulled her into him so that her nipples brushed against his warm skin. The contact felt so good and set her blood afire. He bent so that his breath teased her ear, sending pleasure-filled electric shocks through her body, finishing at the junction of her thighs where the ache had deepened further. 'Skin on skin,' he whispered. 'It feels so good, just like I imagined.'

Sliding his hands down her back, he cupped her bottom, squeezing as he kissed and nibbled at her neck. His movements became faster, rougher. She moaned and let her head fall back, absorbing the sensations radiating through her. Slipping her hands into his waistband, she pushed until his pyjama pants slid below his erection and it sprang towards her. He let the pants slip down and stepped out of them, kicking them aside. He was magnificent. She wanted to touch him but fear got the better of her.

Jason's fingers came around to the front of her linen trousers, and after unfastening them, he dropped to his knees before her and grasped them, tugging away the last remaining barriers as quickly as he could. He gazed up to look at her standing naked before him and shook his head slowly.

'What? What is it?' She was suddenly very self-conscious and wanted to cover her curves up again.

'Just...*look* at you...you have to be one of the most beautiful sights I've ever been lucky enough to behold.'

Her cheeks flushed, and she clenched her hands at her sides. 'Oh stop...I'm ten years older than when you *should've* seen me like this. *Then* I would've been worth looking at, but now—'

'No. Don't do that. Don't take *anything* away from this moment. *Please.* To me...looking at you now...like this... You're perfection. Just as you are.' He grasped her hips and rested his forehead on her belly. 'I had no idea I'd missed you this much. I had no idea how incomplete I was without you. *Please* forgive me.' His words choked as they left his mouth.

Overcome with emotion, more tears escaped and slipped down her face, leaving cold, wet trails in their wake. 'I do forgive you, Jason. But really...there's nothing to forgive. What you did...yes, it hurt...but now that I know why you left, how could I be angry?' She stroked his hair, and his tears dampened her skin as he clung to her.

Once he had calmed, he began to trail kisses all over her from where he crouched. His fingers dug into her hips, and he nuzzled the soft curls at the apex of her thighs and inhaled deeply.

'God, I love your smell.' Horrified at his words, she tried to step back, but his eyes shot up to meet hers. 'I mean it. Don't be embarrassed.' He turned back and nuzzled her again. She began to relax until his tongue slipped between her folds. Her head rolled back, and she couldn't help the groan that released from her throat. 'Mmmm...and you taste amazing too.' He lapped at her until she began to tighten. Her breathing became shallow. Miles had never been able to make her come this way. It had *never* felt this good. It was as if Jason had known the best way to mark her. To ruin her for every other man. She clenched and tugged at his hair as her legs began to weaken.

'Jason...Jason stop,' she whispered desperately.

'It's okay, Stevie...just let go...I've got you.' His voice vibrated deep inside her and pushed her over the edge. She cried out as her legs gave way beneath her and pleasure pulsed from her core all the way to her fingertips and curled toes. He grabbed her body and pulled her against him as he stood.

Once on his feet again, he took her mouth with such fervour that he stole her breath. Their tongues tangled and caressed each other in a passionate duel as their touches gained urgency. Taking what they had lost ten years before.

As he kissed her, Jason backed them towards the bed and tumbled, taking her with him. She was pulled on top of his hard body as he squeezed and moulded her breast with one hand, the other tugging at her hair. His breathing was heavy and fevered, mirroring hers. She broke away from his mouth and nibbled along his jaw, down his neck, making him groan with desire as his hand slipped around to pull her into him. It was as if he couldn't quite get her close enough. She scratched at his chest and back feeling the same urgency making his erection flinch against her, refuelling her need for him.

Suddenly, he moved her so that she was beneath him. He had one leg between her thighs as he trailed kisses down her chest and along to her breast where he drew a nipple between his teeth, swirling his tongue around the peak, making her moan and grasp at his hair to pull him even closer. Heat enflamed her body as her muscles clenched once again. She needed his touch elsewhere. His hand stroked roughly down her body until he found her dampness and began to tease her with his fingers.

As his touch picked up speed, Jason closed his eyes. 'Oh God, I want you so, so much. Please, say yes.'

She reached up and caressed his face until he once again met her gaze. 'I think you already know that my answer is yes.'

Caressing her sensitive flesh again, he made her cry out. He teased her tender nub once more until pleasure shot through her body and she bucked beneath him, her breathing becoming faster. 'Oh, Jason...Jason *please*,' she cried as she soared skyward once again.

'You look so beautiful when you just let yourself go like

that. I love to see you.' Jason caught her cries with his mouth as she clung to him whilst she floated back down to earth. As her breathing calmed, the bed moved. She opened her eyes and looked up to see Jason sheathing himself. He really was staggeringly beautiful. His broad chest glistened with sweat in the dim light, and his bicep muscles flexed and tensed as he moved. Jason naked was certainly one mental picture she wanted to etch into her mind and keep forever.

He leaned back over her again and kissed her deeply, exploring her mouth once again with his delicious tongue and rebuilding her desire for him. 'When I said that seeing you naked before me was the most beautiful sight I'd ever beheld... I was wrong...it was seeing you fall apart in ecstasy like that, in *my* arms. And knowing that *I* made it happen is just... Wow! Words just...fail me.'

She couldn't find the words to respond either at that point. She simply gazed up at him as her breathing calmed, unable to believe how amazing she felt. How connected to him she felt.

He positioned himself between her thighs and hesitated. 'Are you sure you're real? Am I going to wake up from a dream the moment I sink myself inside of you?'

She slowly moved her head from side to side. 'I'm here. This is real.' She hadn't been with a man in a long while and was a little nervous, but she had never wanted to be with any man as much as she wanted Jason.

He thrust himself inside her as a loud groan erupted from deep within his chest. 'Stevie...*my soulmate* .' Tears escaped her eyes at the words she had loved so much before he left. Once he was fully immersed in her, he stopped and nuzzled her neck. He lifted so that he rested above her on his forearms and looked into her eyes. '*My* soulmate .' He whispered possessively as he ran his nose along hers, before kissing her with all the passion and longing ten years apart had built.

She threaded one hand in his hair and slid the other down to his bottom where she kneaded and squeezed, encouraging him to move. It was all the motivation he needed. Picking up his pace, he crashed his mouth into hers once again, urgency and hunger so clearly evident in his heated movements, holding her as his eyes remained locked on hers. She lifted her legs and wrapped them around his waist, inhaling sharply at their deeper connection. She clung to him, never wanting to let him go.

The feeling of him moving inside her was exquisite, like *nothing* she had experienced before. She had always loved sex, but nothing came close to making love with Jason. Because even though there was desperation in his movements, she felt sure that's what this was; making love. She too had fantasised about this moment. And now that it was happening, it was all she had hoped for, and more.

Resting his forehead on hers, he gained momentum, and she tightened again. Soon she was gasping, with her head thrown back and her eyes closed.

'Stevie...look at me...*please*...I want to see you. I need to know this is real.' Jason's pain-filled words pulled her back from the edge. Her eyes snapped open and met the intensity of his. His brow creased and his expression was a mask of myriad emotions. He thrust forward once more, and she shattered into a million microscopic pieces beneath him.

A split second later a guttural roar erupted from his chest as he joined her. 'Stevie!' Her name was a drawn-out sounding cry falling from his lips. '*My soulmate ,*' he whispered once again.

CHAPTER TEN

*J*ason glanced over at the clock. It was almost two in the morning. Stevie was curled into his side with her head resting on his chest. Her breathing told him that she was asleep, yet he continued to stroke his fingers up and down her back, feeling soothed by his own actions.

Making love to her had blown his mind. He'd had plenty of *sex* in his adult life since he left her, but he had *never* connected with anyone like that before. This was *way* beyond sex. He'd felt it deep in his soul. The pleasure intensified a hundred fold just because he actually *cared*. He'd never been a selfish lover, but his partner's gratification was always a means to a selfish end. This, however, had been all about *her*, watching her overwhelmed with pleasure. The fact that he experienced the most astounding orgasm of his life was just a bonus. The way she'd looked when she came... Wow...just *beautiful*. He wanted to experience that over and over again, to hold her and feel her clench as she fell apart just for him.

All for him.

This wasn't how he had intended things to go tonight. He

119

wanted to talk, to find out about her life since he'd been absent. But hearing her talk about sex with another man had sparked possessiveness in him that he had no idea existed. He had *never* felt that way before, but at that moment, hearing her talking about how Miles had made her come every time hurt him so deeply that he suddenly needed her to experience with *him* what he had wanted her to experience all those years ago. He needed to show her how things could be with him.

Seeing her naked had stunned him. Back when they were eighteen they had never gone beyond kissing and holding each other. He had no idea what had lain beneath her clothes, although he was a teenaged guy with a libido like any other teenaged guy. But he had never even touched her breast for fear things would get heated and they'd end up going further. This would have revealed his secret pain to her, and he hadn't wanted that.

But now she was a woman in *every* sense of the word. Her smooth skin and her curves took his breath away. She had been self-conscious, but he had no clue why. She was in no way skinny, but that was such a *good* thing. Women these days were obsessed with being thin. But from experience, he knew there was nothing remotely sexy about fucking a skeleton with skin. Women like that didn't give him a raging hard on like the one he'd had since the day she had re-entered his life. Women were supposed to be soft and curvy to complement the flat, hard planes of a man. Well, of *him* anyway.

Her luscious, auburn hair was still long, something he had always loved about her. And her azure blue eyes still had a sparkle, albeit a little duller than before—he blamed himself for that.

Her nakedness and vulnerability had suddenly floored

him. As he knelt before her and looked up at her earlier, every single feeling he once had for her came flooding back to him. His heart ached and his breath hitched as myriad emotions vied for the surface at once. He'd never cried in front of a woman before, that's for certain. But kneeling there before her, he had been racked with sadness and a kind of grief for the lost years. Years he *should* have been worshipping her but instead he'd been fighting for his country, acting as security abroad, or running an Outward Bounds centre for teens. He couldn't regret the things he had done during their time spent apart, but he *could* regret the fact that they *were* apart.

She stirred beside him, and he reached down and kissed her head. Her eyes fluttered open and she stretched, brushing her breasts again him. His manhood began to waken, and feeling rather ashamed of the automatic reaction of his body to hers, he pulled the sheet over himself.

She ran her hand over his chest. 'Hmmm...what time is it?'

'Just after two.'

She sat bolt upright, fully exposing her breasts in the process. 'Oh shit! I need to go.'

He smirked as he reached up to stroke a finger down the curve that he had been worshipping only an hour or so before.

She slapped his hand away. 'Hey, hands off ma goods, Reynolds.'

'Awww...but they're so touchable.'

She fell silent and picked invisible lint from the sheet. He could tell she was feeling awkward, so he tenderly stroked her cheek. 'Hey, what's wrong?'

'I'm...I'm just not sure that this was a good idea. I mean... what happens now? I think we both need to get real here and realise that—'

'Hey, hey... Will you just stop analysing, *please*?' He

pulled himself upright to face her. His heart had begun to pound in his chest.

She sighed. 'But we need to be clear with each other about where this is going.'

He pulled his lips in for a moment and closed his eyes, dreading the answer to his next question. 'Stevie, are you regretting what we did last night?'

After a pause she answered in a low voice. 'I...I don't know what to say.'

He dropped his head forward onto her shoulder. 'Well, I think if your immediate answer isn't, *No Jason, of course I don't regret it*, then we have a problem.' He turned and placed his feet on the floor, suddenly feeling like he'd made a colossal mistake. 'I don't regret a single thing about it.'

She reached over and stroked a hand down the muscles of his bare back. 'Look, don't misunderstand me, Jason...you were amazing...us together? Mind-blowing. But—'

He stood and grabbed his boxers from the floor, stepping into them quickly and placing his hands on his hips. 'Okay. Just stop. I get it. It was just *sex* to you. You've treated me like a fuck buddy. I get it. I just thought—'

'What?' she shouted. 'How *dare* you accuse me of such a tacky thing? And for your information, unlike you, I've *never* had fuck buddies, you complete arsehole!'

He was breathing rapidly now as anger fought its way to the surface to replace the sadness he had experienced moments earlier. 'Well, what *did* you have? Did they have a fancy name simply because they were having sex with queen fucking Stevie?' he shouted back, but immediately regretted the harshness of his words.

He watched as she silently gathered her clothes and dressed herself. Her face impassive although an errant tear betrayed her calm exterior as it slipped silently down her cheek. He ran his hands over his face. 'Stevie, please stop... I didn't mean—'

'Jason.' She cut off his apology. Holding her hand up, she closed her eyes. 'It's done. Now we both know what we've been missing all these years. Let's leave it at that.'

A lump lodged in his throat. 'Is that it? *We know what we've been missing?* Is that all it meant to you?'

She turned, fully dressed, to face him. 'Don't pretend to be all sentimental now. Especially after how you've been acting since I got here. You've had plenty of meaningless sex. And *you* left *me*, remember? Knowing your reasons only fills in the gaps and helps me to understand *why*. It doesn't change what you did. And sex with you doesn't suddenly heal all of the wounds you left me with. I wish it did. I'd *hoped* that it would. But at the end of this week, I go back to London and you stay here. And as much as I cared about you and about what we had back then, I think a ten hour or more journey every time one of us is feeling horny is just a little much, don't you?' She wiped away another tear that had fallen.

His eyes stung and his heart ached. He'd lost her. He'd been subconsciously trying to push her away since she arrived. She was right about his behaviour, but now that he'd decided to stop doing that, he'd succeeded by doing the opposite. He pinched the bridge of his nose. Leaving her all those years ago had somehow suspended their relationship in time for him. He'd left her physically, but emotionally she was still there in his mind and heart. She was still his...until now.

He wouldn't let her go without a fight though. He had already decided that. He stalked around the bed and grabbed her. 'Hey, before you walk out you need to know that this *wasn't* just sex to me. Okay, I know I've been an arrogant arsehole since you arrived, and I don't have excuses for that... I think it was some kind of...defence mechanism, but this...this was so much more than just a fuck. Why did you think I wanted you to keep your eyes on me? I needed you to *see* me. *Really* see me. I have *never* felt a connection like that with anyone...*ever*. You want to walk out on *me* this time? Go ahead. But you'll be making one mother of a mistake, and I think deep down you know that too.'

She inhaled sharply as he held her eyes with as much intensity as he could muster.

'I have to go,' she said blankly, pulling herself from his grip.

He slumped onto the edge of his bed with his head in his hands as the door closed behind her.

CHAPTER ELEVEN

Day Four of Hell

Stevie awoke around seven after only having a few hours of restless sleep. She had cried for a while when she'd crawled into bed. The urge to run back to Jason and hold him had almost overtaken her, but self-preservation had kicked in just in time. She couldn't give her heart to him again. Admittedly, he had most of it in tiny little pieces under his feet, but the little she still had that remained intact was something she was determined to keep hold of.

She had lied to Jason about the sex. Okay, so she hadn't come right out and said the words, but a lie by omission is a lie nonetheless. She had *hinted* that it had been something she did to find out what she had been missing all these years. That it was meaningless sex. *Stupid, stupid Stevie*. It hadn't been *just sex*. It was in *no way* something she did as some twisted research mission, and she knew she had been very cruel to imply that it was.

Replaying her own words in her mind had made her feel nauseated. She wished she could somehow suck the words back in or go back in time and *un*say them. But as Jason had said only yesterday, 'Hindsight is the bomb.' And now she had to go kayaking and face him. She thought about feigning a migraine, but she couldn't do that to the kids. It wouldn't be fair.

Her phone rang. How come the bloody signal was so good out here in the middle of nowhere? Was there no peace to be had?

She picked it up and hit the answer button. 'Hi, Mum. You're up early.'

'Stevie? What's wrong? You sound...*strange*.' *So very perceptive.*

'No. I'm fine. I've just woken up.'

'Are you sure?'

'Yes, Mum. I was there when it happened.' Her sarcasm was the one thing Dana usually complained about, but not today.

'Okay. Well, I just wanted to check on you. What are you up to today?'

'I have the joys of kayaking.' Her voice was devoid of enthusiasm but not for the reason her mother would no doubt presume.

'Oh dear. Not your kind of thing, is it, sweetie? Well, chin up. It's only for a few more days. Speak soon. Bye, love.'

She frowned. 'Bye, Mum.' Her mother's calls this week were very brief. She wondered why this couldn't be the usual case instead of the hour long chats where Dana told her how much she worried about her. She loved her mother dearly, but her overbearing nature had worsened significantly since Jason's disappearance and then compounded after Dana's diagnosis of a lifelong medical condition had shaken their very foundations. Yet another heartache and worry Stevie could've done without.

After showering, she dried, pulled her hair up into a scruffy bun, and pulled on a pair of cargo pants with a long sleeved T-shirt. The telltale signs of tears shed were all over her face, but she slipped her shades on and hoped that kayaking was an activity that could be done whilst wearing them.

The kids were all in the main hut eating breakfast when she arrived. Her heart almost stopped when she looked directly into Jason's sad brown eyes. *Oh God, no.* He didn't smile. He simply looked away and her heart sank. She was suddenly overcome with the urge to talk to him—to clear the air and come clean about her lies. She acted before the other half of her brain kicked into gear and stopped her in her tracks. He was chatting to Dorcas, who was positively hanging on his every word.

Good grief, pick your tongue up, dippy Dorcas.

She smiled sweetly at the doe-eyed young woman and tapped Jason on the shoulder. 'Excuse me... Mr. Reynolds, could I...erm...talk to you for a minute please?'

He frowned. 'Oh...I'm sorry, *Mrs.* Norton, I'm a little busy at the moment going through the schedule. Can it wait?' His icy tone almost cut through her flesh like a dagger.

She winced, hoping she had done so internally. 'Actually no. It's a matter of urgency. There's an issue. It's to do with the...erm...life-jackets.'

Dorcas' eyes widened. *Whoops.*

Jason was clearly unimpressed with her and his nostrils flared. 'Okay, *Mrs.* Norton, lead the way, *if* it's urgent.' His teeth were clenched and the way he'd said *Mrs.* sent an eerie shiver down her spine.

He took her elbow tightly, digging his fingers into her flesh until it hurt, his anger clearly evident in his flushed face. He led her outside, away from the main hut and continued to walk hurriedly with her. They moved further away from prying eyes, but now he was almost dragging her. She realised he was heading for her cabin. *Shit!* He waited whilst she tried to unlock the door, glaring at her all the while. When she couldn't get the key in the lock through shaking, he snatched it from her and unlocked it himself. He pulled her inside and slammed the door behind them, making the whole cabin vibrate.

'Jason, what if people saw—'

He grabbed her and pushed her against the wall, pressing himself into her and sealing his mouth over hers. She struggled at first, feeling a little taken aback by his aggression. But then she melted into the kiss as his tongue danced around her mouth, sending those little electric shocks to the junction of her thighs.

He stopped abruptly. 'Don't *ever* fucking show me up in front of my staff again, Stevie.' He growled, his eyes blazing.

She frowned. 'But I didn't... What do you mean?'

'You pretty much called into question the safety of my fucking life-jackets in front of little Miss Health and fucking Safety. Do you know how much shit you've caused me now?' He ran his hand over his hair, smoothing back a few strands that had escaped the plain black hair tie securing it at the nape of his rather delicious neck.

'I'm sorry...I—'

'Oh, you're sorry? Well that makes everything fucking better then.'

She had never seen him look so angry. 'Please stop swearing at me. I just needed to talk to you. I needed—'

'Well if you *needed* something, sweetheart, here I am. Take what it is you need.' He stepped back and held his arms out to his sides and nodded towards his groin. 'It's all about *you* in this life after all. What do you need? An orgasm maybe? A quick fuck to see you through the day? Can't get enough of me?' He snorted but his smile was more like a menacing grimace. He was back to the arrogant pig of a few days ago.

She stepped sideways in a bid to get away from him. *Who the hell is he?* 'Forget it. I'm not talking to you when you're behaving like this. This is *not* you.' Her voice wavered.

'Oh but it is, sweetheart. This *is* the *real* me. The prissy fucking wimp died ten years ago. You're looking at a *real man* now, Stevie.'

Tears stung her eyes, and her lips began to tremble at his disturbing manner. 'Well in that case, you need to leave. You're clearly not who I thought you were. I'm done talking now.'

He walked towards her again. 'What, no more talk of life-jackets, eh? Even if that *was* just a ruse to get me alone. Don't think I don't know that. I figured you out straight away.'

'My God, you've reverted back to the cold, arrogant arse-hole that I met when I arrived. What happened?' She gave him an incredulous look.

He clenched his jaw and leaned in so that his nose was almost touching hers. He pointed his index finger in her face. '*You* happened. You turned up out of the fucking blue and made me remember. Made me fucking *feel*. And for what? You gave me the *one thing* I've craved for ten years, and then told me it was *nothing* to you. So that's it...*you* happened.'

She realised she was still backed up against the wall. A million different thoughts seemed to be flying through her mind. Maybe she should scream to get someone's attention. She opened her mouth, but couldn't form the sound with his body pressed so close to hers. She closed her eyes and his rapid breathing heated her face, his heart pounded against her own.

LISA J HOBMAN

'Jason...please...it...it wasn't *nothing*...that's what I wanted to say to you... It was so much *more* than nothing...but now... now I think you just need to go.'

Jason chuckled darkly again. 'You really are a prick tease, aren't you? Little Miss Fucking Prim and Proper.' His fist slammed into the wall beside her. 'You're so damned frustrating!'

Her eyes snapped open to see the fire in his. 'Yeah? Well I guess we know now whose blood you have flowing through *your* veins, don't we?' She immediately regretted her words.

He staggered backwards as if she had punched him in the guts. His eyes were wide and his mouth hung open in disbelief. 'I'm...I'm nothing like *him*... How could you even *think* that? Let alone speak the fucking *words* to me? That was a fucking low and painful blow, but at least now I know how you really feel.' Pain and anguish glowed vividly in his eyes just before he turned away.

She covered her mouth with shaking hands. 'I'm...I didn't mean it... You were intimidating me, Jason—'

Before she could get him to calm down and listen, he pulled the handle and walked out of the door, leaving it wide open. Her chest heaved, and she was suddenly terrified. What had she done? No matter *what* he'd said to her, that was the *cruellest* blow she could have possibly struck. Comparing him to his abusive father was the worst thing to do, and she felt disgusted with her behaviour.

Once her legs regained the ability to function and her brain was once more engaged, she ran after him but he was nowhere to be seen. Panic ripped through her as she ran to the main hut. The kids weren't there and neither was David. She ran out and back to the main clearing and found the bus.

'Oh there you are, Mrs. Norton. Where've you been? Mr. Reynolds can't make the trip now, so we've got Harry instead.

130

He's a qualified instructor, so it's fine. Dorcas said you were worried about the lifejackets, but I said it was probably just nerves...you know with you being a bit new to all this outdoors stuff. Anyway, come on, hop in the bus. We can go now that you're here.'

David's words went in one ear and out the other. 'Oh... David, I'm sorry but I need to speak to Mr. Reynolds very quickly. Do you know where I can find him?'

David leaned in and whispered harshly, 'Mrs. Norton, do I need to remind you that we are here on *school* business? I think your...whatever it is...with Mr. Reynolds will have to wait. Don't you?'

She stared at him, ready to retaliate but clamped her mouth shut. Whatever she said now would only make things worse. And he was actually quite right.

Reluctantly, she boarded the bus, not remembering if she had even closed her cabin door, never mind locked it. Her personal belongings were in there, but she was past caring. She stared out the window as they made the twenty-minute coach journey to their destination.

The Cairngorms National Park was a truly magnificent place. The colours were so vivid. The verdant green of the trees was a striking contrast to the cornflower-blue sky overhead. She could honestly now see the attraction to the place, miles from anywhere but so beautiful in all its Scottish splendour.

The bus and its passengers arrived in the car park at Loch Morlich. Once they had all climbed down and walked through the trees towards the shore of the loch, she paused and looked out at the still water with its mountain backdrop. Her breath caught in her throat as she took in the colours and smells of this most stunning location. The water idled lazily towards the shore, lapping at the shingles as the kids chased around and splashed each other. She inhaled deeply and closed her eyes, listening to the wind as it gently rustled through the lush green giants surrounding her. Yes, she could definitely see the attraction of being here. Suddenly, she thought of Jason.

Oh God, please let him be okay. And please let him forgive my cruel stupidity.

The kayaks were laid neatly by the water's edge in all their gregarious yellow glory, being checked by Harry. He delivered the safety instructions to the students with great competence. Each was issued with a lifejacket and helmet. The kayaks were allocated, too. She had been informed she could sit it out if she'd preferred, but she'd decided that it would take her mind off things and pulled on her lifejacket and helmet, ready to face another new challenge. David seemed impressed.

He made his way over to where she stood, glanced around and then back at her, lowering his voice. 'Look...I wanted to apologise. I have no clue what's going on with you and Jason and it's none of my business... If I'm completely honest, it was jealousy talking. Now forgive me for saying what I'm about to say, as I'm aware that it's highly inappropriate, but I feel it needs to be said by way of explanation for my outburst. I find you very attractive, Stevie, and I'd kind of hoped that us being here together might give us a chance to get to know each other better and that maybe you'd realise you liked me too. I see now that it's not going to happen. And it's obvious that there's something between you and Jason. But...the way *he* looks at you is...well...*odd*. He looks at you like he's known you forever. Like you're the love of his life or something. He looks like he wants to swallow you whole. What I mean is...just be careful, okay? He looks like he could chew you up and spit you out. And...I just wanted to say that I'm here if you need me.'

She was shocked by this latest development and of his description of the looks Jason had given her. But she smiled sweetly and nodded, unsure of what else to say.

Once her spray skirt was fixed in place, helmet on, and her perfectly fine lifejacket was zipped up, Harry secured her into her boat. She joined the rest of the kids as she paddled like crazy getting nowhere fast. Before long she was upside down under the freezing cold water of Loch Morlich. Once she righted herself again, she started the whole cycle over. Paddle like crazy; lose control, roll, repeat. In the end, she gave up and sat stationary in her kayak, watching the others have fun.

Even as the clouds closed in over-head and she was finally subjected to the rain that Scotland was noted for, her thoughts continually drifted back to Jason and his arrogant defence mechanism. There was no wonder he hadn't had a proper relationship in ten years if that was how he behaved. It was as if he was terrified to let anyone get close.

Seeing his eyes this morning filled with a combination of rage and lust was quite frightening and—even more disconcerting—a major turn on. Clearly, he was a man who could be fierce, a trait he had surely picked up along the way. It was certainly not something he was known for ten years ago. Back then he was sensitive, mild and calm, a deep thinker. He had called his former self a *prissy wuss* this morning. That couldn't have been farther from the truth. She had never viewed him that way. But he clearly disdained his past, and that was understandable considering what he had endured.

She shook her head, deciding that mulling over this was a waste of her time. She began paddling once more, but no sooner had she begun than she was under the water yet again.

At the end of a very long and tiring day, the students had all disembarked the bus in the low light of the mid-evening and made their weary way to their cabins to shower and change for dinner. Stevie felt achy and bedraggled. Her hair was a mess and her clothes were still damp from the rain and capsizing countless times, despite the instructions Harry was shouting over the noise of the raucous teenagers.

Once all the students and David were out of sight, she made her way to Jason's cabin. She had no clue what to expect. She had no clue if he'd even *be* there. But something compelled her to go and find out.

CHAPTER TWELVE

The lights were off when Stevie arrived at the cabin. Not letting this discourage her, she walked around to his door to find that it had been left ajar. She pushed it open and stepped inside. The place was silent.

'What do *you* want?' came a gruff voice from behind her. She physically jumped. He stood silhouetted in the doorway, and as it had dropped quite dark outside, his face wasn't visible.

She sighed heavily. 'I came to apologise for what I said this morning.'

'Right. Well you've said it, so you can fuck off back to your cabin now.'

She inhaled sharply as his words cut her. 'Jason...*please*. I didn't mean it. You are *nothing* like your father. It was wrong of me to make such an evil comparison.'

'Nope, you were right. I *have* got his blood running through my veins. I just never imagined it would be *you* who pointed that out to me. Now, please leave.' He stepped aside for her, but she stayed rooted to the spot.

'No, I'm not leaving. Not this time.'

'Suit yourself. I'm having another drink, and then I'm off to bed to try and forget this past few days ever happened.' He walked past her. 'You can let yourself out.'

He walked over to the counter top and flicked a switch which made the under cabinet lighting illuminate. He grabbed a half empty bottle of single malt, poured three fingers of the amber liquid into a glass, and downed half in one gulp, hissing through his teeth after he'd swallowed. He turned to face her, and his eyes were red rimmed.

'You still fucking here?'

She nodded. 'Jason, I don't want to leave you like this.'

'Nah, leaving is *my* job, eh? And I'm fucking good at it apparently. The *best*,' he mumbled, the Scottish tinge to his accent strengthening in his less than sober state.

Tentatively, she walked towards him. 'Are you drunk? You're swearing a lot. Have you had a lot of that today?'

He shook his head. 'Nah. This is only my second...maybe my third...fourth. Why?'

'Because I need to say some things to you, and I want you sober.'

His head lolled back and he groaned. 'Awww, Stevie don't *do* this, okay? Enough. I've heard just about as much as I can take of your fucking judgemental words of wisdom. Save it for your students, all right?' He rubbed his eyes.

Oh great. I've really done a number on him, haven't I?

'Please, Jason. Come and sit with me.'

He puffed out his cheeks and acquiesced as if he had no energy to argue. He slumped down on the sofa while she fumbled with a lamp on the table. She removed the glass from his fingers and grasped his now empty hand in hers. He looked down at their entwined fingers and frowned.

'Jason, I need you to know that what I said was totally out of line. I was just...' She sighed heavily. 'I felt intimidated by

you when you backed me up to the wall. I had a boyfriend...
not Miles...someone else...who hit me a couple of times when
I wouldn't sleep with him, and so it made me feel uncomfort-
able when you—' She was caught off guard by the groan that
left his chest as he leaned forward and punched the sofa at the
opposite side to where she sat. She jumped.

'Fucking *idiot*!' he shouted. 'I always make such a damned
mess of everything! Why can't I just do the right thing, eh?'

She stroked his leg in a bid to soothe him. 'No...no...you
weren't to know, and I know you well enough to realise that
you were just upset and frustrated by my mixed signals. It
doesn't give you a right to intimidate me. I won't let any man
do that to me again. But I know you well enough—'

He snapped his head around to her. 'No, you don't! That's
the trouble! You know eighteen-year-old me, who was all
sweetness and fucking light. Who I am now bears no resemblance to him. I've seen active service in some of the scariest
places on earth. I've killed people. You have no clue *who* I am
anymore. I'm not even sure *I* know who I fucking am!'

Hearing this admission made her heart ache. This already
damaged man had joined the army to put his anger to good
use, but it clearly hadn't worked in his particular case and had
only served to damage him further. She closed her eyes as
tears cascaded down her face.

'Don't cry, Stevie, please. It breaks my heart that you cry
because of me. I used to make you smile...and now look what I
do... I can't bear it, sweetheart...please.' He scrambled closer to
her and pulled her into his lap where he held her to his chest.
'Please...shhh. Please don't cry. Not because of me. I'm not
worth it.' He stroked her hair as she sobbed into him. He
began to kiss her hair and her cheeks where the tears had left
damp trails.

After a few moments, she began to kiss him too. She

cradled his face and kissed his mouth. She could see the moisture around his eyes glistening in the lamplight. She kissed him again, wiping under his eyes with her thumbs, there was no talking, just kissing and caressing. He reciprocated gently at first.

He ran his hands down her back and slid her bottom nearer to him. She kissed him with increasing urgency and thrust her tongue into his mouth. He groaned the same pained sound he had made the night before.

'Jason...make love to me... I want to help you forget what I said... I didn't mean it... I want to prove that to you.' She looked directly into his eyes as she spoke, hoping that her sincerity was evident.

He shook his head. 'No...no...I won't...you can do better than me. There was an element of truth in what you said.'

She took his face in her hands again. 'Jason...no...I was *wrong*. I want you to make love to me. I want to feel how I felt last night...please?'

'No...I can't...not like this. Not when you're feeling guilty. Pity sex isn't my thing.'

She stood from his lap, remembering that she was still damp from the smelly loch water. She held out her hand. 'It wouldn't be pity sex. I need you. Even if you just hold me tonight. Please?' He didn't move as he gazed up at her with a blank expression. 'Come on, we'll take a shower then. I've spent most of the day upside down in the water. You can wash my hair.' She smiled. When he still didn't move, she tugged at the hem of her top and pulled it over her head. Next she kicked off her boots and slipped down her khakis.

She stood before him in her underwear, plain black, every day cotton underwear, nothing fancy—a fact that she regretted now that she was displaying it so brazenly. His expression changed. Biting his lip and with dilated pupils, he stood slowly. She stepped towards him and grasped the hem of his T-shirt. In one swift move it was gone. Next she crouched and lifted each foot in turn and removed his heavy boots and socks. Then his pants were pulled down his long toned thighs, and he stepped out of them. He stood before her in black fitted boxers.

Stunning.

Confidently taking his hand, she led him through the door past his bedroom and into the bathroom. Leaning over, she turned on the water in the walk-in shower. He watched her every move silently. She checked the temperature, and when it was about right she turned to him. Crouching before him again, she tugged his boxers down his legs, freeing his arousal. Gripping his hips, she kissed him there and glanced up to find his eyes closed and lips parted. Standing once again, she unhooked her bra. He opened his eyes again and continued to watch her. She slipped her panties off and grasped his hand once again, drawing him forward to join her under the water.

He closed his eyes and leaned his head back onto the tiles. She found his body wash and squeezed some into her hands. She made lather and spread it slowly all over his chest and down the rest of his toned, muscular torso. She took his arousal in her hands and worshipped him again as he stared at her hands and braced himself. His breathing became erratic and loud until he threw his head back, closed his eyes, and made a guttural noise as he came, grasping her arms and pulling her into his chest. Eventually, he dropped his head back down and looked at her.

Her tears were relentless. 'I'm so sorry that my words hurt you. I'm very angry with myself for what I said. It was wrong. I can't even begin to imagine the things you've done and the things you've seen, but those things were necessary. What I said *wasn't* necessary in any way. I wish I could wash my words away with the soap so they can't hurt you anymore. It's your turn to forgive me now. Do you think you can?'

He nodded as he kept his glassy eyes locked on hers. She rubbed the soap from his body, and while he stood, allowing the suds to rinse away, she washed herself under his watchful gaze.

She let the water cascade over her hair and face, and whilst her eyes were closed, his breath heated her neck as he began to leave a trail of feather-light kisses on her over-sensitised skin. It was as if he had awoken from a trance. She didn't speak or make a sound. She simply brought her arms around him and cradled him to her. He slipped his arms around her and pulled her close, still leaning against the tiles.

He slid down the wall and pulled her with him. 'I'm sorry too...the things I said about fuck buddies—'

'Hey...let's pretend that it all washed away. Let's not keep dragging awful things back up. It's all forgotten, okay?'

He nodded against her neck. They stayed huddled together until Jason began to shiver. 'Come on, let's get you to bed.' She pulled him up and wrapped him in a clean towel that was folded on the vanity unit. She wrapped herself in another and pulled him by the hand towards the bedroom. Once inside she rubbed him down with the towel and then did the same to herself. She pulled back the covers and climbed in naked, holding her arms open for him. He climbed in beside her and immediately nuzzled into her breasts. He stayed there just holding onto her as she stroked his back.

After a while, his breathing changed, and she could tell he was sleeping, so she closed her eyes and allowed herself to drift off too. The last couple of days had been draining, to say the least. Sleep was something she definitely needed.

CHAPTER THIRTEEN

*O*nce again Jason opened his eyes to find that his arms were wrapped around Stevie.

My soulmate .

He thought back to the events of the night before. He was ashamed of his behaviour. If there was a sure-fire way to push this woman as far away as she could possibly get, he'd done it. Yet she had come back to him. She'd comforted him. She'd wanted to take back her hurtful words even though he probably deserved them, and she'd *stayed* with him. If only it was as simple as taking back words to rid oneself of terrible memories.

Last night had been so intimate, even though they hadn't made love, just being washed and pleasured by her and then being held to her breasts and falling asleep in her arms. It was the most intimate night he'd spent with anyone.

Ever.

And now he lay as still as possible, barely breathing. He didn't dare move a muscle, considering that things had gone so terribly wrong the last time he had awoken with her in bed beside him. Instead, he carefully inhaled her scent. Except this time she smelled of him—his body wash at least—and the scent enveloped him warmly like her arms had done, giving him sense of belonging that was long overdue; like she was marked as his for real, even though she really wasn't. In a few days' time, she'd be gone and he would be changed irrevocably. He watched her sleep for a while, trying to commit to his memory the way she looked and felt in his arms. It would be a cruel memory to be left with, but it would be marginally better than having no memory of it at all.

Her eyelids fluttered open, and she gazed up at him. He held his breath. Waiting. To his relief, she leaned up and kissed him, stroking her nose down his tenderly. Pulling herself to a sitting position she pushed him onto his back and began to kiss his chest, his tattoos receiving special attention. He closed his eyes, soaking up each and every sensation.

Smoothing her hands up and down his body, she grasped him again, sliding her hand up and down as she kissed his neck. He remained silent, expecting that any moment he would wake up and the latter part of last night and the whole of this morning thus far would have been a cruel dream. He waited, but other than the wonderful sensations shooting around his body like shafts of light, awakening every nerve ending, the dream remained a reality.

She rose above him and took what she wanted, slowly and tenderly. He gazed up at her to see her head back, lips slightly parted and her eyes closed. *So, so beautiful. And so damned sexy.* She began to move on him, and he slipped his hands up to caress first her waist, enjoying the concave curve down to her hip. This wasn't just sex. This meant something. Knowing this terrified him, but watching her, feeling her, having her here was better than any dream he'd experienced in the time they had been apart. The look on her face was mesmerising. She was lost in bliss. How had he survived all these years without the other half of his soul? The question would no doubt remain unanswered thanks to the brief nature of her visit and he wondered how the hell he would cope when she left if this was how she affected him still.

Leaning forward, she pulled the long veil of her deep auburn hair over one shoulder and placed her hands on his chest, opening her eyes. They were somehow no longer vivid blue but dark indigo. She stared deeply into him as if looking into his soul and moved faster until her mouth was open and her brow was furrowed. He watched her in awe. Never had he experienced such an array of emotions watching a woman come apart like this.

Her nails dug into his shoulders, and she cried out, tears springing from her eyes and down her face, falling in chilled drops onto his heated skin as she kept her eyes locked on his and repeated his name over and over.

Hearing her call his name in her desperation sent him heaven bound as he gripped her waist with one hand and her breast with the other. 'Stevie...oh please...' His garbled and almost incoherent words fell from his lips as he stared into her blue eyes.

She smiled down at him as he began to fall back to earth from somewhere around Jupiter. He tugged her face down to his and kissed her deeply before whispering, *'My...soul... mate,'* again as he caressed her cheek. 'You know...I don't mean to make you cry. You're supposed to feel good.' He kissed her hair.

'I do feel good. In fact *good* doesn't even begin to describe how I feel with you when we're together like this. I've never had such an emotional reaction to...making love like I do with you. So don't take it as a bad sign.' She nuzzled his chest and traced his tattoos with her fingertips. He decided to let the matter drop. She had hesitated before saying *making love* as if she wasn't sure what label to put on it. But the reaction she'd had reassured him that it certainly wasn't *just sex* to her.

They lay snuggled together for another hour. Smiling and caressing but saying very little. Once again worry crept into Jason's mind about what would happen when she left. He fought it away, doing his best to concentrate on the fact that her eyes were sparkling once again and he'd had something to do with that. What he had taken away, he had also begun to put back. It felt so good. He focused on the little flecks of grey that he could see in her eyes. He focused on the way she wet her lips with a flick of her tongue right before she kissed him. He thought back to the intense, earth shattering orgasm that had racked his body, rendering him an incoherent mess. If he wasn't so sated he could feel embarrassed about his cries. But frankly, he would do it all over again...and he *hoped* to.

He traced her arm with his fingers and watched as little goosebumps rose at his touch. 'Today is freedom day, so the kids are allowed to take the bus into the nearby town with my staff as chaperones. It's meant to be of benefit to the kids for their independence, but it's also supposed to be a day when the accompanying teachers get to chill out. So...'

'So, there really is a freedom day? I thought that perhaps Matt at the cycle place had got his wires crossed somehow.'

Jason cringed. 'Oh...yeah...no I just...I didn't want you getting involved with him. He's a bit of a ladies man if you know what I mean.'

She smiled up at him. 'Hmm, a little jealous maybe?'

He chuckled. 'Okay, now who's being arrogant?'

She tapped his chest lightly. 'I *am* not! I just think that you were being a little possessive.'

He manoeuvred to face her. 'Oh? And you haven't looked daggers at Dorcas much at all, have you?' She was silent for a few minutes, and he wondered if perhaps he'd hit a nerve. After chewing on his lip for a few moments whilst he decided how to put things, he spoke, 'I'm going to be completely honest with you, okay? Dee and I...we kissed... once...a long time ago, but I didn't feel *anything* for her and so I put a stop to it. She's like a kid sister to me. I think she has a wee bit of a crush...I admit that. But *I* don't see *her* that way.'

She nodded, looking thoughtful. 'I knew there'd been *something* between you. I have a kind of radar for these things.' She flopped onto her back. 'She still wants you. I'm sure of that.'

'Hey.' He leaned over her. 'She's not getting me, so it's a moot point. Can we just get back to what we're going to do today? I have a few ideas.' He raised his eyebrows playfully.

'Oh yes? And am I to guess that they involve me...maybe staying here...in bed with you...naked?' She smiled. 'To help me chill out obviously...not because you have an amazing body that I may have become addicted to.'

He smirked. 'Well no...*obviously* to chill out...and...you know...*sleep*.'

She bit her lip and nodded. 'Well yes, sleep is *very* important.'

'It is...*very*.' He raised his eyebrows to emphasise his words.

'I mean, they say an average of eight hours a night is a good ball park figure.' She traced the line of his chest tattoo with her fingertips again, acting coy.

He pursed his lips and tried to look serious. 'Eight hours...absolutely.'

She looked up at him through her long lashes. 'And you

know, if sex happened to *occur* at any point during that time...
Well, that's exercise and—'

'Exercise is vital to good health, so that would be *totally*
acceptable.' Jason pulled his lips in, trying not to laugh at her
playful nature. He was loving this side of her.

She nodded, a grin spreading across her face. '*Totally*.'

She giggled, making Jason's insides flip. God she was so
adorable. After a while, he spoke again, clasping his hands in
hers. 'But maybe we do need to talk. You go home in a few
days, and I...I don't know how to feel...what to think.'

She rolled over onto her front and propped herself up on
her elbows. 'We knew this would happen, Jason.'

'Yes, but that doesn't make it any easier. How do we *deal*
with everything? What do you say to people? I...I still don't
want to go back. I *can't* go back, Stevie...*ever*.'

Her eyes filled with sadness. 'I was afraid you'd say that.'

He sat up. 'Look, let's go get breakfast, and then we'll
come back here and spend the day together, eh? We'll figure
this out. I promise.'

'I'd better sneak around the camp the other way so that
I'm not seen. I need to get clean clothes and undies.'

'Hmm, I think I prefer you out of them all together.' He
leaned and slapped her bottom, making her squeal.

'Reynolds! I'll get you back!'

He jumped up and dashed to the bathroom, locking the
door before she could retaliate.

The early morning sun was warm against Jason's skin as he
lowered himself to the sun lounger in his small garden area.
He didn't need a bigger space considering the forests, mountains, and rivers were only just through the trees. He closed

his eyes and raised his arms above his shirtless body, feeling glad that he chose to wear his shorts and make the most of the sun. He didn't know how long Stevie would be before she returned, but he figured now that the picnic was all prepared he could relax for a while.

Before too long he had drifted off.

He opened his eyes on his old bedroom. It was the day of the Leavers' Ball. His mum and the bastard had left for work, and Dillon had presumably gone too, seeing as his music wasn't blurting from his room like it usually did.

Jason glanced around his room. His trophies and medals for various achievements in sport, writing, maths, and chess, were dotted around the space. His pin-board displayed photos of Stevie. His soulmate . Her long dark auburn hair blowing across her face, a beautiful smile fixed in place, and freckles just visible on her nose. They'd been at one of their picnics down by the river. Their favourite place. She looked so happy. But today was the day he would break her heart. Today was the end. The only other way out of this hell was suicide, but he couldn't do that. Not to Stevie.

He had to stay in the world where she was. At least he could take comfort in that even if he wouldn't actually be with her anymore.

He'd had enough of the punishments for ridiculous mistakes. He wasn't perfect. And no matter how hard he tried, he never would be. His father would never accept him for who he was, faults and all. He would never be the doctor his father so desperately pushed him towards being. He had no clue how long the beatings would continue if he stayed, and now that he was older the urge to hit back was stronger than ever. But he refused to lower himself to that level. No. He would rise above it. He would choose his own destiny.

He'd booked a train ticket north and would be joining the

army now that he was eighteen and free to do so. His belongings were packed into a bag along with the certificates he would need to show his grades up to now, his identity, and his date of birth. He pulled the photo of Stevie by the river from the pin board and sat on his bed.

'I'll love you forever, Jason Reynolds. You're my puffin.' She had smiled when she had handed him the little pin badge of the sea bird. He took it with a smile but felt rather puzzled at her choice of gift. He had made her a little silver coloured heart pendant in his metal work class and had engraved it for her.

'Puffin?'

'My puffin,' she repeated as her cheeks blushed the most beautiful shade of pink. 'They...they mate for life...and no matter how far apart they are through winter, they always find each other again. That's me and you, Jason.'

Tears welled in his eyes as he remembered her words.

This was going to be the longest winter.

He placed the photo back on his nightstand. Taking it would only remind him of what he had left behind. Seeing her smile would torment him and drive him insane. Instead, he reached for the little puffin pin badge she had given him. It would remind him without forcing him to look into those clear blue eyes of hers, where he would drown along with his resolve and get on the first train back.

No, he had to make this a permanent exit from his life as he knew it.

No more.

He would take no more.

CHAPTER FOURTEEN

Day Five of Hell

S tevie managed to sneak back unnoticed to her cabin. She flicked on her iPod as she readied herself for a day with Jason. The first track on her random selection this time was a little more upbeat. 'I Caught Fire (In Your Eyes)' by The Used resonated through the room and she danced around, singing along. Trying her best to ignore the meaning of the lyrics and the effect they were having on her, she tidied her hair and slipped on some white lace undies. Dressing in a pair of lilac shorts and a fitted white T-shirt, her mood was happier and she had no idea why. Before the day was over, she and Jason would *have* to talk things through and discuss the dreaded *F* word.

The *future*.

All she wanted to do was live in the moment, but even a dreamer like her knew that this was not something she could do forever. Finding Jason again had been completely unexpected, quite traumatic but...overall...*wonderful*. The sad and terrifying thing was that she knew it couldn't last. There was too great a distance between them, and he would never move back down south. She couldn't possibly leave London and move here. It just wasn't happening.

Three years ago after suffering muscle weakness her mum had been diagnosed with Myasthenia Gravis and Stevie had vowed never to leave her side for any longer than absolutely necessary. It was a condition neither had heard of before and the news had come as a shock initially. Despite Dana's protestations that she could look after herself Stevie had resolved that her life would remain in London where she could be close by should her mother's condition worsen. There were no real definites with MG—each case being quite different—and there was no cure. There were very few people who knew about the diagnosis as Dana was determined to live as normal a life and possible, and for the most part she succeeded. So whilst Jason promised a solution, *she* just didn't see there being one. And to add to that after what she had witnessed of the whole long distance thing, she just *knew* it wouldn't work.

It *never* worked.

She found David sitting on the steps to his cabin, listening to his MP3 player with his eReader in hand. She strolled across and he pulled his ear buds out as she approached.

'Hi Stevie, what you up to today?'

'I'm...I'm...look...can I speak to you in confidence?' She sighed.

He frowned. 'Yes...yes of course. What is it? Has something happened?'

She cringed a little. 'Well, yes...and no...but...mainly yes.'

His tone changed. 'Has this got something to do with Reynolds?' He looked ready to hit someone—namely Jason.

Holding up her hands, she tried to reassure him. 'Yes...but it isn't what you think. Can we go inside for a few minutes?'

'Sure, come on in. Do you want a coffee?'

'No. Thank you, though.'

Once inside the cabin, she sat in the chair in the corner of the room. 'I want to explain something to you about Jason and I...and why the observations you made were actually fairly close to the truth.'

David sat down on his bed. 'Oh?'

'The thing is... And this is going to sound *crazy* but please bear with me... When I was a teenager, Jason was my boyfriend. I was in love with him.'

His eyebrows rose. 'What? How?'

'We were at school together. But when we were eighteen...we...kind of...erm...lost touch. I had no clue he owned this place or I might not have come. He...he broke my heart back then. And seeing him this week completely out of the blue like this has stirred up a whole lot of memories. It's been difficult to see him but amazing at the same time. We have a lot of things to work through. But it appears there are still feelings there on both sides. I have *no clue* where this will go, if anywhere at all, but I wanted to explain why I've been acting so...strange.'

David stared open mouthed for a few moments. He ran his hands over his head and then let them flop to his lap. 'Bloody hell. Seriously? So you came here and had *no clue*? None at all? And then here he was...your long lost first love?'

She nodded. 'Yep, that about sums it up.'

'Bloody hell.'

She smiled. 'David you said that already.'

'Sorry, I'm just *shocked*. It's like something you read about... Like fate or some other such bullshit that I don't even believe in. But here's living proof that I'm probably wrong about that.'

'Well there had to be a first time for you being wrong, eh?'

He grinned. 'So...you'll be spending freedom day with Reynolds then?'

'If you don't mind. We really need to talk.'

'Yeah...yeah...I bet you do. Lots of catching up to do, I bet.'

'You could say that. And please...the circumstances behind all of this are *very* personal. I won't tell you all the gory details but suffice it to say that this has not been easy on either of us. So not a word to anyone, okay? The kids certainly don't need to know.'

David made a zipper gesture over his mouth, turned an invisible lock, and threw the imaginary key over his shoulder.

She smiled warmly. 'Thanks, David. I appreciate this.'

'Hey, that's what friends are for, you know. And look, I *really* am sorry for my attitude about the whole thing yester-day. I was way out of order.'

She made a dismissive gesture with her hands. 'It's forgotten.'

Stevie arrived at Jason's cabin to find him lying on a sun lounger in his garden. He was shirtless and wearing board shorts. There was a serene smile on his face. His eyes were closed and his arms were stretched over his head. She could see every single defined muscle on his torso, and her eyes were drawn to the V, which pointed south. Her heart skipped at the sight. She noticed a silvery scar on his side like someone had gouged a chunk out of his flesh. She wondered if this was one of the permanent reminders of his so-called father's abuse. The thought made her shiver involuntarily as nausea rose within her.

He must have sensed her presence as he opened one eye and a grin spread across his face. 'Hey, gorgeous. You're back and you look sexy as hell. I thought you'd changed your mind.'

'Absolutely not. I wanted to see what you had planned for me on our freedom day. So, are you going to tell me?'

He held his hand out to her and she went to him. He pulled her down so that she sat on him, and he leaned up to meet her face to face. 'Guess what I've been thinking about since you left this morning?'

'Hmm...let me think.'

'Nah...too slow...I'll tell you.' He reached up and cupped her face in his hands. 'In all of my life, I have *never* witnessed a more beautiful sight than *every single time* I see you.'

She scrunched her face. 'Huh? That makes no sense, you crazy man.'

'It makes complete sense. It just means that every time I see you, you look more beautiful than the last time.'

The heat rose in her cheeks as her heart swelled at his romantic words. They were spoken like a man in love. But she didn't dare hope that he was. Her heart was at breaking point already. The tiniest little nudge and it would shatter all over again.

'So what are we doing?'

'Well, I've prepared us a delicious picnic that we're going to take through those trees where a little surprise awaits.' He kissed her deeply, caressing her tongue with his own.

Once he pulled away, she rose from his lap so that he could retrieve the basket of goodies. He took her hand and led her to the bottom of his garden area and through a slight gap in the trees. A beautiful sight greeted her. The cornflower blue sky lay overhead, and the sun cast dancing spots of light along the water. The river looked so clean and the bank they stood upon was covered with wild flowers. The air smelled fresh, and a welcome cool breeze bounced off the water.

'Jason, this is so beautiful. It...it reminds me of...' Her words trailed off as she was momentarily transported back in time to their very own special place by the river.

He lay a blanket out under a large sun parasol that he had already pushed into the ground to shield them from the sun's rays.

He held his arms out wide. 'It's my very own little patch of paradise.'

She took a lung full of the fresh Scottish air. 'Hmmm, you got that right.'

They settled on the blanket, and he took out a bottle of wine and two tin cups. Pouring the amber liquid, he carefully glanced up at her. She tried to stifle a laugh but failed.

'Hey! What's so funny?' He pretended to be hurt. 'Only the best for my gorgeous Stevie you know.'

'Well gee, thanks, Jace. It's good to know you remember how important I am.'

He stopped what he was doing. 'You called me *Jace*.' He smiled. 'No one's called me that in...well...ten years.' He handed her a cup of wine.

'Really? So what *do* you get called? I bet you had a nickname in the army. *Everyone* seems to get a nickname in the army.' She grinned.

His cheeks coloured. 'Yeah...well...let's talk about something else, eh?'

She wagged her finger at him. 'No, no, spoilsport! I think I've hit a nerve! Come on, spill it, Reynolds.'

He rolled his eyes, put his drink down and flopped onto his back covering his eyes with his arm. 'No...it's *really* silly.'

'Exactly! That's why I neeeeeed to know! Come on!' She prodded and poked him in the ribs.

'Okay! Okay! I give in. But you'll never see me the same again.'

She pulled her lips in to stop the grin and held two fingers up to her head in a kind of salute. 'I swear I won't laugh. Guide's honour and all that.'

Jason peeked out from under his arm. 'Well it's clear that *you* were never a Girl Guide.'

She gasped in feigned shock and put her hand over her heart. 'What *do* you mean?'

'Well *that* was not a Girl Guide's salute.'

She gave him a snide look. 'Whatever, Reynolds. Stop stalling and spill it.'

'Okay...at first...I used to get called Rhino. You know cause it kind of sounded like Reynolds, and it was supposed to be ironic on account of the fact that although I was quite buff I was still the smallest and skinniest bloke in my unit.'

'Ooookay...and then?' She bit her lip, eagerly awaiting the thing she could tease him with from now on.

He twisted so that he could point to the scar on his side that had fascinated her earlier. 'See this scar?'

'Oh yes, I was going to ask about that.'

'Yeah...well...I was out in the Middle East. I was on patrol when I got hit by a stray bullet. Fucking hurt like hell. Cracked my ribs but missed all the vital stuff, thank God.' He stopped.

'And?'

He covered his eyes again. 'Oh fuck, I'll never live this thing down.' He huffed. 'After that happened... When I was back out there again... After I'd recovered...which took—'

'Get on with the story, Reynolds. I want the meaty bit!'

'J.R.'

'What?'

'I got called J.R. It became a huge standing joke about the fact that I got shot...and my initials...you know.'

She burst into laughter and rolled onto her back. Tears streamed down her face.

Jason began to laugh too. 'It's still a mystery today, you know, who *actually* shot me, just like the bloody T.V. show. I only ever saw Dallas re-runs, but thanks to that lot I'll never forget it! Someone even bought me a cowboy hat and cigar for my birthday.' He laughed louder at the memory.

She rolled on the blanket so that she was leaning on his chest. Once their laughter had subsided, she spoke again. 'I'm glad it wasn't serious...your bullet wound, I mean. The scar's quite sexy.' She traced the line of it with her fingers.

She propped her chin on her hand so that she could look at his face. He lay there with his eyes closed for a while. 'The first day I saw you...before I knew it was you—'

'When you were ogling me through the trees? Yes, I remember.'

She slapped his chest without any real force. 'When I saw you I noticed the tattoo on your back that looks like script. What does it say?'

'Ah that...I had it done when I was out in the Middle East.' His cheeks coloured and he swallowed. 'It's Arabic, but it roughly translates as *Never alone with you in my heart*. It was important to me to get it done at the time. For the first time, I was beginning to feel a kind of healing...you know... from everything that happened at home. But it was lonely. I'd sit and look up at the night sky and millions of stars were visible. I used to wonder if you were looking up at the same constellations. I'd left you, but I never forgot. I had my memories and even though it was very painful to think about you, I didn't feel quite so alone when I did.'

Tears stung her eyes. 'You had it done for me?'

He smiled. 'Well, I had it done for *me*. But it was all *about* you.'

Pulling her brow into a frown, she tilted her head to one side. 'But why have it done where you couldn't see it?'

He smiled again and dropped his gaze. 'You'll think I'm silly.'

'No...no I won't.'

He sighed. 'I had it done there so that I *couldn't* see it. Like I couldn't see you. But I knew it was there, and I knew what it stood for. And each time I caught sight of it, I was reminded of you.'

A tear escaped and trailed down her cheek. 'That's the saddest and most romantic thing I've ever heard.'

Silence ensued for a few minutes until Jason spoke. 'I don't usually tell people what it means.'

She pulled herself up to sitting. 'What do you say if they ask?'

'I usually spout off some crap about fighting for my country...or my favourite one is to tell them it's a grocery list.' He grinned and sat up.

'And do they buy that?'

'The groceries? Only if I write the list on paper for them. But it has had quite a high success rate, yes.' His laugh was such a warm, beautiful sound.

She shook her head and pursed her lips at him. 'Nutter.'

'Why thank you, Miss Watts.' His expression changed, his smile disappeared, and he closed his eyes. 'I mean *Mrs. Norton.*'

'I've been thinking about going back to my maiden name, actually.'

'Yeah? I think you should. I feel like I'm having some kind of illicit affair with a married woman.'

She giggled. 'Tell me more about what happened to you when you left.'

'Well, I got on a train...went north to an army base in

Cumbria. I'd already set the wheels in motion so they were expecting me.'

'How long had you been planning it?'

He lowered his gaze. 'Remember that day I played 'It's Been Awhile' for you on my guitar?'

She remembered it vividly. She had always felt there was some hidden meaning in that song just for her. Hearing it again over the last few days had been painful. She nodded, feeling a stinging at the back of her eyes. 'I can't listen to that song to this day. When you played it the other night, it really upset me.'

His glanced up at her again. 'That was the day I'd been told I was accepted.'

'But I thought you had to have medicals, interviews and such.'

'Yes, you do. Remember when I said I was going to see my Aunt Celia in North Yorkshire?'

'Yes, I do remember. I missed you like mad.'

'Well, I actually went away for a two day assessment.'

'Shit. Really? But didn't your mum or dad check up on you?'

'Funnily enough on that occasion, no. She has no telephone, and I purposefully didn't take a mobile phone with me, so I just rang them from a payphone. They bought it hook, line, and sinker.'

'I bet you were relieved.'

'Absolutely. Anyway, then I trained up in Cumbria for twenty-six or so weeks. It was pretty gruelling, but I actually enjoyed it. Met some great blokes up there.'

'What did you train as? Aren't there...you know...different roles in the armed forces?'

'Yeah, I was an infantry soldier. I wanted to be right in the thick of it all. And I certainly got my wish. At the end of train-ing, I was deployed to the front line.'

'Bloody hell. That quick?'

'Yeah, but after all the training, you're totally prepared. It's what every soldier's working towards, after all. It's the whole point.'

'Was it frightening being out there and fighting?'

'Absolutely. I saw things that...' He inhaled deeply. 'Let's just say it made me rethink my life in general. I had a shitty childhood, but there are kids that have it so much worse.'

She looked down at her hands, unable to make eye contact for her next question. 'How many men did you kill?'

'That's not something I think about. I wasn't keeping score. I *can't* think about it. I'd never be able to live with myself if I did.' He closed his eyes and dropped his head forward again. It was clearly a difficult subject for him.

'When did you leave?' She was aware she was interro-gating him, but she needed to know, and whilst he was talking she kept going.

'I left the army when I was twenty-three after being in for just over four years.'

'But you weren't a soldier for very long. You left home to join up. Why did you leave?'

'Ahhh...it felt like being a soldier was the answer. And it was at first. But it ended up being a short-term solution for a long-term problem. I knew I needed more, but I just didn't know what that was... Lots of my friends met girls and did the whole marriage and kids thing, but I just didn't know what to do with my life after I signed off. So I signed up with a private company and worked as paid security out in the Middle East for a couple of years, which paid well.'

'What did that involve?'

'It was...varied. I protected an oil baron mainly. He'd had

death threats, and I was assigned to ensure his safety. Another time, I worked with some visiting politicians out in Saudi. I was with a team, and we were responsible for protecting them during their visit. It was dangerous work, but the money was well in excess of anything else I could've earned.'

'Is that what enabled you to buy this place?'

'Yeah...well, with a little help from the nice bank manager. I was a partner for the first year, but Dougie, the owner at the time, took me under his wing. Bless him. Turned out he was ex-army too. In the end, he sold it to me cheap...*very* cheap. His health was failing. He was a really nice guy. Died last year. He was like a dad...a *real* dad.'

She could see the raw emotion bubbling to the surface and reached out to touch his arm. 'Oh, Jason, I'm so sorry.'

He shrugged. 'Yeah, me too.'

CHAPTER FIFTEEN

The sun was still high in the sky in the late afternoon as Stevie and Jason ate crisps and dips and drank their wine from little tin cups.

Feeling completely contented, she sighed. 'Hmmm, this really takes me back to when we used to sit by the river back home. I used to love those times.'

'Me too. I was only thinking about us by the river today. That's what gave me the idea to bring you here. I had so many photos of you that I took at our special place.'

She pulled her brows into a frown. '*Had*? Don't you have them anymore?'

He shook his head, a look of sadness played on his features. 'I do regret it, but I...I left them behind at home. I couldn't bear the thought of looking at you so happy when I knew that I'd broken your heart.'

Her smile slipped away. 'You did break my heart. I can't deny that. But at least I know *why* now.' She leaned over and kissed his forehead.

He slipped his hand into her hair and pulled her closer. 'Come on...let's go back... I really want to make love to you again, and I'm not sure it'd be a good idea to let that happen out here.' His gaze scorched her already warm skin, and his words made her ache for him.

She fought the feelings he was stirring and almost whined at him. 'But it's so *lovely* out here.'

He feigned shock and gasped. 'Since when did you become an exhibitionist Miss Wat...*Mrs.* Norton?'

She giggled. 'I'm *not* an exhibitionist. I didn't mean I wanted to have *outdoor sex*. I just meant it's so beautiful here... It's a shame to go in.'

He folded his arms and pursed his lips playfully. 'Well okay, let me give you a choice then. You either come back with me now or you become *very* much accustomed to outdoor sex and exhibitionism because I'm making love to you regardless. Although I'm guessing the kids will be back soon, and I'm not sure that being found in *flagrante delicto* is such a good career move for such a talented Science teacher.' He winked. 'So what'll it be?'

'But the picnic—'

'We'll leave it for the ants. Come on.' He grabbed her hand and pulled her to stand in front of him. He tucked a stray strand of hair behind her ear. 'I want you, Stevie. I have no idea how many more times I'll have this opportunity to be with you so...please?'

She touched his cheek and nodded. After all, she didn't really need convincing to get naked with this fine specimen of a man. She wasn't *completely* crazy. She reached up to kiss him lightly as a sudden sadness washed over her. He took her hand, and they walked silently through the long grass and wild flowers, through the gap in the trees and back to the cabin.

An hour later and completely sated once again, they held each other in their post orgasmic haze in the kitchen where they had devoured each other on the counter top. She could feel his rapid heartbeat against her ribs. It was in perfect synchronicity with hers.

Jason peppered light kisses on her cheeks and neck. Once again she rifled through her mind desperately trying to figure out a way to be with him after this short break but no solution presented itself. There was no compromise available to them that she could come up with.

The scent of his skin enveloped her just like his warm embrace, and she sighed as sadness began to weigh heavy on her once more. If only it was just lust, something to experience and get out of her system. But once again, as his body heat seeped into her, she was reminded that this was definitely more than *just sex*. She knew that her heart was slipping away and the tentative hold she currently had on it was failing fast.

'Hmmm, I could get used to this,' he murmured into her neck.

She didn't speak. The lump in her throat and the sated fog in her head making it impossible to produce a coherent thought, never mind a whole sentence.

Jason must have sensed her reluctance to speak as he pulled away from her, cupping her cheek. 'Hey, what's wrong, sweetheart? You've gone quiet...did you...wasn't it good...did you not...' Whoops, the inability to make sense appeared to be contagious.

She shook her head. 'No...I mean *yes* it was good...I'm just...I don't know.' She dropped her gaze.

'Come on, if you have something to say, just say it. We need to be honest with each other if we're going to make this work.'

There he goes again talking about making it work! She let out an exasperated sigh. '*Make this work*? But I'm only here for another two days after today, and one of those is meant for travelling. We're not *permanent*, Jason.' Her voice wavered.

He huffed out a long breath and rested his head on her shoulder. 'And here we go with *the talk* I suppose.'

'I just think there are still things that need to be said. We seem to have fallen back into a relationship, which is *crazy* considering we live in two completely different worlds. And as much as I want to live for the moment, in the end, I'll still be going home.'

He placed his hands on her shoulders. 'What if there was a way to get around it all though? Long distance relationships—'

'Don't work. Let's not fool ourselves,' she interrupted harshly.

'We could *make* it work. I *know* we could figure things out.'

'For how long? What happens when one of us *needs* the other and there are hundreds of miles separating us? What then?'

He took her face in his hands suddenly. 'Stay.'

She widened her eyes. 'What?'

'Stay with me, Stevie. Stay *here*.' The urgency in his voice made her heart ache.

She placed her hands over his and removed them from her face. 'Don't be ridiculous, Jason. My life is in London. I have a job...a home...a *dog*.'

'Get another job...up here. We do have high schools you know. Dogs love it up here too. The outdoors and fresh air are exactly what they need.' He seemed excited at the prospect. The conversation was crazy.

'Come on, in reality we've known each other four or five days. I can't move this far north on a complete whim.'

He frowned. 'What? We've known each other our *whole*

lives.'

She placed her hand on his chest. 'If that were true, things would be *very* different. But...you *left.*' She spoke softly, not wishing to sound accusatory.

'But I don't want to be without you,' he whispered as if speaking normally would break him. 'I've waited for this for ten years. I...I just didn't *realise* I was waiting. Ten years I've been lost. But now I know where my place is.' He placed his hand over her heart. 'I know where I belong, and that's inside you. Body, mind and soul.'

She closed her eyes momentarily, trying to summon up the strength to continue letting him down. Thoughts of her mother struggling alone helped forge the much-needed will within her. 'No, Jason, it's not that simple. *I* could ask *you* to come back to London, but I won't because I know that you wouldn't come. This...what we've had here...has been like a holiday romance. Maybe we just need to treat it as such.'

He stepped away, shook his head, and closed his eyes. 'You don't mean that.'

'Yes...I do,' she lied.

She jumped down from the counter top and gathered her discarded items of clothing, putting them on as she moved around the room until she was fully clothed again. The familiar stinging sensation needled at her eyes once more, meaning she daren't look at him.

He disappeared to his room and returned wearing his shorts. She allowed her gaze to trail the length of his body, taking in his thick arms and solid thighs. The ridges of his tight abs and sculpted, tattooed chest, and up until she met his eyes where her own sadness was reflected back at her. Although his body and mind had changed almost beyond recognition, his eyes still portrayed every single emotion he was feeling. Her lip trembled and her stomach knotted. How she was going to walk away after this she really didn't know. How she would carry on her life as normal she had absolutely no clue. What life would be like knowing he was here and she couldn't be with him would tear her apart.

As she stared at him he swallowed hard, ran his hands through his hair, and rested them on his head. 'So you'll leave and I'll stay here and we'll pretend that this never happened?' His voice was breaking, making the water in her eyes blur her vision.

'I think it's for the best, don't you?' she whispered.

He dropped his hands and held them out to her. 'No, Stevie.' He had that urgent, desperate look in his eyes again as he stepped towards her. 'I think you're scared. And I get that. It's all happened so quickly. And when you showed up here I...I was shocked. I was an arse and I'm so sorry. And I think you're scared that I'll run away again. But I wouldn't *do* that. Things have changed.'

She sighed heavily. 'Yes, they have. And *I* have too.'

His nostrils flared as he kept his intense gaze fixed on her. 'But, but there's no reason it couldn't work long distance. Not if we *want* it to.'

'Look, Jason there are *so* many reasons why this wouldn't work. And at the top of the list are the two most important things. One, *trust*. How can we build that with hundreds of miles between us? And two, I don't *want* a long distance relationship. I want to be with someone I can see, hold, touch, and kiss, make love to whenever I want or need them.'

He looked stunned. Like a rabbit in the headlights. His shoulders sagged as he appeared to succumb to defeat. He didn't speak and so she took that as her cue to leave. She opened the door and walked out of the cabin without looking back.

And crack went another piece of her heart.

CHAPTER SIXTEEN

*J*ason watched as the students returned from their freedom day full of fun stories about where they'd been and what they'd seen. It was great to see them enjoying something other than video games, gadgets, mobile phones, and television. But then again, that had been the whole point of running this place—to get kids to see that there was more to life than what they had known and done before and that a whole new world existed outside of their comfort zones. Seeing them animated and excited *without* a chunk of shiny black plastic in their hands brought with it a huge sense of achievement.

'Jason! It's been amazing! We went up the funky-lar railway thing and saw for miles from the top of the mountain!' a boy called Carl informed him. Jason tried to halt the smile from his lips at the boy's mispronunciation. The funicular railway at Cairngorm Mountain was always a popular destination for his visitors, young and old. The views from the top on a clear day were spectacular.

'That's great. Did you take plenty of photos to show your folks?'

'Yeah! And I bought a baseball cap too!' The boy thrust the green hat in Jason's face.

He clapped his hands together. 'Fantastic. Right you lot. Time for dinner. I think it's pizza tonight.'

'Yes!' was the resounding response from the group of eager teens.

Jason shook his head and grinned as they all ran in the direction of the main hut, the smell of pizza drawing them in like a pied piper for their noses.

Once he had changed into jeans and a black Pearl Jam T-shirt, he made his way to the main hut. On arrival through the doors, he caught sight of Stevie sitting with a table full of girls, who seemed to be regaling her with stories of their trip to Aviemore. They were all sporting matching wristbands and enthusing about the various shops they had visited. She looked up and made eye contact. He smiled warmly and she returned his smile, but hers was tinged with a little sadness.

Whilst the students were devouring their cheese fest, Jason stood at the front. He inserted two fingers into his mouth and whistled loudly to stop the chatter in the room.

'Right, you lot, we're going to have a busy day tomorrow. We're going hiking.' A groan traversed the room. 'Awww, come on, you lazy lot! You've had a chilled out day today, but tomorrow we're going to investigate the flora and fauna of this stunning location. We're taking packed lunches and plenty of water, so it'll be a great day. Anyone who suffers from asthma, please make sure you pack your inhaler. It won't be too strenuous, I promise. Then tomorrow night, it's our final night, so we'll have a party here in the main hut.' The room filled with cheers and whoops. 'Yeah, I thought that'd go down well. Anyway, get plenty of rest tonight. There'll be a movie on in here again tonight, but it will finish before ten so get to bed nice and early. We're getting up very early to set off and make the most of your last day here. Have a great evening everyone.'

He grabbed himself a slice of pizza and made his way over to where Stevie was finally sitting alone. He glanced around and then sat beside her. 'Hey, you okay, gorgeous?'

She nodded. 'You?'

He dropped his pizza onto his plate and lowered his head as his stomach knotted and his throat tightened. 'I'm okay... just...starting to feel the pain of losing you again.'

'I know...me too.'

'Will you come over tonight? We don't have to...you know...we can just talk. Hold each other maybe?' He inwardly cringed hoping she didn't think him too soft.

She shook her head. 'I don't think so...not tonight. I need to get some sleep and so do you.'

He nodded, reluctantly acknowledging that she was speaking sense. 'Yeah...yeah. You're probably right. Well, I'll be going. Sleep well, okay? And I'll see you tomorrow.' He stood from the table.

'But you haven't finished your pizza.'

'Yeah, I'm actually not that hungry. Goodnight, Stevie.' He smiled longingly at her, squeezed her shoulder, and turned to walk away.

Back at his cabin, he slumped onto the sofa and ran his hands through his hair. A million different emotions fought for priority in his mixed up mind. A week ago his life had been simple. Work, eat, sleep. A bit of meaningless sex as stress relief every so often, and then the whole cycle would start again. He had gotten to the point where her face was a fuzzy memory. He had gotten to the point where he didn't think about her *every* day. Well, at least that was what he had told himself. But the truth was that the *idea* of her was ever present. There would be a song on the radio that would spark a memory, or a woman with long auburn hair seen from the back, or a movie, or a fragrance wafting through the air.

He had, on occasion, tried to imagine how she would actually look now, what it would feel like to be with her and talk to her again. To just *know* her again. He'd wondered how she would act and what they would talk about. He'd wondered if he would still find her attractive and would she still find *him* attractive? These questions had all been unexpectedly answered in the last few days. But in finding the answers he had received very little comfort. In fact, he felt more alone than ever before.

She was more beautiful than he could have expected and had matured into such a stunning, sexy woman. Although, she still very much resembled the girl he had loved and left. If he was going to get her to see sense and realise that they could make a relationship work, he'd have to act fast. But what could he do?

He stood and paced the floor.

He flicked on his iPod and found 'It's Been Awhile' by Staind. Turning the volume up, he racked his brain, trying to formulate a plan.

Stevie sat on her bed, trying to read the romance novel that she had borrowed from Mollie, but after a while she realised she was reading the same part over and over again. She tossed it aside and paced the floor. The familiar urge to go to Jason was tugging at her insides again. Perhaps she should just go and explain things? Maybe she could say that she would give the long distance thing a try? But then again there had been no talk of *love* between them. There were feelings, for sure. But how deep his feelings ran was something she really didn't know. And of course there was her mother to think about. She couldn't just keep leaving her at the drop of a hat to make the long journey up to Scotland when she missed Jason. And if she couldn't be with him all the time, how could she know things were okay?

He had left her once. What would stop him doing it again when the going got tough? What was to stop him giving up? Perhaps this was simply a combination of nostalgia and lust? She knew how *she* truly felt. That had never changed for her. He had said he didn't want to lose her, but how could she trust his words? She thought back to a conversation she'd had with him only weeks before he'd left...

'Stevie...*when you think of your future, what do you see?*' *Jason lazily trailed circles on her arm as they lay side by side on a blanket in the long grass by the river.*

'*I see you.*'

He smiled but his brow furrowed. '*You see me? Well, I'm glad to hear that.*'

'*What do you see?*'

He frowned. '*I...I struggle to see that far ahead to be honest, but I know what I want to see and that's you and me...happy somewhere...far away though...not here.*'

'*Why not here?*'

'*Dunno...fancy a change of scenery...as long as you're with me.*' *He clasped her hand and intertwined their fingers.*

She pulled herself nearer to him. '*Well, I'm not going anywhere unless you come too.*'

He kissed her tenderly. '*I love you so much, Stevie Watts. Don't ever stop loving me and don't...don't leave me...not even for Eddie Vedder.*'

She had pursed her lips. '*Oooh that's a big ask...but...okay... I'll never stop loving you, and I'll never leave you as long as you promise never to leave me.*'

Weaving his hand into her hair, he pulled her face towards his and kissed her lovingly once again.

Now that she thought back, she realised *he* hadn't promised *her* that he would never leave. However, he *had* said that he wanted a future with her. But he had *still left. Aargh!* Her confused thoughts danced around her head like the angel and the devil fighting for their point to be heard.

Needing a complete distraction, she flicked on her iPod and selected random. 'When You're Gone' by Avril Lavigne was the first track. It reminded her of what she had once lost and was on the verge of losing again.

Her stomach knotted as she thought about how much she had loved him all those years ago and how much she still did. *Why can't things be simple?* She flopped onto the bed, and bending forward, she placed her head in her hands. Tears fell from her eyes and formed wet patterns on the floor beneath her. She wanted nothing more than to be with him, but she also knew that it wasn't possible.

But at least this time, she would get to say goodbye.

CHAPTER SEVENTEEN

Day Six of Hell

*B*leary eyed and puffy faced, Stevie arrived at the main hut for breakfast. It was six thirty, and she surmised that the students were clearly not early morning people due to the lack of conversation and the subdued atmosphere that hung in the air. She made her way over to the hot buffet and piled her plate with scrambled eggs, bacon, and toast. She figured she'd need the energy considering the fifteen-mile hike they were setting out on very soon. Jason had informed David that it would be around seven hours including a break for lunch and breaks for water along the way.

Dressed in khakis and a long sleeved white T-shirt to reflect the heat, she had pulled on her walking boots. Her hair was scraped back into a ponytail, and she had fed the tail through the back of the baseball cap she wouldn't usually be caught wearing. But sunstroke and heat exhaustion were things she could do without and so she had prepared appropriately. She was as ready as she would ever be. David joined her a few minutes later piling his plate with double the amount of food that she had.

She stared wide-eyed at the mountain before her. 'Good grief, David Harris, where on *earth* are you going to put that lot?'

He grinned widely at her. 'Not *on earth*...in my belly! I'm a growing lad, you know. Need the energy for today's expedition.' He winked.

'Hmmm. You'll need a wheelbarrow to carry your belly in at this rate. And as for being a growing lad, you'll be growing rapidly outwards if you keep eating like that.'

'Nah. This is standard for me.' He fell silent as they walked over to a vacant table and sat down. The zombified teens all milled about aimlessly. David was quiet for a while, thoughtfully munching his way through his heap of food. Eventually he broke the silence. 'So...did you and Jason get anything sorted? I...I don't mean to pry...just asking as a concerned friend.'

She smiled. 'Thanks. We talked, but I'm not sure ours is a situation that can be resolved easily.' Her appetite ebbed away.

'No, I can imagine it must be quite difficult. So much history. So much *distance*. Look, I know it's none of my business, but...well...you have a good job. The opening for Head of Science is up after the summer break, and I think you stand a good chance. People have been talking, and it seems you're the favourite for the role. I...I wouldn't want to see you throw that away for some bozo who broke your heart once before. I felt I should say. I hope you don't mind.'

'Thanks, David. I appreciate your honesty and your concern. And don't worry. I'll still be coming back to London with you.' Sadness washed over her as she spoke the words.

At that point Dorcas walked in, as bright and breezy as

usual, and began to gather the teens together to brief them about the hike. Stevie couldn't help the stab of jealousy that bit into her mind as she was reminded that Dorcas would be staying here...with Jason, after she had gone.

Stevie and David finished their food and followed the rest of the crew outside. The sun was already starting to warm the air, and the kids were finally beginning to wake up now that they were fuelled. Dorcas and Harry, who had come in especially for the day, led the way, and David and Stevie brought up the rear. She glanced around to see if Jason was there and was disappointed when she couldn't see him. She wondered if he had decided not to take part in the hike today after all and her heart sank at the unwanted thought.

They had been walking for around ten minutes when Jason appeared out of nowhere and tapped her on the shoulder.

She turned her face and smiled widely at him. 'Oh! Hi. Where did you come from?'

'I was running a little late, so I brought the bike up and parked it just back there. I didn't feel like jogging up here in this heat.' He seemed very smiley and looked divine. His collar length dark hair was pulled back into a ponytail, and he wore long shorts, hiking boots, and a white T-shirt with the WFH logo across the front. Dorcas and Harry were dressed identically—like a uniform.

As if taking this as his cue, David gestured further up towards the middle of the group of students. 'I'll go and check that everyone's behaving themselves.' She smiled and made a mental note to thank him later.

Once David was out of earshot, Jason asked, 'So...how did you sleep last night?' A look of concern etched his features.

She cringed. 'Not too well...so many thoughts whizzing around my head, you know?'

'Oh good, so it wasn't just me then?' He held her arm to pause her as the others walked on. Safe in the knowledge that they were still in view but out of earshot, she stopped. 'Look... tonight's our last night. I'd like to spend it with you. I'm not asking for anything other than your company. I just...I feel that maybe we *need* this. We need to decide on a way forward and this is the last opportunity to do things face to face. I...I... want us to swap numbers. Is that okay? Or at least I want you to have mine. What do you think?'

'I think that's fine. But I just can't think about all that now. Let's talk things through tonight. Right now we're both working.'

Apparently not satisfied with her answer he grabbed his phone from his pocket. 'Look...just get your phone out. Let's do the numbers thing now. Then we can just forget about it.'

She sighed and took out her phone. Jason sent her his number and vice versa. He looked happy and relieved to know there was a tenuous connection between them. No matter how small.

The hike took in some of the most breath-taking scenery Stevie—and the kids by the sounds of the oohs and ahhs—had ever witnessed. The sky was a vivid azure once again, and the clouds that bothered to make an appearance did so in pretty, little white wisps, like the end of a candy floss. The distant mountains reached towards the sky and birds of prey circled on the warm therms overhead. There were several stops for water, top ups of sunscreen, and snacks. Eventually they stopped for lunch in a stunning location off the beaten track and under the shade of the Scot's Pines. The surrounding colours and the pungent, sweet fragrance of the trees made her heart flutter.

This was the life.

This was what God had meant people to experience, not high-rise apartments, traffic noise, exhaust fumes, crime, and war. No; clean air, birdsong, blue skies, and vast mountainous backdrops. That's what life was supposed to be about. She inhaled a lung full of the balmy, fresh air and smiled widely.

'It suits you.'

She looked up into the handsome face she had once been besotted with. 'What does?'

'The great outdoors.' He opened his arms out to his sides and moved as if to showcase that very thing. 'I caught you smiling, Mrs. Norton. You're loving this.'

She couldn't help giggling. 'Ahhh...caught red handed. Yes, it really is stunning.' He sat beside her. 'So...you have a motorbike? I would never have imagined you on a two wheeler.'

'No? Not even with the hair and the tats?' He sniggered. 'I love my bike. So much freedom.'

She snorted. 'So much *danger*, more like.'

His expression became serious. 'The danger only becomes an issue when you take stupid chances. I choose to stay alive instead.'

She pursed her lips for a moment. 'I've never been on a bike,' she said thoughtfully.

'Never? Shame. I bet you'd look a damn fine sight in leathers.'

She couldn't see his eyes, thanks to his shades, but she could imagine they were mischievous, rather like his half smile.

She scrunched her face. 'Hmmm. I'm not so sure about that.'

He nudged her shoulder. 'Come on... I'll have to take you for a spin sometime.'

'Well, considering I'm going home in less than twenty four hours, I'm guessing that won't be happening any time soon.' She immediately regretted her words.

His smile disappeared. 'You have to keep reminding me, don't you?'

'I'm sorry but it's the truth.'

Suddenly, there was a loud scream and a commotion coming from a small cluster of rocks a short distance away where some of the girls had been sitting.

'Oh shit! What's happened?' She rose and rushed over, closely followed by the rest of the staff.

'Miss! Miss! Jess has fallen, and I think she's broken her leg or something!' a rather panicked girl shouted and waved her arms as the staff approached.

The girl in question had fallen from the rock where she was sitting and had landed badly. She was laying at the foot of the large boulder screaming in agony. Stevie glanced down at the poor girl and her stomach lurched. Her foot appeared to be facing in the wrong direction at the ankle and memories of her conversation with Mollie sprang to mind, creating the visual she'd been avoiding. Jason deftly made his way down to where Jess was and examined the girl's leg. He tried to calm her down but she was more than a little distressed.

He called up to where everyone was gathered. 'It's a nasty break. Can someone ring for an ambulance please? Quick!' he shouted. Dorcas got right onto it. 'Stevie, can you get down here? We can't move her, but I think she'd feel better if you were here.'

With Harry and David's help, she clambered carefully down to where Jess was sobbing and clinging to Jason's hand as her friends looked on, some of them crying too. When she reached the girl, Stevie held her hand and stroked her hair, talking calmly and trying to reassure her that help was on its way.

'The ambulance will be about fifteen minutes. They've said not to move her but to make sure she is shaded and given water to keep her hydrated,' Dorcas called from above them. Water was passed down and a makeshift shade was constructed roughly using twigs and picnic blankets.

Fifteen minutes later, right on time, the paramedics made their way to where Jess was laying injured. She was given something to ease the pain, but agonised cries still rang out through the trees as her leg was straightened and fastened into a splint. Once she was strapped to a backboard, she was carefully lifted back up to where the ambulance had stopped.

'Am I okay to come with her?' Stevie asked as Jess clung to her hand.

'Of course...that's no problem.' The paramedic smiled warmly. She climbed into the back of the ambulance and gave a reassuring wave to Jess's friends and the rest of the staff.

'Call me when you have any news!' Jason called just as the doors were closed.

CHAPTER EIGHTEEN

Day Seven of Hell

*I*t was three in the morning when Stevie finally arrived back to camp with Jess, who was now sporting a cast that reached from toe to thigh. Thankfully the break was clean and didn't need surgery. She had been very brave, and her only bother seemed to be that her favourite jeans were now ruined thanks to her nasty fall and the need to cut them from her legs. Stevie helped her get into her dorm where her friends helped her change and get into bed. The poor girl was exhausted and desperate to get home to her mum. There had been talk of getting her home straight away, but after a call to her mum by one of the doctors at the hospital, it was decided that it would be easier if she could travel home with her friends, the proviso being that she was given ample room for her cast.

She arrived at Jason's cabin without thinking. It was as if her heart and body were set to autopilot mode. Luckily, he had been expecting her and had left the door unlocked. She stripped down to her underwear and climbed into bed beside him. He enveloped her in his arms and mumbled in his sleep. The chance of a last night had been taken from them through no one's fault. Overwhelmed by sadness at being held in his arms this way, she swallowed hard and tried to fend off the threatening tears. They had fallen asleep this way so many times when they were innocent teenagers—fully clothed and just holding each other. But this was different. This was the last time.

This was goodbye.

Tomorrow...or rather later today, she would say the word to him for the last time, to the man who she had given her heart to ten years ago and had lost it to all over again in the last week.

This was the end of Stevie and Jason.

'Love...my soulmate ...love you,' came Jason's mumbled voice as he nuzzled her hair. His words spoken whilst unconscious were her undoing, and the tears began to flow relentlessly.

Stevie awoke a few hours later. Jason's arm was still wrapped around her, his chin resting on her head. She stretched to see the clock. It was seven already, and she still had to pack. Slowly and carefully, she lifted his arm, slid out of the bed, and placed it back down. She grabbed her clothes and hurriedly dressed as she reached the kitchen.

Dashing back to her cabin and managing to do so unseen, she began to pack her bag. The coach was picking them up at eight, and breakfast was being served early today. Once she had packed, showered, and dressed in the clothes she had left out, she made her way to grab a quick bite.

David made a beeline for her. 'Hey, thanks for yesterday. I

think it was best that you went. I'm just not sympathetic enough. Kids get sports injuries and I'm all *Oh, stop whining, you big wuss*, but something tells me that approach wouldn't have quite hit the mark with Jess.'

She laughed. 'No, I think you're right there.'

'The coach has arrived anyway. The bags are being loaded up. We'll be ready for the off pretty soon.' He gave her a knowing sad smile.

Dorcas thanked everyone for joining them at WFH and said that she hoped the accident on the hike hadn't spoiled it for them. She was given a rousing applause, which seemed to set her mind at rest.

Jason was nowhere to be seen.

Once the kids were all accounted for and Jess was secured in her seat, David and Stevie thanked Dorcas and Harry for all their help.

Still no Jason.

David climbed aboard the bus and Stevie followed. Anger bubbled inside of her. *After everything that's happened this week, he hasn't even got the decency to come and say goodbye.* She stared out the window as the bus began to pull away. The kids waved frantically at Dorcas and Harry, shouting their thanks and goodbyes.

Suddenly, Jason appeared from the direction of his cabin. Her heart lurched in her chest. He was dressed only in his shorts and had nothing on his feet, despite the stones and dirt beneath them. He was running towards the retreating coach, waving his arms; a panicked expression across his face.

"Erm...Geoff...Geoff, stop the bus, mate.' David called to the driver. The bus came to a halt. He leaned over and whispered. 'Stevie, I'm guessing it's not me he's after.' He gestured in Jason's direction. She nodded and gulped down the lump of emotion lodged in her tight throat.

Shakily, she climbed down from the bus and walked towards Jason, who was now bent double resting his hands on his knees.

'God...I may...be fit...but...I'm no...fucking...*runner*...that's for...sure,' he gasped as he stood there, and she mused on his ironic choice of words given their last parting.

She gave him a moment to catch his breath and glanced up at the back seat of the coach where David was just telling off the boys in the back for making kissy faces at them.

'Please...can we just talk for a second...out of view of the bus?' Jason's breathing calmed. She glanced back at the bus where David was gesturing that she had five minutes. They walked towards a clearing in the trees where they would have more privacy.

Coming to a halt, she turned to face him, pointing in the direction of the coach. 'I could lose my job if one of those kids says something about this.' Her anger returned. 'You wait until I'm almost out of sight before you *bother* to turn up and *then* you make a huge scene and show me up!'

Jason held his hands up in surrender. 'No...no...I set my alarm, but for some reason the battery died and so it didn't go off. I was exhausted from waiting up for you until gone two this morning, and I overslept as a result of that, and I'm so...*so* sorry. But you *have* to know that I meant what I said when I asked you to stay. Please? Or...or go home and sort stuff out, and then come back here and we'll work this out...please?'

His voice was filled with desperation, and she wanted to run into his arms and scream, 'Yes!' at the top of her lungs.

But she just couldn't do it.

Her mother needed her and long distance relationships just didn't work.

Pulling her lips in to stop them from quivering, she closed her eyes, trying hard to compose herself as so many conflicting emotions fought to escape. Eventually she spoke. 'Jason... We've been through this. *My* life is in London. *Your* life is here. *This* was temporary. We were *never* meant to be. We have to accept that now.' She opened her eyes, and he was standing too close for comfort.

His eyes widened. 'Stevie, no. We were *always* meant to be. I just...I thought I could get over you...I was wrong...so, so wrong. I realise that now. We were *always* meant to be. Even when we were eighteen. I should *never* have left without you. I need to tell you something. Remember when we talked that time and I asked where you saw yourself and what was in your future?'

She frowned. 'Yes...I was thinking about that yesterday.'

'Well, I was going to ask you to run away with me. I was on the verge of telling you everything. But I couldn't do it. I couldn't *do* that to you... It would've been so selfish of me. I didn't want to drag you into the mess that was my life back then. What the hell did I have to offer you? But I *wanted* you with me, so, so badly. I've missed you so much I felt physical...*pain*, Stevie. You've got to believe me.'

Tears spilled over and cascaded down her face as her heart ached. 'I do believe you. But back then, all I knew was that you were gone. I lost my heart and I lost the most precious thing in my life, Jason. I lost *you.*'

His lip trembled and his beautiful, warm, brown eyes filled with tears. One escaped, trailing a wet path down his unshaven face as he gazed pleadingly into her eyes and reached out to cling to her arms. 'None of that matters now. I'm here. I had my reasons to leave, yes. And I *felt* I had no way out of things... L-like I've said before...I was...I was *lost* for a while that's all...and lost things *can* be found. This week has proven that. Please don't leave. We need more time. Please don't go.'

His voice broke as he tried to get the words out. He gazed down at her. 'I can't lose you again. Please...I love you, Stevie. I've never stopped loving you. Without you, I know now that I'm just a shadow. It was like I was walking through life searching for something to make me whole again and to fill the hole inside me where my heart should've been. What I didn't realise was that *you* were it...*you* were my heart. There's a reason I'm nothing without you. I know I was an arse to start with when you arrived, but that was...that was just self-preservation. The happiness I've felt in the last few days has far outshone anything I've felt in the last ten years. That's got to count for something...it *has* to *mean* something...hasn't it?'

She reached out and touched his damp face. 'I'm so sorry, Jason.' The feeble sentence was all she could manage. She pulled away and turned to leave, but remaining where he stood he grabbed out for her arm again.

'Stevie, I'll do anything you ask...*anything.*'

She turned to gaze at him standing there, looking desolate, and knew the very question she needed to ask, as much as it would hurt to hear the answer. 'Jason, will you come to London with me?'

He let go of her arm, hunched his shoulders, and covered his face with both hands as he began to sob. A heart-wrenching sound filled with the pain and anguish that would stop him from answering.

'I didn't think so...and that's okay. I really *do* understand. Goodbye, Jason. Take care.' She walked towards the bus on legs that had all but turned to jelly, not daring to look back.

David gave her sad smile and patted her arm as she re-boarded. Once she had taken her place, the vehicle began to move again. She looked through the glass to see a defeated and broken looking Jason watching her leave.

And crack went the final piece of her heart.

After the coach was out of sight, Jason trudged back to his cabin with a dull, heavy ache in his chest. His lip still trembled and his eyes were still damp. So much regret, so much sadness lay like a lead weight on his shoulders. Seeing Stevie after all these years had sent him into meltdown, but at the same time had filled him with a sense of hope again. Hope was something he hadn't felt since *long* before he left her ten years ago.

He hadn't told her how he felt until time had run out. But how could he? After all, she had made it clear on more than one occasion that this was nothing more than a fling for her.

She was over him.

And now that she had experienced with him the *one thing* they never had shared before he left—making love—she was *still* willing to walk away. Yes, she had shown emotion, but looking back now, he realised that was probably a little nostalgia.

Seeing her get on that bus had torn what was left of his heart out. Knowing he probably wouldn't see her again felt like someone had stamped on his heart whilst it lay, still beating on the floor.

Leaving her the first time had hurt like hell. But *losing* her this time was *far* worse. Losing her this time had been a choice he'd had no control over. *She* had chosen to walk away simply because she didn't love him. She hadn't said it, so she can't have felt it.

He sat on his sofa in his quiet, empty cabin. The silence was deafening and so he leaned over and turned on his iPod. He flicked through the tracks and found the one he needed to hear. Listening to the words would torture him. He knew this. Yet he still pressed play.

'Here Without You' by 3 Doors Down filled the room and his auditory senses as he sat alone listening to the poetry of the lyrics and wishing he had just said *yes* to London. But he knew deep down he could never go back. Not to stay. And even though she knew his reasons for this and understood them, she'd made her mind up. He hadn't been her choice. But he couldn't blame her. He leaned forward resting his fore-arms on his knees as the tears came. His chest ached and his shoulders shuddered as her name fell from his lips in a sad and desperate plea.

He sat there for what seemed like forever, just staring at the vase of wild flowers in the middle of the table. They had made her smile. He was dragged from his memories when there was a knock on his door.

His heart leapt as adrenalin spiked in his veins and he dashed to open it. 'Stevie?'

Dorcas cringed. 'Oh...sorry, Jason, it's just me.'

'What do you want?' he snapped harshly, stomping away from her into the middle of the room.

She stepped inside. 'Just to see if you're okay. Are you? You looked...devastated when she...when Stevie left.'

He turned to face her, his heart hammering in his chest. 'Really? You think? Well is there any fucking wonder? She fucking ripped my heart out, Dee! She ripped it out and fucking *stamped* on it. I laid myself bare for her and for what? For *nothing*!'

She flinched. 'Maybe she'll see sense, Jason. Maybe if she loves you—'

He let out a derisive laugh. 'Ha! That's just it. She never *said* she loves me!' Anger rose up inside him as he grabbed the vase of wild flowers from the table and threw it at the wall. It smashed on collision, sending droplets of water and petals flying to the floor and making Dorcas physically jump. 'She says she doesn't want a long distance relationship before she's even given us a fucking chance! I had no say in *any* of it. Maybe she was getting her own back for what I did. The bitch!'

Dorcas began to back away. 'Look, I'll leave you to calm down—'

'Calm down? Calm the fuck down? Really? I need to follow her, Dee. I need to get her to admit it. She does fucking love me! She must! You don't share what we shared if you don't feel something!'

Grabbing the scrunched up T-shirt he had tossed on the sofa the night before, he pulled it over his head. Grabbing his boots he yanked them onto to his feet and tied the laces quickly. He grabbed his helmet and his keys from the counter top.

'Jason, please don't ride angry. Please calm down before you do anything stupid.'

'I've already done the most fucking stupid thing of my life, Dee. I left the *one woman* I've ever loved behind ten years ago and then I let her walk back in *and* out of my life within the space of a week. I'm a fucking idiot!'

He stormed past her and out into the clearing where his bike stood. Dorcas followed and watched with wide, fear-filled eyes as he mounted his bike and kicked away the stand. He turned the key in the ignition and set off hurtling down the long driveway, leaving a cloud of dust in his wake.

Although it was a warm day, the breakneck speed at which he travelled sent cold blasts of air across his skin. He exceeded the speed limit as he hurtled down the A9 putting his own life and the lives of others at risk. The further south he travelled, however, the more rationality overtook emotion.

The more calm overtook the rage that had been burning inside. Numbness, apathy, and acceptance began to settle over him. As this happened, he began to slow the bike until eventually he pulled into a layby at the side of the road and came to a halt.

He removed his helmet and sat there, staring down the long, empty road, his chest heaving as a sense of defeat washed over him. Alone again. He would go no further. How could he? She had stated her case clearly. And she wasn't a bitch. She was just being sensible and making an adult decision based on her own needs. There was nothing wrong in that. He slotted his helmet onto the handle bar and rubbed his hands over his damp face. As much as he didn't see the problem of the five hundred and thirty two miles that would lie between them, she obviously did.

So as hard as it was and as much as it would hurt, he would have to let her go.

CHAPTER NINETEEN

*S*itting on the coach and staring out of the window, Stevie fought the tears that threatened to betray her once again. The memory of his face as the coach pulled away hurt so much. It was one memory of Jason that she would very much like to forget but doubted that she would any time soon. She wondered what he was doing as she gained distance from him. Was he upset? Was he angry? Both, she guessed. And who could blame him? She had given nothing but mixed signals, despite the words she had spoken. She had no one to blame for her sadness but herself.

Slipping her ear buds in, she hoped to be relieved by something that would lift her mood, but of course every track had subconsciously been put on there because it reminded her of her first love. She pulled the buds out again and thrust the device back in her bag, vowing to wipe the damned memory and start afresh with a batch of new songs when she got home.

Glancing out of the window, she realised the sky had darkened just like her mood. A thick, heavy, grey expanse sat above the road and pelted the coach with fat raindrops. The clouds were crying the tears she couldn't allow to set free. The journey seemed endless, and David had thankfully seen fit to leave her to her melancholy mood. As the mountainous backdrop receded into the distance, so did her feelings. Numbness took over, proving to her that she had in fact left the remaining pieces of her heart back in Scotland.

Back in the little leafy London suburb, she unlocked and walked in her front door at nine o'clock after retrieving Rowdy from her neighbour. He was so excited to see her that he almost knocked her off her feet. Once safely ensconced back in her comfort zone, she fell to her knees in front of the over excited canine and buried her head in his fur, finally giving in to the emotions that she had been keeping locked away for the last ten or so hours.

'What have I done, Rowdy? What have I done?'

The next morning, Stevie lay on the sofa with Rowdy on the floor beneath her when her front door rattled. She sat bolt upright hoping beyond hope that it would be Jason, which was ridiculous and deep down she knew it. He had no clue where she lived.

'Stevie, darling! Are you up yet? I've missed you,' her mum's voice called from the hallway.

'In here, Mum,' she replied unenthusiastically.

'You're still in your pyjamas, sweetie. It's almost eleven o'clock, you know. We said we'd go for lunch today.'

Stevie shrugged. 'I know...I just...I don't feel like it.'

'Goodness me! I was going to take you to Marco's for ice cream! You love Marco's. What has that trip *done* to you?'

Stevie pondered for a few moments, wondering what she could and *should* say to her mum to explain her poor mood. Eventually, she sighed. 'Mum...sit down...I have something to tell you, but you can't tell a soul. Do you understand? Not a *single person*. I mean it.'

Dana's face grew pale. 'Oh my. What's happened, love?'

'You're going to be shocked when I tell you. Come on... come and sit down.'

Dana did as instructed and clasped Stevie's hand in her own. 'Sweetheart, what's happened? Come on love, out with it.'

Stevie proceeded to tell her mother about bumping into Jason on the trip and about the feelings it brought. She left out the parts about the hot sex, thinking it may seem a little inappropriate. She found it hard to keep her emotions in check however and cried rather a lot whilst her mum just sat there open mouthed.

'Oh, sweetie. I knew there was something. I *knew* it. You just didn't sound yourself on the couple of occasions I spoke with you. I can't quite believe you saw him. And he was *well*. And what his dad did to him.' Her eyes glazed over with sadness.

'This is why you must tell no one, Mum. Please.'

Dana looked directly into her eyes. 'Stevie, I'm your mother. You should know you can trust me. But I must say that I don't understand why you can't make a go of things with him if you still love him and he clearly still loves you.'

'Because, Mum, there is the small matter of over five hundred miles between us *and* the fact that he ran away once. What's to stop him doing it again? Only this time he wouldn't need to run would he? Because he'd already be as far away as bloody possible. I can't do long distance, Mum.' She began to sob. 'I just can't.'

Taking a deep breath Dana tilted Stevie's chin up and peered into her eyes. 'Has this got anything to do with my illness? Because if it has please don't throw this away because of me, darling. I'm perfectly fine. My medication is working great, and I'm getting around just like anyone my age. I can't have you throwing your life away because you're worried about me. I just can't.'

Stevie closed her eyes for a moment, hoping to make her next words ring true. 'No, mum. It's the long distance thing. I...I can't do it. I've seen it fail so many times and I just can't put myself through it.'

Dana seemed satisfied—for now—and pulled Stevie into her arms. 'Okay, sweetie, shhh, okay. No one understands your reasons more than I do, honey. I just want you to be happy. Maybe if *I* call him he'd see—'

Stevie sat up. 'Don't you dare! Don't you *dare* ring him, Mum!'

'Okay...okay. I'm just worried, sweetie. The last time I saw you like this was...ten years ago.'

'Yes, well I got over it then, and I'll do the same now. I have to. I just *have* to. What we were doing up there was stupid anyway. It was always going to end. We were in some kind of denial if we thought it'd work out differently.'

Dana smiled knowingly. 'Love will do that to you, darling.'

Getting back to normal was hard. Stevie cried for the first few weeks at the smallest of things. Her mother was understandably worried about her but didn't pressure her to talk. She appreciated that. Dana told Stevie on more than one occasion that she wanted to pick the phone up and call Jason, beg him to come and rescue her daughter from her heartache, but Stevie had made her promise yet again that she would do no such thing.

She had to stop listening to music, as every track seemed to be taunting her. The final straw came when she turned on the radio and heard Duran Duran's 'Ordinary World'. After a few moments of being drawn in by Simon Le Bon's emotion-filled voice singing of losing someone he loved, she switched off, deciding that a world without music would have to suffice until she was stronger.

If that ever happened.

She had heard nothing from Jason, which was both a disappointment *and* a relief. She'd half expected him to turn up on her doorstep, but thankfully she had underestimated his strength.

Her own, however, was waning.

Sitting on the sofa marking a mid-term assessment, she reached down and dragged her fingers through the soft hair on Rowdy's back. He was such a big softy, even though his tough-looking exterior would have you believing otherwise. His bark was loud and he'd always made lots of noise when anyone came to the door. He was her guardian, and she was grateful for his company, especially since she had been so down lately.

Her ex, Miles, had been in touch far too often for her liking, and she'd tried to keep him away but he was so persistent. He'd convinced her to go out for dinner with him on several occasions, and she was so lacking in energy that she couldn't be bothered to argue.

Life after Jason—once again—was proving to be hard. In fact it was hard*er* the second time around. After searching her soul for hours, she had come to realise it was because of sex.

This was an added issue that she had never had to deal with before. She'd never made love with someone she was actually *in love* with. But being with Jason...the connection...it was something she couldn't forget. Okay, so it was passionate and heated, but she knew that for *her* it was filled with love. She just didn't believe that Jason felt that too. Even though he had expressed his feelings for her, she had put it down to desperation. A last ditch attempt to get her to stay or come back. Well, she wouldn't.

It was over.

She stared blankly at a completed Chemistry answer sheet. She had always preferred Biology. But being so talented in both topics was a huge help when the Chemistry role had been released at the school she had wanted to work in.

The phone rang.

'Hello?' Her voice was akin to a deflated balloon.

'Hi...erm, Stevie?' *Jason! Oh my God!*

She cleared her throat. 'Y-yes?'

'Hi, Stevie. It's Dillon.' Her mind had played a cruel trick on her. *Oh...Dillon...not Jason.* 'Look, I'm so sorry to bother you, but it's my dad... He's had a stroke. He's in the hospital, and I thought you should know. He's...he's probably not going to make it.'

She let out the breath that had caught at her first assumption. 'Oh, Dillon, I'm so sorry. I'll come right down.'

'No...no, it's fine. He's unconscious. Come tomorrow if you can though, please. I just... You're the closest thing I have to family, and I just...with Mum gone I needed to tell someone.' His voice wavered, and her heart ached for him.

'I understand. I'll be there tomorrow. Is he in the general?'

'Yes, ward nine. Bye, Stevie, and thank you.'

'No problem. Take care. Call if you need me.'

She hung up the phone. She needed to contact Jason. But

what would she say? Should she contact him at all? Would he care? Would he even want to know? So many questions scrambled her already addled brain. She grabbed her phone and called her mum. Dana would know what to do.

'Hi, sweetie! I was just thinking about you, isn't that spooky?' Dana answered breezily.

Stevie took a deep breath. 'Mum...something terrible has happened.'

There was an audible intake of breath. 'What? What's wrong darling?'

'Mick Reynolds has had a severe stroke and is in hospital. Dillon rang earlier. He...he says Mick isn't going to pull through.' Silence ensued for what felt like an age. 'Mum? Are you there?'

'Y-yes... Sorry, sweetie...You must ring Jason.'

'That's what I was wondering about. But...he hates Mick. I don't know if I should tell him or not? If I hadn't seen him in Scotland he wouldn't be any the wiser.'

'He has a right to know, Stevie. It's his father regardless of what's happened. You know how upset he was to hear Shirley had passed away.'

'I just don't know what to do, Mum. This is different than the news about Shirley. He adored his mum. I feel stuck.'

'To be honest darling, I think you *have* to ring him. I know it'll be difficult for you, but knowing this and not telling him would be wrong. Give him the option to do something about it if he chooses to. But if he decides not to come, at least you've done your part in informing him.'

'Yes...yes I see what you're saying. I just... I honestly don't know how he'll react.'

'Call him now. Get it over with. Let me know what happens.'

'Okay, Mum. Oh and Mum?'

'Yes, sweetie?'

'I... I love you so much.'

'And I love you, Stevie. More than anything in this world.'

The call ended. Dana was right. She *had* to tell him. What he did with the news was down to him. She flicked through her phone's contact list until she located Jason's number. It was now or never. From what Dillon had said, time was of the essence.

She pressed the dial button on the screen with a shaky finger. Her heart hammered in her chest. It rang for a while but then went to voicemail. Relief washed over her. After weeks of trying to get back to normal, the last thing she needed was to hear his real voice. The recorded message was still difficult to hear but far less personal, and so she could handle that.

'*Hi this is Jason. I'm not available right now so leave a message.*' The beep sounded.

When she spoke, she felt foolish and stumbled over her words. 'Erm...ahem...Jason. It's me...erm, Stevie.' It appeared to be just as hard talking to his inbox. 'I'm sorry to bother you. I wouldn't have called, but...and I don't know if you want to know what I have to tell you... Okay, now I'm rambling. I'm just going to say it, and you can do with the information whatever you see fit. It's your dad...erm...it's Mick...he's had a stroke. Dillon says he's not going to make it. I just thought you should know. He's in the general in ward nine. I'm sorry...bye.'

Hearing Stevie's voice sent Jason's heart racing. But hearing the news she left for him to deal with sent it to a grinding halt. He sat on his sofa and ran his fingers through his hair. *What*

the fuck do I do now? He was torn between going down to London to make sure that the old man actually died and staying put and letting it happen where he would be none the wiser.

The longer he sat, the harder the decision became. He realised after a couple of hours that he only had a small window of time to make any decisions. No matter what he chose to do, he would probably regret the decision he made. Damned if he did, etc.

He picked up the phone. 'Dee? Hi. I have to leave for London. Something's come up...a family thing. We have no kids due in for three days, and I'm guessing I'll be back soon, but if not, can you contact Mel, Joe, and maybe Matt and get them to come in for me to help you and Harry?'

'Of course, Jason. Is this to do with that woman? The one from Wilmersden High School?'

'Indirectly, yes. But it's not what you think.' He frowned. Why did he say that? It was nothing to do with her.

'Oh...erm it's none of my business, Jason. It's just that I was just so worried when she left and you—'

'Yeah, yeah, look, I have to go. Call me if you need anything, but you know how to run the place without me if necessary.'

'Sure...no worries. Ride safe okay?'

'Will do. Bye.'

He went to his bedroom and grabbed his rucksack from the cupboard, filling it with the essentials needed to take a trip down south. His heart thundered in his chest. This was *not* good. He didn't want to make this journey at all, let alone for *this* reason.

He pulled on his leathers and made his way outside. The sun was beating down, and he already had a sheen of sweat covering his skin. Straddling the hunk of shining metal, he kicked it off its stand and put the key in the ignition, but didn't turn it. Dropping his head, he hesitated, contemplating his rash decision to dash down to the place he had nicknamed *hell. And here we go again. The fucker's messing with my head even when he's unconscious*. He rubbed his hands over his face.

The man who had ruined his childhood, the man who had pretty much ruined his *life* was seriously ill. The parent he was actually bothered about, the one who cared was already gone. Did he care if this man died without seeing him one last time? He wasn't so sure. He slipped on and secured his helmet, turned the key in the ignition, and slowly pulled onto the long driveway that led to the main road.

Stevie felt like she was somehow betraying Jason by being at the hospital bed of his dying father. The man had caused Jason such pain and suffering and here he lay, frail and small, attached to machinery that was keeping him alive. Dillon sat opposite her, clinging onto his father's hand, looking pale and drawn. The shadow of stubble on his chin and the dark circles around his eyes told of the stress and worry that this young man was going through. He was oblivious to the pain and humiliation his brother had experienced at the hands of the man before them. To him, his father was his last remaining beloved relative.

Keeping her discovery a secret was so hard. She wanted to tell Dillon he was no longer alone, that his brother was alive and well. But it wasn't her place to do that. Jason still wished to remain out of sight. He hadn't returned the call she had made over twenty-four hours ago, and she presumed he wouldn't. All she could do was secretly hope that once the inevitable happened and Mick was gone Jason would contact Dillon and resume being a big brother. He would be needed. But would he step up?

There had been no positive change in Mick's condition. Dillon had been told it was only a matter of time. He looked so forlorn, and she felt helpless. She sat silently, and every so often she checked her phone for messages, each time coming up with none.

Leaving Scotland was hard for Jason. It had been his home for such a long time now that he felt homesick as soon as he crossed the border into England. But the further south he rode, the more and more uneasy he became. It had been just the same after he tried to follow Stevie.

It was a long ride, and he made as few stops as possible, only making the time to refuel either himself or the bike. As soon as he stopped, he began to feel the heat soaking through the black leather he wore, but thankfully once he set off again, the breeze blowing against his body cooled him down.

He decided to stop at a hotel chain around five miles from the village where he grew up. He would be better equipped to keep his anonymity this way. After checking in, he removed his leathers, showered, and collapsed onto the bed. Sleep came quickly, but he was soon in the midst of a painful dream...

'You're worthless, you know that?' His father's voice rang out.

Eighteen-year-old Jason stood cowering in the corner of the old run down shed.

'You ruin everything. Everything! All you needed to do was pass the Oxford entrance exam and you would now be doing

something worthwhile for once! Then I wouldn't have to look at your face every day. I don't ask too much. Just for you to try, Jason. That's all I ask. But nooo. Jason thinks it's funny to fail exams on purpose. You still continue to ruin my life. It's almost as if you enjoy knowing how much you hurt me.'

Knowing what was coming, Jason grabbed something heavy from the floor and raised it ready to strike...

He awoke with a start, sitting bolt upright. His body covered in sweat. His chest heaved as he flopped back onto the bed and wiped his hands over his face. This was the first nightmare where he was about to retaliate. Lowering himself to that man's level, even in a dream, scared him half to death. *That's what the man did to me. Why the hell am I even here?* He slammed his fists into the mattress beneath him and closed his eyes again. He lay awake for a long while, but eventually found himself in the midst of another scene...

He was standing outside a restaurant on the main street in Wilmersden. The windows were steamed up. He rubbed a patch clear so that he could look through the glass. There she was. His soulmate , Stevie. But she was sitting opposite another man. Anger bubbled inside him. She leaned across the table and stroked the man's arm lovingly. Jason saw the glint on her left hand. An engagement ring? No!

The man was clean-cut and handsome. Just what Stevie deserved. He looked so happy there with her. In fact, they both looked happy. Had what they had shared in Scotland meant absolutely nothing to her? He banged on the window. His heart raced. They didn't hear him.

He looked around for something to hurl at the glass. He needed to smash through. But there was nothing within reach, and he couldn't move anyway. He was cruelly frozen to the spot. When he looked back through the window, Stevie and the man were kissing. Nooo! They were surrounded by people who seemed to be congratulating them. She looked over and made eye contact with Jason. He waved frantically to try and get this situation to stop. She was his! He needed to get to her. He banged on the window frantically again and again, but she wouldn't take notice. She just smiled and turned away.

Once again, Jason awoke in a panic. He'd lost her. *No, it was a dream...it was a nightmare, that's all. Okay, no more sleeping. Not worth it.* After allowing his breathing to calm, he sat up.

Realising he was soaked in sweat, he jumped in the shower again and let the hot water melt away the memories of both dreams, feeling his muscles begin to relax as he stood under the cascade.

Once out of the shower and dry again, he checked the time, seven o'clock. It was Saturday morning and he was at a loss. Should he go to the hospital? Should he get back on his bike and leave? He didn't know what to do for the best. He ordered room service, but when it arrived, he looked at the plate full of food and his stomach turned. After trying a couple of mouths full, he decided that perhaps he should just admit defeat and he pushed the plate aside.

After pulling on his leathers, he made his way downstairs. There was something he needed to do, and there was no time like the present.

CHAPTER TWENTY

*T*he little village of Heaton in the leafy London suburb was still as pretty as Jason remembered. There were more shops on the high street now in addition to the butchers and general store. His mum's best friend had opened her own salon, and he could see her through the window as he drove by. She was bent over an elderly lady fixing curlers into place. Her bright red lips were still her main characteristic from what he could see. She had been his mum's best friend for many years. He remembered her coming to their house to cut the family's hair. He used to hate having his hair cut, probably the reason for its current length.

He continued to the end of the village past the old doctor's surgery and turned left down a little track that led to St. Cuthbert's church. He hadn't been there in so very long. Reverend Greenough had been a nice man, and Jason had often thought about going to ask for help but had never plucked up the courage. Looking back, he felt sure that the kind-natured soul would have helped him. But as he had once, rather cheesily, said to Stevie, 'Hindsight is the bomb.'

He leaned the bike on its stand and made his way over to

the plot where his grandma and grandpa's ashes were interned. Sure enough, beside their plot was a flower-covered grave with a stone that read, *Here lies Shirley Margaret Reynolds. Loving mother and wife. Forever in our hearts and minds.*

Jason dropped to his knees before the stone and placed the small bunch of wild flowers he had gathered from the churchyard entrance where things had become a little over grown. He had always preferred wild flowers and remembered that his mum had too. He would bring her some back each time he returned from a picnic by the river with Stevie. Her face would light up, and she'd hug him tightly, telling him what a wonderful son he was. He didn't feel very wonderful at the moment, here in the present where his mother lay in the ground beneath him.

He traced the lettering on the headstone with his fingers. 'Hi, Mum. I came back. It's only a flying visit though. Mick is ill and I felt I had to come and... Oh, I don't know... God, I hate the word closure but...' He gazed skyward. 'Oh heck, I'm sorry God. I didn't mean to use your name in vain like that... Anyway, as I was saying, I suppose closure is what I need.

'Mum...I missed you...*so* much when I left... I thought about you all the time. The way you'd hug me and tell me everything would be all right. If only you'd been right about that. I missed your hugs...your encouragement...the way you used to smile at me and kiss my nose when I brought you flowers.' Several tears escaped his eyes and trailed down his cheeks.

A sob escaped his chest. 'I'm so sorry I wasn't here for you in the end. I hope you didn't suffer. I would've hated to see you suffer, but I should've been there... I should've helped...I...' He wiped at the salt water as it overflowed. 'I just couldn't stay. I hope that deep down you understood why I left...why I had to go. I couldn't stand it anymore, Mum. I thought maybe you knew about it, but maybe not... I don't know anymore. All I know is that I lost so much thanks to that...that *man*.' He clenched his jaw as anger rose to the surface once again. 'I lost my family, my home, my friends...Stevie.' He rubbed his hands over his face.

'She came to Scotland, you know. I was so shocked... Seeing her there was just...*mind* blowing. She's so beautiful. Completely stunning...just like I remembered. But then you knew that. She said she'd kept in touch with you when I'd gone. I'm so grateful to her for that, but the thing is... I still love her, Mum. I broke her heart and left her and she should hate me, but I plucked up the courage and told her why and she forgave me... But in the end, she couldn't love me back. I tried...I begged her to stay with me, but well, she couldn't, and so I lost her all over again. I lost her, Mum... What am I going to do now?' He looked skyward again for a second as if expecting the answer to be made known to him.

Silence ensued.

He huffed out a long, shaking breath. 'You'd love Scotland. The fresh air, the wild flowers. So many wild flowers... the dramatic scenery that can change at the drop of a hat. I mean it, Mum. One minute bright blue skies and the next raging thunder storms. It's so beautiful. I wish I could've taken you. I wish you could've come to live there with me. You'd have been so happy.'

He wiped his eyes again, his lips trembling as he spoke. 'I hope he never did to you the things he did to me. I hope he never hit you. You were so lovely and just didn't deserve that. I worried for so long about you and Dillon, but I had to leave. Please forgive me Mum, please... I'm so sorry.' Relentless hot tears streamed down his face as his shoulders shuddered under the force of the myriad emotions he was trying so hard to come to terms with.

He sat for what seemed like hours in the peaceful tranquillity of the old graveyard. The wind rustled through the bowing branches of the trees, and he closed his eyes, wishing he was back home, sitting outside his cabin in the Cairngorms instead of sitting by his mother's grave.

He suddenly sensed a presence and opened his eyes to see an elderly man wearing a clerical collar standing over him. He clambered to his feet without speaking, and the man smiled warmly at him.

'Jason, you've returned.'

'Reverend Greenough...you...you recognise me?'

The man looked much the same apart from a full head of grey hair instead of greying brown.

'Young man, I would know that face anywhere.' He held his hand out towards Jason, who gripped it firmly and shook. 'How are you? Are you well? Please, come in for a cup of tea.'

'Oh, I should really go...but...'

'I understand, son. I'm guessing this is only a fleeting visit. Is it because of your father?'

Jason nodded. 'But I have no desire to see him. You don't know what went on... I...shouldn't be here.'

'Jason, I knew there had to be a very good reason why you left so suddenly. I felt so very guilty for so long. I prayed for you often...still do. I wish I'd made it clearer to you that you could turn to me in your hour of need. I would've liked to help you. But whatever your reasons, I know they were valid.'

Jason nodded again. He walked towards the church gates and Rev'd Greenough walked alongside him. 'Did you see my Mum much after I'd gone?'

The reverend smiled sadly. 'I did. She came here every Sunday without fail. She lit candles for you. You were on the intercession prayers list right up until she passed away. She felt sure you'd return one day. And I'm so glad you did. You proved her right. And the faith she had in you too.'

Tears stung his eyes again. 'Two years too late, though.'

The reverend placed a hand on his shoulder. 'Your mother wouldn't have seen it that way. She blamed herself. She wished she could've done more...known more. But things were hidden from her too. Please know that. She was oblivious to how you felt until it was too late. The relationship between your mother and father suffered terribly when you'd gone. Even now, I don't know what happened and I don't need to know, but back then...with you gone there was nothing anyone could do to prove that things were amiss. Not that anyone was *angry* with you for leaving. People were just very worried.'

'Thank you...thank you, Reverend Greenough. I think I needed to hear that. It doesn't take away the guilt, but nothing will I don't suppose.'

'Give it time, son.' He turned to walk towards the vicarage. He glanced back at Jason. 'And whilst you *are* here, I really think you should consider visiting your father. This will be your last chance to say goodbye and to put to rest the wounds you still carry. Think about it, Jason. Take care. God bless you.' He turned and walked away, leaving Jason staring at his retreating form as he disappeared from view.

He climbed back on his bike and glanced up the lane towards the main road. The hospital was a ten-minute ride away, and he sat there weighing up whether he should just go and get it over with. Although the man was unconscious and wouldn't be able to answer his questions, perhaps just seeing him and talking *at* him for a while would be cathartic enough. He switched on the engine and set off, but made a turn for the river at the last second and found himself in the spot where he and Stevie used to spend many hours together.

The place was still beautiful. It wasn't Scotland, but it was still a place shrouded in memories. Some wonderful and some tinged with sadness and pain. He climbed off the bike, walked down towards the water's edge, and sat for a while with his forearms resting on his knees. He closed his eyes, breathing in the familiar smells of his surroundings...of his past...and imagined that he was a teenager again. He thought back to one of their conversations that had stuck in his memory. It took him back to a happier time when Stevie was always beside him...

'Do you think every couple goes through this?' she asked as he gazed down into her vivid blue eyes. The sound of the river flowing gently just below them was a tranquil soundtrack to their chatter.

'Through what?' He was lazily running his hands through her hair as she lay sprawled out on her back with her head on his lap. His floppy fringe kept getting in the way, and he kept swiping it back. Stevie had joked that he needed a headband or braids.

'This...' She gestured back and forth between them. 'You know, wanting to spend every possible minute together. Do you think it's...I don't know...normal?'

Jason laughed. 'What's normal? Not sure I'm familiar with the concept.'

She slapped him lightly. 'Be serious! Tell me what you really think.'

He leaned forward and kissed her lips tenderly. 'I think it's as normal as things get. You and me...we're like...cheese on toast...we're just...meant to be.'

'Cheese on toast? Couldn't you think of anything more

romantic as an analogy than cheese on toast?' She poked his leg, feigning annoyance.

'Okay...' He looked skyward, pursing his lips whilst he contemplated.

'I think we're like Romeo and Juliet...only without the angst and death,' she offered.

He laughed at her suggestion. 'I was thinking more like Bonnie and Clyde...only without the crime spree and murder.' They both laughed.

After a while, he shifted to lay beside her on the blanket they always took with them. 'Do you know though...I think the best thing is...that we're just...us. Stevie and Jason. Together... always and forever.' He pulled her into his body, held her face gently, and kissed her lips like he needed her more than anything in the world...more than food...more than air...more than life itself.

CHAPTER TWENTY-ONE

Stevie hung the last item of washing on her line and carried the empty basket inside. A motorbike rumbled outside and her heart leapt. Was it him? She stopped in her tracks and waited, holding her breath. The bike continued on its journey. *Dammit.* She closed the door behind her and grabbed a bottle of water from the fridge.

It was another warm, sunny day, and once again she had no clue whether Jason had even received her message. She contemplated calling him again, but decided she'd done all she could. Anything more and she would sound like she was nagging when she had no right to do so. Especially not now that she knew everything.

She had promised Dillon she would visit Mick again either tonight or tomorrow. He seemed to appreciate her going to visit his father, and so she was happy to go now that school was finished for the summer. She had mixed emotions about the man now, however, and wished he was awake so she could ask him why he had treated his son so badly.

She picked up her phone and flicked through the

messages to make sure she hadn't somehow missed a call or text from Jason. But no. There was nothing.

Jason stepped into the hospital and his nostrils were immediately assaulted with the smell of disinfectant and bleach, making him slightly nauseated. He had always hated hospitals; ironic considering the career his father had tried to force upon him. Slowly, willing one foot in front of the other, he made his way to the nurses' station of ward nine when all he wanted to do was to turn around and leave.

'Hello, can I help you?' The grey-haired lady behind the desk smiled as she spoke.

Jason cleared his throat and looked around feeling rather inconspicuous. 'Oh...yes...I believe my father is in here...erm... Michael Alexander Reynolds...he...erm, had a stroke.'

'Oh yes.' She frowned. 'But his son, Dillon has already been in. Who might you be?'

He cleared his throat again. 'I'm his *other* son...kind of... what do you call it...estranged? I'm Jason.'

'I see...I see. Well, he's very ill. I'm not sure how much you're aware of, but...I'm so sorry. Perhaps you'd like to speak to the doctor? I know that this isn't something you'll want to discuss out here with me.'

'No, it's fine. I'm aware there's little chance of his recovery. I just...need to see him.'

The lady smiled kindly. 'Of course you do, dear. He's in room five, down the corridor and to the right.'

He began to walk towards the room, counting down until he arrived at room five. The door was closed, and after taking a long, deep breath, he opened it and walked inside. He was greeted with the sight of a frail looking man, eyes closed, lying flat on a bed attached to all manner of bleeping and flashing machines. The man was grey-haired and pale. He bore very little resemblance to the man Jason had once known and feared. You could have been forgiven for thinking that *this* man had no malice in him. No anger. No aggression. But he knew different.

He tentatively stepped towards the bed and looked down at the unconscious man. He wanted to feel something. *Anything*. But all he felt was numbness in his heart...or the space where one used to be. A nurse walked in and checked over the machines, marking on a clipboard chart, smiling at Jason.

'You can sit with him. You're family. It may help for you to talk to him,' the nurse offered before walking out and leaving him alone with the man once again.

He walked over to the chair and sat down. 'So you're on your way out, are you, old man?' His voice was croaky and his mouth dry. 'This is the second time today I've spoken to a dead parent...although *you're* still clinging on I see. I have no clue why I'm even here. I owe you nothing, Mick. But you... you owe me *so much*.' He sat silently for a few moments as tears of anger welled in his eyes. He chewed on the inside of his cheek and clenched his fists in his lap.

'I wish you could just answer my questions. I've got so fucking many. Why'd you do it, Mick? Why did you treat me so badly? Was I such a fucking disappointment? Did I show you up so badly that you had to hit me...punch me so fucking hard? Did I really deserve that? I was a little kid when it all started. All I wanted...all I *needed* was for you to be proud of me. All I wanted was for you to tell me you loved me and to mean it. Okay you said it in front of Mum and Dillon, but what about when it was just us, eh, Mick? Would it have hurt you so much to just show me some love? I can't even bring myself to call you *dad*.

'I left my home...my friends and my whole life thanks to you...beating me whenever I did the slightest thing wrong. I was a *kid* for fuck's sake. No kid's perfect. But no kid deserves that. Dillon wasn't perfect, yet you never hit him with a belt or a stick, did you? You never punched him so hard he threw up. What did *I* do that was so fucking bad? I just don't get it. I don't get any of it.

'You ruined my life. I wanted to *marry* Stevie. I *would* have married her, Mick. I would have been a good husband too. Well, I would have tried my best, that's for sure. But you... you took that away...you took my *future* with her away!' He raised his voice at the man lying still and unaware before him. 'Now she won't let me into her heart again. Why? Why did you do it? Wake up and fucking tell me the answer, Mick!' He stood and towered over the oblivious man.

He calmed himself and sat again. 'Were you happy, eh? When I left? Was it what you wanted? Me out of the way? Were you happy that I walked out on everything and everyone that I loved just to get away from you? Well I hope you found it easy to live with yourself after what you did. I *loved* you. I would have done *anything* to have you love me back. I looked up to you. But you had to spoil things.'

He dropped his head in his hands and let the tears flow. 'I want to forgive you. I really do. I'm trying so hard. The thing is...you can't hurt me anymore. All the damage has been done. You can't break what's already broken. So I suppose the only thing I can do is be the bigger person, eh? I'll do what you could never do... I'll forgive you.

'I'll never know your reasons...if you even had any...but today this ends, Mick...no more. It's over. I forgive you.' He reached out and grabbed the cold hand that lay still before him. 'I can't forget but I can't live with all this hate inside me either... I forgive you, Dad. So if that's what you were waiting to hear, I've said it. You can go now.'

He sat there for a few moments still clutching Mick's hand. He stood to leave, and as he did so one of the machines intermittent beeping stopped. A flat line appeared on the screen.

Mick was gone.

Jason walked out of the room as two nurses rushed in. With tears streaming down his face, he walked past the nurses' station as one of the nurses who had entered his father's room jogged after him.

'Mr. Reynolds! Are you all right?'

He wiped his eyes. 'Not really, but I'll live.' He smiled sadly and walked through the doors.

Overcome with nausea, he took some time in the men's restroom to splash water on his face and calm himself. After walking away from his father's room, a sense of panic had washed over him. He was suffering palpitations, and he knew that part of it was down to just being *here*, in this area again. He longed to go back to Scotland. Back home. But now his father had passed, he knew that returning home would most probably be delayed.

He had no idea how long he'd been standing there, staring at his reflection in the mirror over the sink. Thankfully, no one else had entered. After taking a few deep breaths, he left the rest room and made his way towards the hospital's exit.

'Jason!' He looked to his left just as a fist connected with his face.

CHAPTER TWENTY-TWO

*J*ason staggered backwards with the force of the impact. He hit the wall with his back and the air left his lungs in a whoosh. Bending double, he gulped desperately trying to pull air back in, but as he looked up, he could see the fist ready to strike again. It came towards him again, this time hitting him in his side.

'You bastard! You fucking disappear off the face of the earth for *ten years*, and then you come back like nothing's happened! And *you're* the one who's by his bed when he dies! You selfish, spineless bastard!'

Jason recognised his brother's voice, albeit more mature than he remembered. He didn't retaliate. He stood up and the fist connected with his face again. People walking into the hospital stared and gave the pair a wide berth. Someone shouted for security, and two large, burly, uniformed men came to grab for Dillon. Through blurred vision and the blood seeping from the corner of his eye, he could see that Dillon had filled out quite a bit. He'd always been a scrawny kid. His mousey brown hair was in a fashionable short crop, and his eyes mirrored Jason's in colour, but that was where the similarity ended. And there was something else burning in there too.

Hate.

He wore loose fitting jeans and a fitted white T-shirt, which was now spattered with Jason's blood. He watched as the two security guards lunged forward. Holding up his hands, he yelled, 'No! Leave him. He's my brother.' The two men glanced at each other in confusion.

'Don't go playing the fucking big brother card with me now, Jason. I have no brother! Not after what you did!' The pain and anguish was audible in the younger man's voice, and he lurched forward again delivering another blow to Jason's body, making him crumple to the floor. '*You* killed them, Jason! You killed Mum first when you left and never said why. You just up and left! How could you *do* that to her?' Another punch, this time to his back. 'And now you've killed Dad! I've lost *everything* because of you! No one was the same after you left. I got the scraps of everyone because *you* decided to do a disappearing act! How could you? Did *I* mean nothing to you? Did *we* mean nothing to you? And what about Stevie, eh? You left her too!'

Another punch made contact but with less force. Dillon appeared to be tiring himself out.

Jason sat in a crumpled heap, blood streaming down his face and his eye swelling as he was motionless, slumped against the wall.

The two security guards grabbed Dillon. 'Oy! Enough, sonny Jim!' One of them shouted right in Dillon's ear. 'You're upsetting the other visitors. You pack it in right now, or I call the police, capiche?' He strained against the men who were twice his size. After tugging and resisting, Dillon finally held his hands up in surrender.

The men let him go and stepped back but hovered in case

he decided to attack again. Jason looked up and waved the men off. 'It's fine...we need to talk...thanks for your concern though.'

He pushed himself up and felt his nose. There was so much blood. An elderly lady skirted around Dillon and passed Jason a handful of paper towels without speaking a word. 'Thanks, love. I appreciate that.' He did his best to smile as the lady gave him a sympathetic look and Dillon a scowl before walking through the hospital entrance. The security guards backed away and left the men alone.

Jason looked up into Dillon's face to see an expression, which was a combination of fear, anger, regret, and sadness. His chest heaved up and down. His hair was damp with either sweat or the fact that he had rushed here after a shower.

Panting like he'd run a marathon, Jason addressed his brother. 'Do you want to go inside, and I'll wait here for you?'

Dillon's face contorted with confusion. 'You didn't fight back...you just...you *let* me hit you. Why didn't you fight back?'

'Because you're my *brother*, Dillon, and as much as you have *no idea* why I left, you are obviously upset and have every right to be so. So I didn't *want* to hit you. I *don't* want to hit you. I know I have a funny way of showing it, but I do love you. I always did. I'm not here to fight with you.' Jason blew out a long huff of air and dabbed at his cut lip. 'Look, go on inside. Say your goodbyes. I'll be here when you come out.'

Dillon still looked confused and shook his head. He pointed a finger at Jason accusingly. 'You owe me some answers, Jason. But I don't want to talk to you right now. I'm so angry all I want to do is punch you as soon as I look at you. Now fuck off back to wherever you crawled out from. We'll talk when *I* want to. On *my* terms.'

Jason nodded. 'Okay, little bro. That's fine.' He took out

his wallet and removed a business card. 'My mobile number is on this card. Ignore the other stuff, it's my business up north. I'm staying at the Sure Stay...the one just off the motorway. Room forty. I'll wait to hear from you. We have lots to discuss, and there's some stuff that you need to be prepared to hear. It's not pretty.'

And with that, Jason thrust the card into his brother's hand. 'Now you've got my contact details, it's just how you want it...on *your* terms. I'll wait to hear from you.' And with that, he turned and walked away.

'He's fucking back! I can't believe it, Stevie. He must have some kind of telepathy. I don't know how he dares to show his face around here after what he did.' Dillon's disembodied voice sounded distressed and pained down the line.

Stevie's heart almost stopped. 'Jason? He's here?'

'Yeah, he fucking is... Jesus, I'm so sorry for swearing... and I shouldn't say Jesus either...but fuck. What do I do now?'

Her heart drummed out an erratic rhythm in her chest. 'When did you see him?'

'He was just coming out of the hospital when I arrived. They'd rung to tell me Dad had passed away, and I rushed to get there. They said my *brother* was with him when he passed, but *I* should've been there, Stevie. *Me* not *him*.' A sob travelled down the line, making her heart ache for him. Regardless of what she thought of the man, he had never harmed Dillon.

'I'm so sorry about your loss, Dillon. I really am.' She rifled through her thoughts, trying to make sense of Jason's unannounced arrival back in their hometown.

'But why is *he* here? Why would he come back now, Stevie? He didn't come back for Mum. I just don't get it.'

She began to sweat. She was either going to have to tell him everything or she was going to have to lie. Neither option sat well in her gut. A split second decision brought her next words. 'I saw him, Dillon. About a month ago. I was helping on a school trip that happened to be at an Outward Bounds centre up in the Highlands. It turned out that Jason owned the place.'

'What? This...this Wild Front Here place on his business card? You went *there*? You saw him but didn't think to tell me?'

She swallowed the ball of anxiety lodged in her throat. 'Look, Dillon, there are *so* many things that you don't know. Jason asked me not to tell you, or anyone for that matter, that I'd seen him. He *needed* to stay away and had very good reason to do so. You have to believe me when I tell you that. What he did...when he left...he did it because he *had* to. I can't tell you any more than that. Please trust me.'

Dillon snorted. 'How *can* I trust you? You lied to me by keeping it from me. A lie by omission is still a fucking lie, Stevie. I could've gone to see him. I could've spoken to him.'

'But like I said, he wanted to *stay* disappeared. He thought I'd tracked him down at first. He wasn't happy to see me initially.'

'*Initially*? So what happened when he got over it and found that you were as shocked as he was?'

'Dillon...that's...it's complicated.' She sighed heavily.

'You fucked him, didn't you?'

She inhaled sharply at the bitterness and choice of words. 'Dillon! It's none of your business! And there are very deep feelings between Jason and me. He still cares for me, and I for him. It's not about sex...it's...it's—'

'What, Stevie? *Love?* When he left you ten years ago and disappeared without saying a word?'

'Stop it, Dillon. Stop it right now or I hang up and don't speak to you again. You're not in possession of all the facts. When you are, you *will* understand. I'm sure that now he's here he'll talk to you.'

'He won't *be* here. Not after today.'

'Why? What happened today? When you saw him, how did you react?' Silence followed her question. 'Dillon? What did you do?' Panic washed over her.

'I hit him repeatedly. He deserved it. But he...he wouldn't fight. He just let me hit him.'

'No! No! Oh God no, Dillon. He really didn't need it. Oh God. Where is he? Did he leave again?'

'Ha...well for all I know, he did. It's what he does best, after all.'

'Dillon!' She lost her temper and shouted. 'Where the hell is he? Did he say where he was going or *anything*? *Anything* at all? Tell me right now, or so help me I'll—'

'He said he was staying at the Sure Stay...room forty. But why do you care? He dumped you remember? He left *you too!*'

'Yeah and like I said, he had good reason. And here in the real world, Dillon, shit happens. You deal with it and you move on. Some things are worth forgiving and some aren't, and I hope very soon that you realise the difference.' She slammed the phone down and grabbed her car keys and bag. She rushed for the door and once outside, slammed it behind her.

CHAPTER TWENTY-THREE

*J*ason called into the pharmacy in the grounds of the hospital on his way back to his bike. He picked up gauze squares, antiseptic ointment, and painkillers along with fabric wash, toothpaste, and other things necessary to clean up after a beating. This was the first time his face had been involved, and when he caught sight of himself in the reflection of a shop window, he winced at the image staring back at him. His eye had begun to blacken and his cut lip was swollen.

All chances of leaving as soon as possible and heading back home were now scuppered. He knew now that he would need to remain in London for the foreseeable future and deal with the fall-out from seeing his younger brother, Dillon. He would also need to help sort his father's affairs out. A job he did *not* relish the thought of.

Back at his hotel, he cleaned up his cuts and washed his face before taking a long hot shower. Once dried, he pulled on a pair of scrunched up pyjama bottoms. His leathers thankfully covered his T-shirt, and so there was no blood on it, but it needed a rinse through. Once he had washed and rinsed it, he hung it over the shower rail and examined his bruised ribs in the mirror. Dillon had certainly done him over good. His whole body ached. And he was completely drained from the encounter. He couldn't be bothered to go through the agony of pulling on another T-shirt. Raising his arms, he had discovered, was too painful a task, that one thing was certain.

He pulled the drapes closed and gingerly lowered himself to the bed. Sleep would be good. Sleep was healing, so they said. Unless the dreams returned. He got himself settled and had just closed his eyes when there was a knock at the door. *Fuck it.* Was Dillon here for round two? He groaned and rose slowly from the bed again, feeling every muscle expand and contract painfully as he moved.

With more than a little trepidation, he opened the door a crack and peered out. Worried blue eyes stared back at him. He pulled the door wider.

Her hands flew to her face. 'Oh Jason, no!' Tears overflowed in waves from her beautiful but sad blue orbs, and she reached up to touch his face. 'Look at you. I can't believe he did this'

He frowned at her words. 'You know? How?'

'He called me to tell me you were here. I told him that I saw you up in Scotland. He wasn't happy and said some cruel things.'

Anger rose within Jason, and his heart began to thunder in his chest. 'Right...now I'll fucking hit him.'

'No...no...please...he doesn't understand. Can I come in?'

Jason stepped aside. 'Of course, sorry, come on.' He flicked on the light, hurting his sore eyes in the process.

'Are you...are you okay? Do you need to go to the hospital? Can I get you some ice from the restaurant downstairs?'

Jason shook his head. 'I'm fine. I've dealt with worse. At least there were only fists involved.' He tried to smile.

'He said that you *let* him hit you. Why didn't you defend yourself, Jason?'

'How could I? He thinks I left out of some twisted need for attention or to cause him harm. He's angry. He said that I killed Mum and Dad. Maybe he's right... I spoke to Reverend Greenough, and he said that Mum was never the same after I left. Maybe she died of a broken heart, Stevie.' His voice cracked. 'And I can't hit my own brother...well, not over that. I'd hit him for upsetting you though. That's different. What did he say to hurt you?'

She touched the bruise just under his eye. 'Never mind that. It's really not important. I dealt with him and he apologised. Did you let him hit you because you felt you deserved it? Because if that's the reason, you should know that you're wrong. You didn't deserve any of that.' She held his face in her hands. 'You did what was right for you. It was what you *had* to do.' She caught a tear with her thumb as it trailed down his bruised cheek. 'Dillon will understand when you tell him.'

Jason shook his head. 'I can't, Stevie. I can't tell him. How could I do that to him? It'd be like killing them all over again. I can't replace his happy memories with that shitty mess. And who's to say he'd even believe me? He hates me right now. Why would he trust anything I had to say?'

She stroked his cheek. '*I* believe you. And so will he.'

Jason stepped away and walked over to the bed. He sat heavily and ran a shaking hand through his damp hair. He sniffed and wiped his eyes. 'Can I ask you to do something for me?'

She gingerly stepped towards him. 'Anything...what is it... what do you need?'

'I need *you*...please? I just want to hold you and have you hold me back, that's all. I just want to feel something else... something other than pain and fucking anger for just a while.'

With a trembling lip, she switched off the overhead light, kicked off her shoes, and walked over to the bed. She climbed on and lay back, opening her arms to him. He crawled over to her, holding himself stiff due to the soreness of his body and curled into her, burying his face in her neck, pulling her as close as he could get to her. She stroked his hair and held him.

He moved his face to rest on her chest and inhaled her scent feeling comforted by her closeness. Her embrace was the one place that made sense to him. It made sense of all the nonsensical, dramatic, crazy things in his life. He listened to her heart beating out its soothing rhythm against his cheek.

After a while, he lifted his face to look at her. He could see her watching him in the dim light that shone into the room from the small en-suite bathroom. *Beautiful.*

'What? What's wrong?' She looked worried again.

'I'm just feeling very sad. Today has been so hard, and the only thing that's felt right is lying here with you. But I know that this is temporary. We want different things and to be in different places. I can't stay here. And you can't leave. I just wish… I wish there was a way to make it work for us, but I'm trying so hard to accept that there isn't one.' He rested his head down again and stroked her arm with his fingers.

'We've been through all of this, Jason. Let's not fight over it now…please.'

She was right and Jason didn't have the energy to fight with her over this anyway. She had made up her mind and clearly nothing he could do or say would change it. He would just take what he could get of her whilst he was here. Not in a selfish, demanding way. No…only what she was prepared to give him. And right now, her time and her comfort were all he needed.

≈

Stevie lay there enjoying the familiar feeling of Jason cuddled up to her. It was reminiscent of so many times they had fallen asleep in each other's arms as teens. The pleasant sensation of his weight half atop her body was new but felt good nonetheless. It brought back bittersweet memories of her visit to Scotland.

He was such a strong man, physically, but he had such a tender, damaged heart. The trouble was she had already fallen again. It happened all those weeks ago when she saw him for the first time in ten years. She'd tried to keep her fragile heart intact, but it was a futile exercise.

Jason was her first love, her only love if the truth was told. Being with him was the most natural thing ever, like breathing in and out. There was little conscious effort involved. It just happened and it felt right. But therein lay the problem. They lived completely different lives now. Over five hundred miles apart. And he still wouldn't fight for her. Not really. Not that she expected a knight in shining armour or any such fairy-tale crap. No. She just wanted a real man with real feelings, who she knew belonged to her, forever and always, a man who wouldn't just give up. Jason had been that man once. But he had also given up once.

The sad part to all of this was that she knew that she would never feel about another man the way she did about Jason. She had been ruined in that way. Although they had lost so many years, they still had the connection that made them two halves of the same soul. She could find a handsome man, a kind man, a man who adored her. But none of that would matter one single bit.

Because he wouldn't be Jason.

She stroked his hair, feeling overwhelmed with a sense of melancholy that once again her time with him was limited.

She wanted to spend time with him whilst he was here but feared that she might break again when he left.

'Will you come out on the bike with me whilst I'm here?' His question came out of the blue.

She laughed. 'What? Are you kidding?' *Me on a bike? No chance.*

He shook his head against her chest. 'Nope, I'm perfectly serious. Don't you think it'd be a massive turn on clinging to my body with a huge roaring monster between your thighs— and I mean the bike by the way—and us travelling at, oh, say around a hundred miles an hour?'

She somehow knew he was grinning even though she couldn't see his face, and knowing that made her grin too. 'Hmm. You do know that exceeding the speed limit is actually *illegal* don't you? And I haven't got a clue how to even *be* on a bike. I'd be terrified. And I might scream like a pathetic girl or something equally as ridiculous.'

He lifted his head and looked at her with a serious expression now fixed in place. 'But you'd be with *me*, so you'd be perfectly safe.'

Tell that to my heart. 'I don't know. I'll think about it. But that's all. I'm not saying yes.'

With a mischievous twinkle in his eye, he replied, 'But you're not saying no, which is good enough for now. I'll just work on you with my masculine charms until you say yes.'

'I bet you will. Hey, changing the subject completely, have you eaten?'

He raised himself up carefully and eyed her with a playful grin. 'Very subtle, Wattsy. No, I haven't eaten. Are you hungry for something other than me?'

'As surprising as that may seem to you, yes, I'm bloody starving. Shall we go out somewhere? Grab a bite to eat and get a drink maybe?'

'Sounds like a plan. Or we could grab a takeaway and go back to yours. I'd like to see where you ended up living. And then I'd get to meet this canine companion of yours.'

She cringed. 'Rowdy? Oh, I should probably warn you he doesn't like men. He's very protective of me. Well, actually he's as soft as a brush, but he *can* be protective. It depends if he sees you as a threat.'

He laughed heartily. 'What kind of name is *Rowdy*?'

She giggled. 'Ah, all will become clear when you meet him.'

He nodded thoughtfully. 'Okay, and what do you mean a threat? Like if he thinks I'm going to steal his biscuits?'

'Durrr, no. Like if he thinks you're going to steal *his* Stevie.'

'*My* Stevie,' Jason mumbled sulkily, his voice only just audible.

She smirked. 'Sorry what did you say? I didn't catch it.'

He pouted. 'Nothing. Let's go eat.'

Jason carried their bag of Chinese food back to Stevie's car, and she unlocked the red convertible with the push of a button on her key fob.

He looked over the car admiringly. 'I still can't quite believe that *this* is *yours*,' he stated with raised eyebrows.

She placed her hands on her hips. 'Why do you sound so surprised?'

'Oh, I don't know... I just thought you'd drive something more...*practical*, I suppose.'

She rolled her eyes. 'Gee thanks. I'm twenty-eight, not *sixty*-eight.'

Jason climbed into the passenger side. 'Yeah, I know. It's just quite...*sporty*. I'm impressed, don't get me wrong.'

'I *am* quite sporty, thank you very much, and I don't really care if you're impressed or if you aren't to be honest.'

Jason made a face at her, making her giggle. She had the most beautiful laugh. She pulled out into the early evening traffic and headed towards her town house on the outskirts of Wilmserden.

'Are you sure you want to go back to mine? Wouldn't you rather go out somewhere?'

He gestured to his battered face. 'Looking like this? No thanks. I hate being stared at and talked about. I'd rather just stay in and chill with you, if that's okay? I can get a cab back to the hotel later.'

She smirked. 'But *I* might stare at you. And I *have* been known to talk to myself, so I may just talk about you too.'

Jason smiled widely. He loved her playful side. 'You *think* you're funny, but you're sooo wrong.'

'Oh *really?* So why are you smiling?'

'I'm not smiling.' He smiled wider still.

'You are *so* smiling!'

'Oh shut up and drive woman. It'll be time for me to go back to my hotel before I get a chance to eat at this rate.'

'Yeah? Well that'd mean there would be more food for me. I've seen you eat remember. The phrase *a potato more than a pig* springs to mind.'

Jason gasped. 'You cheeky sod!'

The pair laughed together and it felt so good, and secretly Jason hoped he wouldn't be going back to the hotel tonight at all.

CHAPTER TWENTY-FOUR

*R*owdy the dog started barking excitedly as soon as Stevie turned the key in the lock. 'Urgh, that dog is so bloody—'

'Rowdy? Yeah I get the reason for the name now.' Jason grimaced at the loudness of the bark and wondered if the dog was as menacing as he sounded. He was about to find out and wasn't exactly happy at the prospect.

Once inside the door, the huge fluffy canine growled and lurched for Jason pinning him to the wall. His teeth were bared and his paws rested at the top of Jason's chest as he snarled at the intruder. 'Fuuuck! Oh shit...oh no. He's massive, Stevie. I think he's going to kill me!' Jason's voice wavered with fear as he stood wide-eyed and frozen to the spot.

'Rowdy no! Down! Bad boy!' she shouted as she yanked at the dog's collar. 'Nah...you'll be fine. Just don't make any sudden movements.' The dog, seemingly reluctant to do so, jumped down but kept a watchful eye on Jason as he backed away slowly towards the living room.

He swallowed hard. 'I...erm...I really don't think he likes me.'

She pulled her lips in. 'No, you're right. He doesn't. I'd say he pretty much hated you on first sight.' She smirked. Jason was aware that he must look ridiculous with his six-foot plus frame cowering and eyeing the dog warily, but he simply didn't dare take his eyes away.

'Can you open the wine, Jace? There are a couple of bottles in the fridge. Or if you prefer red, there's some in the wine rack.

'I would...but...the dog is kind of...watching every move I make, and I daren't move very far right now. He looks ready to take my head off...or...or worse.'

She laughed. 'What's worse than him tearing your head off?'

'Well at this precise moment he looks primed and ready to bite me in my...erm...*goods*.'

She threw her head back and guffawed loudly. 'In your *goods*? That's hilarious!'

'Considering I'm on the receiving end of both *your* ridicule *and* the hungry looking dog eyeing up my meat and two veg, I'd say *hilarious* is not a word I would use right now. Can you please do whatever it is you do to get him to go away? Mind tricks, hypnotise him, drug him, or something...whatever, and just get him the hell away.'

Pursing her lips together and obviously trying not to laugh any more, she clicked her fingers. 'Rowdy...come on...out.' Once she gave the dog the command, he skipped off merrily, leaving Jason to heave a huge sigh of relief.

'*Now* can you open the wine, you big baby?' she teased as Jason walked through to the kitchen on rather shaky limbs.

He gaped open mouthed at her. '*Big baby*? Have you ever

been on the receiving end of teeth like that in your nether regions?'

'No, I haven't! And he didn't even bite you, you big wuss. He's a big softy.'

Jason cocked his head to one side and narrowed his eyes at her. 'Oh yeah...snarling teeth and sharp claws...very cute and cuddly. Just like a teddy bear.'

After rolling her eyes for what seemed like the millionth time, she served up the food and carried two plates over to the small dining table at one end of her kitchen.

He brought the wine and sat opposite her, glancing around his surroundings. 'It's a really nice place this. Very...*you*.'

She frowned at him. 'Why did you say it like that?'

He chuckled. 'I didn't say it like anything. I just meant that it's you...you know...modern yet cosy...very tidy...very, *very* tidy...on the verge of OCD tidy.' It was his turn to tease now.

She threw a napkin at his head. 'I do *not* have OCD. I just like things neat that's all. Everything has its place. There's nothing wrong with that.'

'No...no nothing wrong. I'm just wondering how long it will take you to straighten all the tins in your cupboard that I've mixed up.' He sniggered.

She gasped as her eyes widened. 'You've messed up my cupboards?'

'Only the one with the tins lined up alphabetically with the labels all perpendicular... Well, they're not anymore.' He wiggled his eyebrows, and she looked around her. He presumed she was looking for something else to throw. Instead she huffed and carried on eating. Smiling to himself he vowed to check the cupboard again before he left.

~

Once they had finished with their meal, they moved through to the lounge and Rowdy was put to bed; much to the dog's apparent disappointment. Jason could have sworn that he actually heard the dog grumble, 'That's not fair,' as the door closed on him. But he was decidedly more relaxed knowing that the wolf...sorry...*dog* was safely tucked away in the kitchen behind a wooden barrier. Although he was sure that if the dog was so minded, the flimsy door wouldn't be much of a barrier at all.

After a few moments, she broke the silence that had fallen between them. 'So what are your plans for going back home?' She sat on the lounge floor. *Crash* by The Dave Matthews Band played in the background, and Jason had his eyes closed.

He opened them and looked over to her. 'Sick of me already, eh?'

'Don't be daft. I...I just wondered how long you were staying.'

'Well, that all depends on Dillon, I suppose.' He took a large gulp of his wine. 'I'm not sure what to do. I feel on the one hand that I should tell him everything...he should know... but I'm also scared of spoiling the memories he has of Mum and Dad. Plus there's the added issue that he may not believe me. Like I said before, he was under the impression that my reasons for leaving were selfish, which I suppose they were, but not intentionally.'

'I think he needs to know. It would help him to understand, and you're each other's only remaining family now. You'll need each other. *You* may not think so, but *I* do.'

'That's true... It's just not something I want to talk about *at all*. I found telling you so, so hard. I just don't know how he'll take it.'

'Well, you won't know until you try. When are you seeing him?'

'He hasn't called. Probably expects me to have gone back to Scotland. I want to prove to him that I won't run again.'

'I think he'll appreciate that once he knows everything.'

They sat in silence for a while. Jason closed his eyes once again and listened to the compilation CD that she had selected. Each track had a kind of melancholy quality. 'White Flag' by Dido floated through the air as the two former lovers sat close enough to touch but neither reached out.

As Jason listened, a lump of emotion lodged in his throat. The lyrics resonated deep within him and he opened his eyes. Her eyes were closed and her face was damp.

He reached over and touched her arm. 'Stevie?' His voice cracked with emotion.

'This song always gets me. Every. Single. Time.' She wiped at her eyes and puffed her cheeks out, blowing the air from her lungs. 'It makes me think of when you left. Even though I was the one left behind, I lived by the lyrics for a very long time. I was determined not to give up. I was determined to wait for you. Even though everyone around me was telling me to move on. I couldn't. I *wanted* to wait for you.'

She glanced over to Jason, who listened intently. 'And I did...for so long. I felt sure that you'd come back soon after you left. It's crazy, but I still felt connected to you somehow. As time wore on, I realised that I'd been living in some kind of denial. You *weren't* coming back. I think I'd somehow stopped living. And then one day, I decided enough was enough. But I still listened to the song every so often. I felt closer to you when I did.'

His eyes stung. He had been a blubbering wreck ever since she had come back into his life. Every raw emotion hidden deep within was gradually making its way to the surface once again. Things he had suppressed for so long. He wanted to say the right thing. To apologise again but what good would it do? Apologies wouldn't bring back the last ten years. He stroked his hand up and down her arm. His chest ached.

'I had...well, *have* a song like that too. It tears me up to hear it. I'd sit wherever I could and stick my ear-buds in and listen to it when I was alone.'

Her eyebrows rose. 'Really? Which song was it? If you don't mind me asking.'

'It was... It came out after I left but...the words spoke to me.' He cleared his throat as if just thinking about it made him emotional. 'It was 'Here Without You' by 3 Doors Down. There's one particular verse that just...well, you can probably figure it out.'

She stood and slowly walked to the stereo system. She pressed a few buttons, and then the familiar sound of a guitar and the voice of 3 Doors Down's Brad Arnold broke through the silence. She strolled back across and held her hand out to Jason. 'Dance with me?'

He gazed up at her for a moment. She looked so beautiful. He slipped his hand into hers and pulled himself up carefully, feeling the strain in his ribs. The stinging sensation returned to his eyes as he cupped her face and bent to kiss her forehead. Pulling her close into his chest, he wrapped her in his arms and let those damned raw emotions of the past few days...the last month and the past ten years...overflow. The grief for the loss of his best friend and first love...the grief for the loss of his mother and his pain and anger towards his father all poured out.

Suddenly he was sobbing. His body shuddering as the tears spilled from his eyes, soaking into her clothing as she held onto him. At the particular verse that got to him the most, he pulled away and stared into her eyes as if to convey the message within the lyrics directly into her soul. The message that no matter where he'd gone when he was away for all those years, no matter how difficult times had become, the love he felt for her had never faded.

She tiptoed and covered his mouth with her own. Kissing away the pain and anguish. He held on tight to her, never wanting to let her go. Why could this not work? Why could they not figure this out? He wished he knew why she was so reticent. But then he remembered the words she had spoken only minutes before, and he had his answer. Regardless of the reasons behind his leaving, the fact that he left and was gone... lost for so long that it had broken her. Not just her heart, but her trust and her spirit too. He sobbed again, leaning his face into the crook of her neck as she stroked his hair.

'I want to make this better, Jason... I want to help but I don't know how.'

Jason knew what he wanted. He wanted to be with her. To hold her. To make love to her and to get lost in her again. To forget the fact that this was temporary. To forget that the last ten years had been spent apart. For tonight he wanted to just *be* with her.

Pulling away he gazed into her eyes. 'I understand why we're temporary...or why there is no we. I know what I did hurt you too much. But...just for tonight, let me love you. I just want it to be you and me...for however long we have... even if it *is* just tonight. I want to stop thinking about all the bad stuff. I want to love you... I *do* love you...so much.' He stroked her hair as he poured his heart out.

She took his hand and silently led him towards the stairs and up. Jason wiped at his eyes as he followed her. She opened a door and led him inside her pretty bedroom. He glanced around but his gaze soon came back to her. She stepped closer to him, and he caressed her cheek with his thumb. Bending to kiss her, he closed his eyes and breathed in her scent.

CHAPTER TWENTY-FIVE

Stevie pulled at Jason's T-shirt and he bent forward, lifting his arms stiffly. Once she had removed it, she dropped it to the floor and smoothed her hands over his chest tracing his tattoos with her fingertips. He watched her as she moved her hands over his taut skin. She bent and kissed the bullet scar and bruising at his side and continued to trail kisses back across his stomach and up to his pecs. He closed his eyes and inhaled, expanding his chest under her touch. He really was stunning.

When his eyes were locked on hers once again, she took hold of the hem of her own shirt and lifted her arms over her head, removing the item and discarding it on the floor. She unfastened and stepped out of her jeans and stood before him in just her pale blue satin underwear. They had seen each other undress when she visited him in Scotland, but this was more intimate, emotion hanging thickly in the air between them as they gazed at each other longingly.

She took control once again, freeing Jason from his jeans and pushing them to the floor so that he could step out of them. Kneeling before him she continued to cover him in gentle kisses as she gazed up at his dark, hooded eyes. While she caressed him with her tongue and clung to his hips, he closed his eyes and inhaled deeply through his nose as he clenched his jaw. He ran his hands over her hair as she revelled in the taste of his skin. Suddenly, he grabbed her and pulled her to standing again without speaking but winced as he moved, the bruising clearly giving him some discomfort

She pulled her brows into a frown. 'Why?'

'It felt too good and I want this to last as long as possible,' he whispered. She closed her eyes as she smoothed her hands up his muscular back and he unclasped her bra and pulled it down her arms, discarding it along with everything else. Tilting her chin upward he placed a tender kiss on her lips; his were still wet from the tears he had shed. The taste of salt water mingled with the taste of the wine he had drunk not so long before. The last remaining clothing was removed and left wherever it fell.

Stepping back, she pulled him with her and they lay together caressing each other and placing feather light kisses wherever they touched. Her fingers caressed him gently where the purple hue of bruising scarred him temporarily. He touched her cheek and kissed her forehead tenderly without speaking. Carefully, she pushed him onto his back and strad-dled his torso, staring down at his toned, muscular chest and thinking to herself that even bruised and battered she had never seen such an erotic, breath-taking sight as Jason's body and his lust filled gaze staring back at her.

She bent to kiss the bruises at his side, his chest, his neck, and then his mouth, where she lingered cautiously for fear of hurting the cuts that were only just beginning to heal, running her hands through his shaggy hair. Her tongue explored his mouth, teasing and tasting as it moved and eliciting a deep moan from within him. He didn't seem to care about his cut lip as he kissed her back with increasing fervour.

She broke the kiss, reached over to her nightstand, and opened the top drawer. She was sure she still had protection hidden in there but was beginning to think she was wrong when her fingers eventually touched the edges of a small box. Finding what she needed, she silently opened the packet, moving back slightly so that she could cover Jason's arousal. He hissed air in through his teeth as she touched him, and he closed his eyes. When he opened them again, he pulled her face down to his, once again ignoring the wounds he carried, and took her mouth in a hungry kiss that set her skin on fire, one hand in her hair and the other squeezing her bottom and hip as if he couldn't get her close enough.

Manoeuvring herself so she could take him in, she did so, slowly and without taking her eyes away from his. He smoothed his hands up her thighs to her hips and continued up until he cupped her breasts, kneading them and toying with the pink buds that were already peaked. As she moved on him, she relished the feeling of being connected so intimately to, and filled by, the man she had always adored. He closed his eyes as she placed her hands over his and slid her hands down towards his shoulders where she gripped him as she began her ascent to ecstasy. She tried to focus on locking her eyes on his, wanting him to see her and wanting to see him too as they made love, but the pleasure coursing through her body made it difficult.

She leaned into him, and he pulled himself up so that he was sitting, to meet her in another needy, urgent kiss, their breathing a mirror of each other's desire as they climbed and soared skyward together. Their bodies, now slick with sweat, slipped over each other, and she glanced down to where they were joined, watching in awe and thinking how amazing they looked connected in this way. Jason reached down between their bodies and massaged her tender spot making her cry out as she moved on him, taking him deeper.

As she climaxed and clenched around him, Jason followed close behind. They clung to each other desperately, mumbling heartfelt words of love and adoration. She held him and he enveloped her in his arms. She could feel his heart pounding against her body as he held her close. She stayed in his arms with him still buried inside her until they calmed, floating back to earth and sharing tender kisses and touches.

Jason lay there with Stevie curled into him as she traced his tattoos again. They seemed to fascinate her and it made him smile.

He inhaled deeply and kissed her head. 'Thank you.'

She propped herself up on one elbow looking down at him. 'For what?'

'Taking my mind off all the crap in my life. It felt good to concentrate on you and me for a while.'

She kissed his shoulder. 'It was a purely selfish act.' She grinned and blushed.

He pulled his brows into a frown. 'How so?'

'Because you're really good in the sack, Mr. Reynolds. I mean *really* good.' Her mischievous smile was contagious, and he couldn't help returning it with a wide one of his own.

'Oh *really*? Well that's good to know. Maybe you'd like to write me a reference.'

She pretended to think, looking to the ceiling and tapping her chin. 'Hmmm, we could build you a website and offer your services out. I could write a testimonial.' She giggled.

He chuckled. 'Oh yeah? Thanks, but a career change into

becoming a male escort is one I think I'll pass on... I think I'll stick to running my camp.' He turned slightly, cringing at the pain as he moved. 'Seriously though...thank you.' He touched her cheek with deep tenderness. 'When I'm with you...when we...make love...it's...there's this connection... I know I've said it before, but it's the truth. It's like the rest of the world ceases to exist whilst we're joined to each other in that way.' Heat rose in his cheeks, and he rolled his eyes, covering his face for a second. 'God that sounds *so* bloody corny and a bit too deep for me.' Embarrassment curled around his gut as he watched for her reaction hoping she didn't laugh.

She shook her head. Her face was completely serious. 'No...it's not corny, Jason. I feel it too.' Her voice was just above a whisper as if it pained her to admit it.

'When you were with Miles...was it ever this good?' He cringed as soon as the words had left his mouth. 'Shit, I'm sorry, that's none of my business. Scrap that question. Forget I asked.' He closed his eyes, wishing he could take the question back.

'Jason, look at me.' He opened his eyes again cautiously and hers were locked on his now with such clarity.

'Nothing has *ever* been as good as this. No one has *ever* made me feel the way you do. I've never experienced pleasure like that with anyone else. Only you.'

Deep sadness reflected in her eyes back at him. 'You don't sound too happy about it.'

She turned her face away from him. 'That's because I'm not. If it was *just* sex I'd know that I'd be able to walk away with my heart intact...well, what's left of it anyway, but now I somehow doubt that I will.'

Feeling encouraged by her admission, he cupped her cheek. 'Then *don't* walk away, Stevie. I want you. And I get the feeling you want me too. We'd be so good together. We always were. Can't we just see where this goes? There's so much history between us, and I feel like we *could* do this together. I mean…it'd be difficult admittedly, but I think—' He was on the verge of begging but stopped in the nick of time, biting his tongue.

She reached up and touched the bruising under his eye with her fingertips. 'Please…can we *not* talk about this now? Can we just *be* together? We know where things will go if we set foot on that road again and…I can't…not now.'

Jason nodded reluctantly again. He sat awkwardly holding his side and wincing. 'Okay. Look it's late…I should get a cab—'

'Just stay. It's silly to leave now. And you were comfy. I'll cook breakfast for you later, and you never know, Dillon might call. He only lives a short distance away from me. It seems silly to go all the way back to the hotel when you could walk to his flat from here.'

In his mind, Jason fist bumped the air victoriously. He didn't need to be convinced. 'Okay, if you're sure.'

'Absolutely.'

Jason lay back down, pulled her next to his body again, and closed his eyes. It wasn't long before sleep took him.

CHAPTER TWENTY-SIX

*J*ason awoke to the delicious aroma of bacon and eggs permeating the floorboards into the bedroom where he had slept wrapped around Stevie for the remainder of the night. His stomach growled in response, and his mouth watered in readiness. He began to stretch but stopped when pain stabbed his side—a stark reminder of the events that had transpired the day before. Grabbing his clothing, he quickly called into the bathroom to examine his purple tinged features and flinched at the battered face that peered back at him from the mirror. He shook his head and turned to make his way downstairs.

He could hear music floating through the air from the kitchen, and as he made his way quietly there, she was leaning against the counter top with her back to him. Her head was hanging down as the lyrics of 'Already Gone' by Kelly Clarkson tugged at his heart. He paused, taking in the words and watching as Stevie's shoulders shuddered. This was her way of mentally preparing herself for his departure, he surmised, as he listened to the words that were affecting her so deeply. His heart sank as he ran his hands over his face and walked away. He couldn't bear to see her this way. Especially when all he wanted was to be with her and she clearly wanted to be with him.

What a crazy situation.

Before she could turn to see him standing there, he silently made his way back upstairs and sat on the bed. As he waited for her to call him down, he tried to think of something to say to ease her pain. He knew that pretending he hadn't seen her crying would be better, and that this way she would be ready to see him and wouldn't feel awkward about being caught. But he still racked his brain to try and come up with something, anything that he could do to make the pain go away. He came up blank. Eventually, after another five minutes or so, she appeared in the doorway looking fresh faced. Her hair fell over her shoulders, and a strong urge compelled him to go over and run his fingers through it as he told her he had come up with a solution for them. But it would've been a lie.

'Hey, I was wondering if you were going to surface at all, sleepy head.' She smiled.

'Yeah, sorry, I haven't been awake long, but the smell has got me all hungry, so I was just contemplating coming down. Are you...are you okay, Stevie?' He wondered if she would confess to being upset.

She frowned and shrugged her shoulders. 'I'm fine, why wouldn't I be?' *No confession then.*

'No reason...just checking...you know, after last night.'

She grinned and blushed. 'Like I said, purely selfish.' He smiled back. It made him happy that he had turned her on too.

She turned and walked towards the stairs, giving him a fantastic view of her gorgeous arse in her tight jeans. *God, Jason you're such a bloke.* He was about to follow her when a faint ringing came from under the bed. Carefully crouching to poke his head under the covers that hung down, he discovered that his phone had somehow ended up under there. Once he retrieved it, the ringing had stopped. He checked for a missed call and didn't recognise the number.

Shit. Dillon.

He dashed down the stairs and into the kitchen. 'I've had a missed call from a number I don't recognise. I think it could be Dillon. I should ring him back.'

'Oh gosh, yes. I'll put your breakfast in the oven to keep warm. Go and call him.'

He nodded and made his way into the lounge where he hit the return call button. It rang and rang but eventually a male voice answered. 'Hello?'

'Oh...hi. I've just had a missed call from this number...this is Jason.'

'Oh...right...yeah Jason, it's Dillon. I was ringing to see if you'd done your usual disappearing act yet.'

Jason clenched his jaw. 'No, Dillon, I said I'd stay until we'd talked and I meant it.'

'Yeah, well forgive me for not believing you.'

Jason exhaled heavily. 'Look Dillon, I'd really like to talk to you. I need to tell you some stuff—'

'More lies?'

'No, what I have to tell you is going to be difficult to hear, mate, but it's not lies.'

'Yeah, well, I'm not your mate so you can stop calling me that right now. As far as I'm concerned, we share some genes and that's where our connection ends. The sooner we talk and you say whatever it is you want to say, the sooner you can fuck off back under whatever Scottish rock you crawled out from.'

The harshness of his brother's words cut him deeply, and he closed his eyes at the physical pain in his stomach. 'Whatever, Dillon. Name your place and time and I'll be there. I'm at Ste...I'm not far away from you at the moment.'

A humourless dark laugh reached his ear. 'Well recovered, dickhead. The only sad part is that I knew you'd have manipulated her to get in her knickers again. What other way would you have found out where I live? You couldn't just leave her alone could you? You had to fucking have her, didn't you? I just can't believe she'd be so stupid as to let you in.'

Anger began to bubble to the already fragile surface. 'Stop it *right* now. I won't stand for you talking about her like that. It's disrespectful and she doesn't deserve that. Not from you after all she did for Mum.'

'Oh yes, sorry, I forgot she meant the world to you...that you loved her so fucking much. I'm guessing that will have been why you *left* her ten years ago.' Sarcasm oozed thickly down the line.

Jason's jaw ticked. 'Time and place Dillon.'

'Meet me at The Jolly Roger on McMillan Street in an hour. I'll be the one who doesn't give a shit.' The line went dead.

Jason walked through to the kitchen again feeling a little shell shocked by the venomous way in which his brother spoke.

Stevie looked up from the magazine she was pretending to read when he entered the room. 'How did it go?'

'Oh you know, Let's just say that surgery without anaesthetic would've been less painful.'

She cringed. 'Oh, that bad, eh?'

He nodded. 'I'm meeting him in an hour at the pub on McMillan.'

'Come and sit down to eat then. You'll need the strength.'

He sat at the small table, feeling his appetite retreat

following the unpleasant few minutes he had experienced and dreading what the next few hours would bring.

Jason stood outside the large oak doors of The Jolly Roger, plucking up the courage to enter. He inhaled a deep, calming breath and pushed on the doors. He walked straight to the bar and ordered a Jack Daniels, neat. After knocking it straight back, he ordered another. He felt eyes burning into him and turned around to see his brother with a rather menacing look in his narrowed, dark eyes. With a clenched jaw, he walked over to the corner table and sat opposite Dillon.

'Hi, Dillon.'

'Just get on with it. I'm not interested in small talk. I want you gone. And the sooner you talk, the sooner that happens.'

Jason flared his nostrils, clamped his jaw down, and spoke through gritted teeth. 'I get that you don't like me very much, but just cut the fucking attitude. You have *no clue* why I left. And so you need to stop being so fucking judgemental and aggressive.'

Dillon snarled. 'Like I said dick-wad, just get on with it.'

Jason's fists clenched as he tried to calm the storm raging in his blood. His voice dropped to a low rumble. He spoke only loud enough for his brother to hear but not loud enough to be overheard by other patrons. 'Right... I was hoping to do this with a little sensitivity, but I can see that will do no good, and so I'll just come out and say it.'

He inhaled deeply once again and wiped his sweating palms on his jeans. 'He...*Mick*...used to hit me, Dillon. That man you called Dad. And I don't mean a few petty slaps around the head when I didn't tidy my room. I'm talking canes, belts, bits of wood...his hand...his fist. Whatever he could get his hands on. Whenever I did anything that he disapproved of or that fell below his high and fucking unrealistic standards, he would *beat* me. I spent so many days avoiding being alone with my own father...avoiding any type of competition or test that would involve me failing, I avoided things that would mean me having to take my shirt off—'

Dillon's eyes grew wide. He lurched across the table and grabbed a hold of Jason's T-shirt, his fist held high in readiness. 'What a load of utter shit. How fucking *dare* you come back down here and make up such lies?' His tone was incredulous, his expression pained.

Jason held his hands up in a surrender pose. 'Hit me again, Dillon, if it helps, but think about what you're doing. You're behaving just like him. Is that what you want?' Dillon let go and sat down heavily in his chair again.

Jason sighed in relief. 'I was stupidly hoping you'd believe me straight off, but I also knew there was a chance you wouldn't, and I can't *make* you believe me. He was good to you. I know that and so I do understand why you wouldn't believe me...but it's true.'

Dillon shook his head. 'You're a liar. What the hell would make you spout off such crap? That man was your *dad* and he *loved* you. If we weren't in a pub right now I'd kick your fucking head in.' He clenched his fists on the table. 'He spent loads of money buying you books and shit. Taking you places for your fucking pathetic chess tournaments and such. How can you say things like that about him?'

'Spending money on me doesn't mean he loved me. He took me places, so that if I lost he could smack me around on the way home without you or Mum seeing him do it. I'm so sorry, Dillon. I hate telling you all this...I really do, but you have to try to understand my reasons for leaving. That was the hardest thing I've *ever* done...until now...but it's all true...'

Jason's emotion filled voice wavered, and Dillon just stared blankly at him for a few minutes.

Dillon's voice became a whisper, and he shook his head. 'I would've known...and he would've hit me too. He wasn't like that. I would've seen it.'

Jason leaned towards his brother, desperate to comfort him but didn't dare reach out. 'I can't explain why that didn't happen, but I was *so* glad it didn't. I would've...I wouldn't have *let* him hit you.' He ran his hands through his shaggy, long hair. 'I stood it for so long...for a hell of a long time... And the only reason I left is because I knew you weren't getting the same treatment. You were his pride and joy, and I was jealous of that for so long, but I loved you, and I didn't want you to go through it too.'

'I...I don't believe you.' Dillon stood to leave. 'I'm not staying here to listen to you anymore. Just fuck off back to Scotland and take your lies with you.'

'Okay, I understand why you think all that, but...please... think about it... Do you remember all the times you wanted me to go swimming with you and I refused?'

Dillon snorted. 'Yeah, of course I do. You were a wuss, that's all. Always saying you were scared of the water and couldn't swim, which is pathetic...*you* were pathetic.' He pointed his finger in Jason's face.

He looked up at his little brother. 'It was nothing to do with that. I was covered in bruises.'

Dillon clenched his fist in front Jason's face. 'No...no that's a lie. You're lying.'

Jason slowly shook his head. 'I'm sorry, but it's the truth. Remember how I'd always get ready for bed in the bathroom?'

'Again...wuss...God only knows what you thought you had to be ashamed of.'

Jason closed his eyes briefly. 'Bruises, Dillon. That's what I had. Bruises.'

Dillon folded his arms over his chest defensively. 'But you did footy at school. If what you're saying is true, how did you get changed without someone seeing?'

'I always wore a T-shirt under my school shirt. And he used to be clever about hitting me so that the marks were on my back most of the time.'

'But...*why* would he have done it?' The rhetorical question hung in the air between them like a poisonous gas. Dillon's face was contorted, and he was avoiding eye contact.

'I honestly don't know. He used to say I was a disappointment and he regretted the day I was born. He'd go on about how much I hurt him and my mum and spoiled everything. I never understood. I don't think I'll ever know the real reason why he had so much hate for me...well, not now he's gone... but I had to leave. I was ready to retaliate, Dillon. I was getting bigger and less willing to take his shit, but I was so determined I wasn't going to lower myself to his level. Plus I was scared I wouldn't stop if I hit him back. I have scars, Dillon. Not huge ugly ones thankfully...he was clever...but I have physical scars to go with the mental ones he gave me too.'

'It can't be true. Not Dad. He'd never do that. It just can't be true.' He looked pleadingly at Jason.

'I swear to you on my own life...it's all true.'

Dillon's eyes widened, he stood up and ran his hands over his head. 'And I fucking did the same...at the hospital...I did just the same. I beat you up. No wonder she was so angry with me.' Dillon's eyes became glassy and he backed away. 'I've... I've got to get out of here. I...I...need some air.' He stormed towards the door only pausing to allow a young loved-up couple to walk in.

Jason followed close behind, pausing whilst the couple's

friends followed them in scowling as Dillon barged through the middle of their group. Once outside, Jason looked up and down the street, but there was no sign of Dillon. In a panic, he walked to the alleyway that ran down the side of the pub. Dillon was by the garbage bins, bent double, throwing up onto the dirty concrete beneath him.

'Dillon...are you okay, mate?'

'Do I *look* okay?' Dillon shouted. 'You've just told me that my dad was an abusive son of a bitch, for fuck's sake! What the hell am I supposed to do now, eh? How do I deal with this? Cause I'll be damned if I know!'

Jason looked on as his brother hurled the contents of his stomach onto the alley floor. Suddenly, Dillon stood and ran towards Jason, grabbing at his shirt and almost knocking him off balance. 'If I find out you're lying! If I find out this is all bullshit I swear to God...' Dillon's chest heaved.

Jason remained silent and waited for his brother to calm himself, keeping his stare locked firmly on Dillon's and hoping that his eyes said enough to make him finally believe.

He tentatively placed his hand on his younger brother's shoulder. 'Come on...let's walk down to the park at the end of the road, Dillon.'

The younger man nodded and followed. 'Did Mum know?'

Jason shrugged. 'Honestly, I really don't know. I used to think maybe she did, but then surely she wouldn't have let it continue. I know that she loved me. I just...again, I'll maybe never know.'

The colour had drained from Dillon's face. 'She was heartbroken when you left, Jason. She just...fell apart. She talked about you constantly, and it caused arguments between her and Dad... She'd...she'd just cry... She used to sit on your bed and cry for hours. She sometimes cried herself to sleep on your bed. It tore me up, Jason. I felt like *I* lost her back then.'

A familiar lump lodged in Jason's throat on hearing of his mother's heartache. 'God, Dillon, I'm so sorry for that. It broke my heart to leave. I can't express how much it hurt. I mean, physical pain, but I *had* to go. I hope you can forgive me.'

'You know the cane and the plank of wood that he had in his shed that I tried to nick to build my kart? He shouted at me for trying to take them... Were ...were they...'

Jason nodded. 'I'm sorry.'

Dillon halted in his tracks. 'Stop fucking apologising!' he shouted, clenching his fists.

Jason nodded again and they continued walking until they arrived at the small park and began to stroll slowly around the boating lake.

Without making eye contact, Dillon continued. 'And how often did this all happen? Daily? Weekly? What?'

'Several times a week some of the time. It depended on how well I'd done in tests and things most of the time, you know...whatever excuse he could use, but other times it was because I'd apparently looked at him with the wrong attitude or I'd been off with Mum. He'd wait until he got me on my own and then he'd insult me...call me a waste of space...tell me what a shit excuse for a son I was. I began to believe him. He told me I'd ruin Stevie's life too.' His voice cracked at the memory.

'He said she could do so much better...that she didn't deserve to have me dragging such a nice girl down and making her life crap. I think that was part of the reason I stopped myself from asking her to come with me. I wanted to so much, Dillon. I loved her so, so much. She didn't know about any of this until I saw her at the camp a month or so ago.'

Dillon huffed the air from his lungs through puffed cheeks. He grabbed Jason's arm to stop him from walking. 'Are you telling me the truth? Or is this your way of getting out of disappearing now he's dead and can't defend himself?' The question was sincere by the look in Dillon's eyes.

'It's all true, mate. I'm sorry to have to do this to you, little bro.' The sting of tears prickled behind his eyes again. 'I lived through fear, Dillon. When I was old enough to get out, I joined the army.'

Dillon snorted. 'You? The army? Are you having a laugh?'

Jason managed to smile. 'Funny, Stevie had a similar reaction. And no, I'm not joking. I needed some way of venting and the training helped. I couldn't see a counsellor as they'd have reported him, and he'd have been put away. I didn't want to take *your dad* away, Dillon...you were safe. He was a *real* dad to you. I couldn't take that away from you. You're my little brother...I loved you...still do.' Jason's lip trembled and his voice wavered as he swiped at the tear that had betrayed him and escaped down his stubbled cheek.

Dillon's eyes were filled with so many emotions. Pain, anger, fear. He shook his head. 'I...I can't believe we had two completely different versions of the same dad, Jace.' He swallowed hard. 'I don't get it... I don't know why he'd do such things. You were such a bright kid. I heard him bragging to his mates so often about you. I was always so jealous at how easy you found studying and at how proud he seemed to be of you. I used to get poor marks, and he'd ruffle my hair and say shit like *better luck next time, son*, but you...you'd fail and he'd get violent on you. My God, Jason, I'm so sorry.' And with that, Dillon flung his arms around Jason and hugged him hard, right there in the middle of a busy London park as his tears began to fall in earnest.

CHAPTER TWENTY-SEVEN

Stevie had been looking forward to relaxing during the school summer holidays. She had intended to use the time to get away and clear her head of the Jason fog that had descended during her visit to the Highlands. That was clearly not going to happen now, especially seeing as the Jason fog had descended in person to cloud her mind and take over her senses once again. She sat in the garden with a glass of fruit juice in her hand, untouched, as she wondered how things were going with Dillon. Would Jason call in afterwards? Would he feel like talking? She had no clue.

Rowdy began to growl at her feet. Glancing down at the grumbling animal, she realised he was poised, ready to pounce, his eyes peeled on the entrance to the house.

'What's wrong with you, Rowdy? You daft mutt.' There was a loud knock on the door. She raised her eyebrows. 'Bloody hell...a dog with foresight. I could make millions.' She ruffled the dog's fur and immediately went to answer the door. Pulling it open with a smile that fell as soon as she saw the broken man before her.

'Hi...I'm sorry to bother you. Can I come in? Please?'

She stepped aside without speaking. She followed him inside and stood in front of him. 'What do you want, Miles?'

'We need to talk, Stevie. I had to see you...to talk to you.' He stepped forward with his arms reaching out to her. 'You haven't been in touch since we went for dinner a couple of weeks ago and I've been so worried. Stevie, there are things I need to say, so please just let me speak.' He inhaled as if to gain strength. 'I love you...but...I realise now that we're over and nothing I can do will make you love me back. I thought we could get through this if I said I didn't care about having kids, but the truth is... I want to be loved by someone. *Really* loved. And I accept now that you can't give me what I need. And I'll never be what Jason was to you...is to you. So... regardless of how I feel I need to move on. I've...I've met some-one. I wanted to tell you when we went for dinner last time, but...you were so broken up it didn't feel right. I will always love you, Stevie. Always. But I know it's time to let you go. To let us go.' His lip trembled and he swallowed hard.

She scrunched her face. 'I see...well...that's great. Great that you've met someone. I'm happy for you.' Sadness washed over her at the way she had treated him. 'I'm so sorry things didn't work out between us. I really am. I always loved you, you know.'

His responding smile was tinged with sadness. 'Yeah, like you love that dog of yours.'

'It's the eyes.' She smiled.

He chuckled and shook his head. 'Are you okay? I mean really okay? I just want you to be happy.'

Her eyes began to sting and she closed them briefly. 'I...I don't really know. But I'll get there.'

'If he hurts you again, Stevie, I swear—'

She held her hand up. 'I'm a big girl, Miles. I can take care of myself.'

He pulled his lips between his teeth and nodded. 'Well... see that you do.'

'So who is she?'

'Just someone I met at a... good grief this is embarrassing... I met her at a Salsa class.'

'You? Salsa?' Stevie couldn't help giggling.

'Hey, I've got rhythm I'll have you know. Anyway, her name is Charlotte...Charlie for short. I think things could really go somewhere with her.'

Stevie reached out and touched his cheek. 'I'm so happy for you.'

He stepped closer and stroked her cheek. 'Thank you. I hope that you and I can still be friends. We were in each other's lives for so long...' Something sparkled in his eyes and Stevie realised that they were filled with life once again. Guilt seeped through her veins at the heartache she had inflicted that had caused his eyes to lose that sparkle she had loved.

'Of course we can be friends. I'd miss you if you weren't around.'

Miles smiled as he gazed into her eyes. Where his eyes used to be filled with adoration they were now filled with acceptance. 'Are you still hoping you'll end up with him? Jason I mean? After all he's done to you?'

She closed her eyes briefly as the memories of the night before came flooding back. 'I...I honestly don't know. Things are difficult. With Mum and...'

'He doesn't know about Dana's illness?'

She shook her head. 'I'm not going to guilt him into moving here. But he is here...in London.'

Miles smile disappeared. 'Oh. And you've seen him?'

She nodded again.

He shook his head and clenched his jaw. 'He'll hurt you again, Stevie. You do know that, don't you? He has no heart. I just don't get why you love him so much but couldn't love me after I treated you right.'

She sighed and her shoulders slumped. 'Miles...please...we've been through this. There are things you don't know. Things that happened—'

He took her by the upper arms and stepped closer. 'You've slept with him haven't you? You've let him manipulate you again, haven't you?' He rested his forehead on hers. 'Why, Stevie? Why do you continue to let him hurt you? I would never have hurt you like this.'

'Look, it's none of your business, Miles. We're divorced and we're both moving on, remember? You said we could be friends and that you'd met someone, so let's just leave it at that, okay? And anyway, he's not staying...we're not together... but...look I think you should go. He may be calling around, and I think it's best if you're not here.'

'So he knows about *me*? About *us*? Does he love you like I did? Can you honestly say that he's good for you, Stevie? Look deep inside yourself. Can you be sure he won't leave without a trace again? I can't stand by and watch you let this happen. It tears me up that he damaged your heart so much that you can't give it to someone who deserves it.' He pulled her into his chest and wrapped his arms around her. 'All I wanted to do was protect you. All he wants is to use you.' He pulled away and moved his hands to her cheeks, pleading with his eyes. 'Even if we're not together, Stevie, you mean so much to me. Please, please don't let him hurt you anymore.' He crushed his lips into hers and held her there for a few seconds. She didn't reciprocate the kiss and he didn't attempt to make it more. His mouth stayed closed along with his eyes and he inhaled through his nose.

'She covered his hands with hers and removed them from her face. 'I think you should go now,' she whispered.

He nodded and hugged her once more.

Jason stood frozen to the spot as he observed the scene through the window. He watched as the copper haired man stroked her cheek, kissed her, and held her to him. His heart was being ripped out all over again. *So this is why she wouldn't stay in Scotland with me. This guy. Who the hell is he anyway? And why did Stevie make love to me if she's in a relationship? Is this who she is now? A cheater? A liar?* He watched even though he knew it was doing him no good. Suddenly, she looked over and noticed him standing there. He shook his head, turned, and began to walk away.

'Jason! Jason wait!' She shouted from inside. 'Please wait!' Her door opened and hit the inside wall with a resounding thud.

He stopped and turned to face her. 'Why? So you can rub my face in it a bit more? I get it, okay? I get that we're nothing. You've made that very clear.'

'How the hell have I made that clear?'

'Oh, give me a sodding break! I saw you kissing him, holding him. I'm not blind, Stevie. I saw how you looked at each other.'

'Not that it's any of your damn business, but what you actually saw was *him* kissing me goodbye...*him* holding me out of concern...*him* looking at me with sadness. If you'd have given me a minute to explain you would've understood!'

Miles appeared beside them. 'Is this him? Good, now you can tell him the truth about us. Tell him...go on...tell him everything.'

Pulling her fisted hands up to her head she screamed,

'Argh! Miles, just go! We've said all there is to say! Just go home!'

Ah so this is Miles. The ex-husband.

Miles' eyes were wild with determination. 'Tell him we're back together then...go on...tell him you still love me. He deserves to know the truth and you deserve better than him.'

Jason contorted his face in disgust. 'You're *back together*?' He ran his hands through his hair. 'I'm such an idiot!' His voice was a strangled noise he didn't recognise as himself.

Miles' grin was sinister. 'We were on our way upstairs, mate. We'd be together in *our bed* right now if you hadn't showed up!' he barked at Jason only inches from his face.

'What?' Jason widened his eyes and stared at her.

She lunged at Miles and pushed him with as much force as she could. 'Why are you doing this? Tell him you're lying! Tell him we just said goodbye and that you've moved on! Don't do this to me, Miles! If you care for me like you say you do, then don't *do* this to me! Please tell him!' Desperation filled her voice and she clung to his coat.

Miles smiled evilly. 'Sorry, mate, it's true. We've been sleeping together for weeks...working things out like married couples do, you know.' He made a patronising running gesture with two fingers. 'So you'd better run along on back to God knows where you came from and get on with *your* life, because she's mine!' His face was beet red, and saliva shot from his mouth like a rabid dog as aggression oozed from every pore.

Jason laughed humourlessly, shook his head, and turned to walk away. She slapped Miles hard across the face. 'You idiot! After everything you just said to me in there! Why are you doing this now? To prove a point? There are no points to prove! What about Charlie? You admitted we were over! We are DIVORCED and it's MY bed! I *hate* you right now! If you loved me like you say you do, you would never have done such a cruel and heartless thing! You'd just let me go instead of clinging on and making my life a misery. Because that's what you do, Miles. You make me *miserable!* Just leave and don't *ever* come to see me again! If you do, I *swear* I'll get a restraining order against you!' she sobbed. Jason carried on walking, but her bare footsteps slapped on the pavement as she jogged after him.

'Jason! Please!' He stopped again. The thought crossed his mind that perhaps Miles *was* lying to get him out of Stevie's life. Her reaction had been so dramatic. Was it an elaborate cover up? She reached him and pulled his body around so that he would face her. 'Jason, he's lying. I swear to you. Please. He came to tell me he's met someone else and that he knows we'll never get back together. I don't love him anymore; that's why I divorced him. There is *no way* I'm getting back together with him. He's just trying to protect me in his own stupid way...that's all. He doesn't want me to get hurt again and thinks if you're not here that I won't. I don't want him, Jason. I need you to know that. Please, come back to the house.' She cupped his face in her palms.

He could see the truth like a beacon of light in her eyes. But it changed nothing. The sad, painful realisation had hit. His jaw ached from clenching. 'The stupid thing is, Stevie... You may not be *his*, but you're not *mine* either. We're...temporary...a fling. It hurts too much, and I have enough to deal with right now.'

'Look, you've just been through a very emotional talk with Dillon. Just come back and talk. Or just sit and don't talk. Either way...please, just come back.'

Jason glanced back towards her house where Miles still stood, anger rolling off him in almost tangible waves. 'He loves you so much. Why don't you just give him a chance? He's fighting for you. And he's here in London permanently. I'm not.'

'I don't care, Jason. I don't love him. I never really did and he knows that. He's met someone and he's moving on but he still cares about me and doesn't want to see me hurt. But I want to be here for *you*. Even if this *is* temporary.' Well, she had confirmed it again.

Temporary.

She hadn't contradicted him like he had hoped. But he had no fight left in him anymore. The long talk with Dillon had taken every ounce of emotional and physical strength he had left and had flushed it down the nearest drain. He was spent. He began to walk back with her.

As they got closer to the house, Miles shook his head, turned, and began to walk away. He stopped and turned back to face them. 'The thing is, mate, *I'll* be the one here when *you've* gone. And I *know* you'll be leaving. It's what you do apparently. And I'll be the one who gets to pick up the pieces. I did it before and I can do it again. Just remember that.' He turned and left.

Back in the house, Jason could see that she was still shaking. He slumped onto the sofa and rested his head in his hands.

She sat beside him but didn't touch him. 'How bad was it? With Dillon I mean?'

'Like I said earlier after the phone call, open heart surgery without the anaesthetic would probably just about sum it up.'

'Oh dear. Did he believe you?'

'Eventually. Not at first, but the more I talked, the more he understood. Be honest with me...*completely* honest...do you still love your ex-husband? Because he clearly loves you fiercely, and I don't want to be the guy to break that apart. If you love him I'll walk—'

'Stop. I told you about me and Miles. I *don't* love him. And I don't want to talk about him. I want to hear how *you* are. I want to make the most of being with *you*.'

'But if you have nothing...no one here. Why can't you come with me? Why can't we try to make *us* work? I don't understand. It's not like we're continents apart. It's a few hundred miles. It's *nothing*. Not if we love each other.'

She sighed heavily. 'Jason, we've been through all of this. I don't *want* a long distance thing. They simply don't work. And it's over *five hundred* miles. It's not *nothing*. Plus my mum n—erm...is here too and I love my job. I love *being* here. London is an amazing place. You could love it too if you gave it a chance. You could sell up and move back here now that... now that Mick's gone.'

'And do what? My business is in Scotland. My *home* is there. I *belong* there. I don't belong here. I never really did.'

'But you said you belong with me. Doesn't that count for anything?'

'Of course it does. But just being here...it's...I can't...'

Her face lit up suddenly. 'Let's go out. Let me show you how things have changed here. All the things you ran from have gone now. Don't you see that? Let me try...please?'

He shook his head. 'It won't change my mind, Stevie. This place isn't home for me. But I'm happy to spend time with you. Every second with you is precious. I sincerely hope you know that.'

She smiled. 'So you'll let me show you *my* London?'

'On one condition.'

'Oh? And what might that be?'

'That I take you on the bike.'

CHAPTER TWENTY-EIGHT

*T*he following day, Stevie sat on her sofa nervously picking at her nails. Jason was due to arrive any second. He had requested that she wear old jeans with leggings underneath, a thick jumper with a T-shirt under that, and a thick jacket too. She felt trussed up like a turkey on Christmas day. She had tried her best to get out of being Jason's pillion passenger. Her favourite and *best* excuse was her lack of helmet. He had laughed heartily and told her it was no issue after all.

Dammit!

He hadn't said much about the talk he'd had with Dillon. She got the impression he would talk when he was ready, and so she hadn't pushed him. She knew that the situation had pained him and then witnessing the débâcle with Miles had just about finished him off. Thankfully, she had been able to convince him that the whole scenario was Miles' back to front way of looking out for her. Not that any of it mattered. At some point, he was determined to go back up north.

The roar of a motorbike engine rumbled outside, and her heart almost leapt out of her chest. *Oh no...oh no...why did I agree to this?* The anticipated knock on the door came loud and clear, and she nervously made her way to answer it.

Jason stood beaming at her in his black leathers, looking incredibly hot—in all senses of the word. His hair was tied back in a messy ponytail at the back of his head and sweat beaded above his brow. She wanted to lick it off and peel him out of his clothing. Her nipples stood to attention, but luckily it wasn't obvious, thanks to the number of layers making her feel like the Michelin Man. *Good grief, Stevie, get a grip!* She forgot how to speak for a moment.

He grinned at her knowingly, and her legs almost gave way beneath her. *Probably nerves...nothing to do with that smile...or lust...or the fact that under those leathers he's toned... tight...tempting...oh shit.*

He gestured to the bike. 'You ready to go?'

'Erm...I can't do this, and besides I told you yesterday I don't have a helmet so—'

'Ta-daaaa!' Jason held out a brand new helmet complete with teddy bear ears.

She stared open mouthed, but this time it was at the ridiculous item he was presenting to her. 'You've got to be kidding me. I'm not wearing *that*!'

'Oh, come on. I thought it was really cute. Try it on... please?' He pouted and fluttered his eyelids, and of course, she melted like an ice-lolly in the sunshine. Seeing him looking so excited made her adore him even more. She surmised that she would have ridden a ravenous tiger down the street if it got this reaction from him. His chocolate eyes sparkled as he stood there waiting for her.

She rolled her eyes and turned to lock the door behind her, chuntering under her breath about being treated like a five-year-old. She reluctantly grabbed the helmet from his grasp and pulled it down over her ears. She felt like her head was in a vice and glanced up to Jason, who stood there with a look of pure pride on his face.

'Awww, my Stevie, the bike virgin. You look so cute. But like I said before, add a set of leathers and...' His words trailed off, and she could pretty much read his smutty mind, thanks to the fact that he bit his bottom lip and then licked it as he raked his eyes over her denim clad body.

'I feel like I've been bloody mummified. All these bloody layers.'

'Hmmm, think of the fun we'll have peeling them off later.'

Ignoring his mischievousness, she continued. 'And I'm scared to death, Jason.'

He stepped towards her and rested his forehead on her helmet. 'You're perfectly safe with me, but only because you're not wearing leathers.' His slow smile made her squeeze her legs together. He took her hand and led her to the huge hunk of metal he called a bike and climbed on.

He held his hand out to her. 'Climb aboard, gorgeous, and I'll give you the ride of your life.' He grinned at her as she took his hand and swung her leg over to straddle the bike. He glanced over his shoulder at her. 'Get comfy, sweetheart, and hold on tight.' His accent sounded more Scottish than usual and her heart and stomach did simultaneous somersaults. He pulled his helmet over his head and strapped it in place. She slipped her hands around his waist and held on for dear life. 'Erm...Stevie...I know I said hold on tight, but breathing is quite imperative to riding safely. Can you let up a little?'

She giggled and loosened her vice-like grip. 'Whoops... sorry about that...nerves.'

He patted her hand where it lay across his stomach. 'Relax. You'll be fine. Trust me.'

He turned the key in the ignition and hit the accelerator.

Stevie let out a high-pitched squeal, and tucked her head into Jason's back, clenching her eyes shut. She could feel Jason's chest vibrating. *The rotten shit's laughing at me!*

Eventually, she began to relax and the whole thing was quite exhilarating. She dared to lift her head up and realised that Jason had taken quite the scenic route to get into the part of London she had mentioned to him the night before. Around thirty minutes later, they pulled up in a small car park off the main road of the leafy suburb she loved so much. She climbed from the bike and pulled off her helmet shaking her long, auburn hair out and running her hands through it.

'Oh. My. Word. That was bloody *fantastic*! I was terrified at first, but wowee, when I relaxed...words fail me. Bloody helmet though...don't know why I even bothered doing anything with my hair today.'

Jason removed his own helmet, and whilst still straddling the bike, he pulled her towards him. 'Ah, but you have the sexiest head of helmet hair I think I've ever seen.' He leaned in and kissed her tenderly.

As always, the spike of desire heated her right down to the junction of her thighs as she became a jellified mess in his arms.

'You really enjoyed it then?'

Her smile was wide. 'It was such a thrill! It felt amazing. I never expected to feel that way.'

He shrugged. 'Well, I'd say I told you so, but I'm not that immature.'

She stuck her tongue out at him.

He smirked. 'Clearly the same can't be said for you.'

Kissing Stevie had become Jason's favourite pastime since

arriving back in his version of hell again. The name he had applied to the city of London since leaving had stuck in his mind, but now that he was here, it wasn't quite as hellish as he remembered. Perhaps that had something to do with him reconnecting with Dillon...or putting the horrific memories to rest. Or perhaps it was just the fact that Stevie was here. All that said, he still could never live here again. He would never hack it in the big sprawling metropolis now. He was used to breathing the clean Highland air and being surrounded by the vast open spaces back home.

He followed her along the main street that she was so keen to show him. He knew deep down that this would change nothing, that he would undoubtedly be returning to Scotland after the funeral and house clearance. But he went along with things and tried his best not to let sadness take over their day together.

After a short walk down a bustling main street, they arrived outside an old bookshop. Jason glanced up at the sign. *The Book Depository. Cool name. Wouldn't it be funny if the owner was called Lee Harvey Oswald?*

She turned to him. She had a gleam in her eyes that melted Jason's heart. 'Oh I just love this place. They have books dating back to before the First World War...probably even older than that actually. Come on in.' She pushed the door open and stepped inside. The little old bell above the door jingled as they stepped in and was greeted by the fusty smell of old books.

'Stevie, darling! Bloody lovely to see you! I thought you'd moved away. It's been too bloody long!' A dashingly dressed man greeted Stevie with air kisses. His tweed jacket with elbow patches and his bow tie were perfectly befitting of the English Gent he appeared to be.

'Charles! It's good to see you too. This is my good friend,

Jason Reynolds. Jason this is Charles Oswald, the owner of this place.'

Jason couldn't help the grin that spread across his face. 'Oswald? Cool. Nice place you got here.'

Charles blushed and patted his hair. 'Why thank you, young man. Very nice of you to say so. That's not a local accent is it? Where are you from?'

'Ah, well, I *am* originally from London, but I moved away quite a long time ago. I live in the Highlands now, so I guess I've picked up a little of the accent.'

'The Highlands, you say? Bloody hell. I'm thinking there must be something pretty bloody spectacular up there.'

Bloody hell this bloke says bloody *a lot!* Jason bit his lip to stop from sniggering.

'Why do you say that, Charles?'

'Oh, a good friend and former employee of mine, Jim... You remember Jim, Stevie? The scruffy haired one... Oh, no offence, Mr. Reynolds.'

Jason smirked. 'Oh, none taken.'

'Yes, well, Jim was originally from Scotland, but he studied at Oxford and stayed here with his wife. Got divorced...terrible mess...and moved up to a little place called Shieldaig a few years ago. He loves it there. Fresh air...open spaces. He runs a little campsite and shop now. Sounds like a bloody idyllic life to me. His girlfriend, who was from London too, moved to be with him not so long ago. I think I'd jump at the bloody chance too if it wasn't for the business. I've visited and it really is stunning. Very tranquil and so picturesque.' He made a dramatic flourish with his hands.

Jason looked over at Stevie and raised his eyebrows as if to say *I told you so.* 'Sounds to me like your friend has good taste, Charles.' He spoke without taking his eyes away from Stevie's.

Her cheeks flushed and she looked away. 'Are we okay to

have a browse, Charles? Jason is more of a rugged outdoorsy type, but I'm determined to get him into paperbacks too.' Jason knew she was changing the subject deliberately. He feigned hurt at her comments about his reading habits and poked her in the ribs, gaining an elbow in his own in return.

'Absolutely, darling. Go ahead. Give me a shout if you need anything.' The telephone began to ring, and Charles excused himself and went to answer it.

They spent a long while thumbing through the books, and Jason bought a couple to prove a point to her that he wasn't a complete philistine. He had stood and watched her perusing for a while, loving how her mouth moved as she read to herself. *That beautiful mouth.* She glanced up and caught him watching her, but he just smiled and watched as the pink hue rose from her neck to her cheeks. *She's just so bloody cute. Whoops. Spent a bit too long in the presence of this shop's owner!*

After looking around the Aladdin's cave of a bookshop, Stevie insisted they go to a small coffee shop just along the road, claiming it was the best coffee she had *ever* tasted. They sat at a table in the window where they could look out over the busy street and do a little bit of people watching. Shoppers sauntered by carrying colourful bags, wearing summer clothes and wide smiles. It seemed like quite a chilled out location, nothing like the London he remembered. Central London was no doubt *exactly* as he remembered it. Frantic people in business suits without a single conversation in them, keeping their heads down as they made their way along the hectic streets. Cars and taxi's whizzing by, horns blearing, people shouting, fumes from myriad different vehicles, and people suffering road rage. A positively stress-inducing atmosphere. No, here was different. Calm. Serene in a way.

But it wasn't home.

He devoured a huge slab of carrot cake with cream cheese frosting as she sipped her latte from a tall glass. Closing his eyes, he savoured the sweet, melt-in-the-mouth texture. When he opened them, he handed a fork full to her.

She closed her mouth around the fork. 'Hmmm.' The noise she made had him twitching in his leathers. He looked up at her to find her watching him again. 'You see...*this* London is not at all like the London you envisaged is it?' She cocked her head to one side.

'No, quite right. The shops are far more quirky around here, and the bookshop was a real gem. I've enjoyed today...thank you.'

'But?'

Jason frowned. 'What do you mean?'

She pursed her lips for a moment. 'It sounded like you were going to say *but* and follow it with something negative.'

'No, not at all. It's just.' He placed his fork down. 'I don't know...I miss home...*my* home up north.'

Her eyes took on a tinge of sadness. 'But you once looked on London as your home.'

'Not really...if I'm honest. When I talked about being lost it applied to me being here too. I was misplaced here. I never felt at home. Not in the true sense of the word.'

'You travelled a lot when you left though, so how do you know what *home* really is?'

He thought for a moment. 'That's just it. I think I discovered what home *is* by first finding out what it *isn't.*'

She shook her head, and her forehead creased at his cryptic response. 'What do you mean?'

'I mean that... Well, everyone usually thinks of home as where they grew up, but that wasn't the case for me. I'm sure you can understand why. And then I thought that being in the army would mean I found my home abroad maybe...or maybe being on the move all the time would feel right. Maybe I didn't need a base as such. But when it came down to it, I missed being in *one place*. So the security job gave me that for a while. Warm weather, sunshine, etc...but even then I didn't feel at home. When I settled in Scotland things just clicked... for the most part.' He shrugged.

She leaned forward. 'Only for the most part?'

Jason dropped his gaze to where his fingertips played in a pool of sugar granules on the table. 'Yeah, it seems I lost something else when I left all those years ago...along with my sense of home. I...I left my heart behind too.'

She snorted. 'Good grief, Jason...can I have some crackers to go with all the cheese?'

Sadness overtook him at her reaction, but it was clear from the blush in her cheeks and the water in her eyes as they looked anywhere but at him that she didn't *really* feel that way. What he'd said had hit a nerve and self-preservation mode had kicked in.

He leaned forward and looked into her eyes. 'Stevie, I left my heart because, as I said to you up in Scotland, *you* still had it. I thought I could leave you behind and forget. I'm not sure who I was trying to kid. I was delusional to think I'd ever get over you. And seeing you again made me realise and admit to myself that I hadn't forgotten at all. All I'd done was push the feelings I had into a little box on a shelf in the deepest recesses of my mind.'

She fiddled with the long stemmed spoon on her saucer. 'Oh.'

'Seeing you again made me open that box and dare to peer inside. And what I saw terrified me.'

'In what way?'

'Because from day one of you turning up at the camp I've known...I've known that we should be together. We should have *always* been together and I ruined that. And now...now you won't or can't give me a second chance.' He dropped his gaze back to the swirls of sugar on the table.

'It's not as simple as that. And it's not because I don't care. You have to understand that I have a life *here*. I simply can't just uproot myself. What would I do if things didn't work out? If you got scared and ran again? I'd be alone up there. I would have moved hundreds of miles away from everything I know and love for *you*. But what would I have for *me*?'

He gazed up at her once again. 'But you know my reasons for leaving now. That wouldn't happen again. And you could get a job, you'd make friends.'

'All on *your* terms. I've made bad decisions before, Jason. I married Miles because *he* wanted me to. It didn't work out. I can't repeat the same mistake again.'

He leaned forward. 'But who's to say it'd be a mistake? You set off on something like this with a negative attitude and you're dooming it to fail. I just don't get why we can't try. *I want to try.*'

She sighed heavily and slumped in her seat. 'I've witnessed first-hand what long distance does to people—'

'But I'm not Jed. I know what he did to your mum. I wouldn't do that.'

'You say that now...just like he did. I...I'm sorry but I can't look beyond here and now, Jason. I can't.'

'You mean you won't.'

She heaved a long sigh. 'Okay, you're right. I *won't*. I don't *want* to do that to us. I don't want to sit at home spending my time wondering what you're doing and who you're with...or if you're still as interested in me when I'm hundreds of miles away and can't touch you or talk to you face to face. Phone calls are not the same. We both have needs that can't be met by someone who's so far away. And I don't just mean sex.'

'So, we really are at an impasse then.'

A sad determination appeared in her beautiful blue eyes. 'No, Jason. We have to accept this for what it is. At the end of it we *have* to move on. I've never lied to you. I've been honest about this from the start. Your business is up in Scotland and my job is here. Neither of us can afford the time or money to trek up and down the country all the time. I'm...I'm just trying to be realistic.'

He laughed humourlessly and shook his head. 'Are we both just too stubborn?'

'No, we're both making sure we have what we need to get by in life.'

He listened to her words as his chest ached. They really had reached an impasse, despite her unwillingness to admit it. He was willing to try but she wasn't. Nothing else could be done.

That was that.

CHAPTER TWENTY-NINE

*T*hey left the coffee shop and began on their way again. Stevie was on a mission to try to convince him that London *could* be home for him again. They walked along together browsing in the quirky little boutiques and second hand shops. They tried on silly hats and disguises in the old joke shop and took photos on their phones.

The good old-fashioned record shop was Jason's favourite place. He searched for what seemed like hours through old vinyl LP's that reminded him of happier times in his child-hood. They laughed at some of the seventies album sleeves and had a competition to see who could find the funniest. Later, they listened to Led Zeppelin's 'Ten Years Gone' in the close confines of the cramped listening booth, their heads pressed together to share the headphones.

The music oozed melancholy, and the irony of her song choice wasn't lost on him. Leaning so closely to her was stir-ring him up again. Their eyes were locked for most of the track as their foreheads touched and their breath mingled. Despite the desperate desire to do so, he didn't kiss her. The look in her eyes and the way her lips remained parted told him she wanted him to. But he managed to restrain himself.

Only just.

The little dress shop next to the record shop is where she had spent the longest. All the clothes were handmade by the shop's owner Maria Marcone. She insisted to him that Maria was destined for greatness, as her designs were so beautiful and the fabrics she used were, according to Stevie, the most stunning textures and colours. She ended up spending two hundred pounds on a new outfit, which she insisted was a bargain for individually designed clothing. Jason nodded and secretly yawned and rolled his eyes when her back was turned, but it earned him a punched arm and twisted nipple when he was finally caught in the act.

Although he wound her up about being bored, he secretly loved watching her trying on what seemed like a million different outfits. She looked gorgeous in each and every one. And all he wanted to do was take her back to her house and undress her again. Although what he felt wasn't all about sex, he really did want to make the most of being with her that way. For all the good it was doing him. But he figured he would be leaving here with a broken heart regardless.

She took him to a little patisserie owned by a cool Frenchman called Michel LaPierre. Michel had moved to the area from his home in Normandy almost twenty years ago to be with his girlfriend, whom he had met whilst she was on holiday near his hometown. His pastries were divine, and Jason managed to munch his way through a large selection whilst they walked in between shops.

She even resorted to taking him to the largest inner city park in the area, where they sat and finished the last of the pastries. She seemed determined to prove that there *was* an abundance of fresh air here too. Jason loved her all the more for it. But they both knew it would change nothing.

As they sat watching a mother duck and her chicks swim around on the pond, she nudged him. 'See, we even get fresh air in London.'

He smiled and nudged her back. 'Okay, touché.'

'Do you know where else we should go?'

'I know exactly where we should go.'

They strolled towards the bike, and once they were ready, they set off to visit their special place down by the river. Once they arrived, they walked hand in hand to their favourite patch of banking and sat.

'I came here before I went to visit Mick. It was strange being here again. It's even stranger being here with you now.'

She glanced up at him. 'It's like we've travelled back in time somehow.'

'Do you think if we knew then what we know now we'd have still done things the same?'

'Hmmm...I would've tried to help you if I'd known what I know now. I would've tried to stop it. Maybe then we wouldn't have lost ten years.'

He dropped his gaze to the long grass that surrounded them. 'Where do you think we'd be now? I mean, if you'd been able to stop it all? Would we still be together?'

She smiled and turned her face away, discreetly trying to wipe away a stray tear. But he'd already seen it trickle down her cheek.

'Hey, I'm sorry, Stevie. I didn't mean to upset you.'

She turned back to face him. 'I know. I just...this is the first time I've been here since you left, and even though you're here...I still feel like I'm alone.'

He leaned forward and took her chin between his thumb and finger. 'I thought of you every day. Even when I didn't realise I was thinking about you. Looking back now, I know that... I'd catch a fragrance...hear a song...see a girl with long auburn hair...and they would all be you. I dreamed of you. I missed you every day.' His voice had lowered to a whisper.

He kissed her then and pulled her down in the long grass just like he used to when they were teenagers. He cradled her head with one hand and her cheek with the other as she ran her hands through his hair. This kiss wasn't lust filled or urgent. It was tender and innocent, filled with love and adoration, and it made Jason's heart ache just a little bit more than it already had.

After spending an hour sitting in each other's arms, they left the riverbank and made their way back to her house. Jason parked, removed his helmet, and checked his watch. *Six thirty.* She pulled off her helmet with bear ears and ran a hand through her hair. He stifled the groan fighting for release. She had no idea how sexy she was and how the smallest of things she did affected him so deeply.

Pulling her into his arms, he kissed her chastely and said goodbye, then watched her as she walked away from him and opened her front door. She turned around and waved with a sad smile as he looked at her with what he was sure was the same amount of sadness in his eyes. His mobile phone rang as he was about to put his helmet back on and ride away, but noticing it was Dillon calling, he answered.

'Hi...Jason, it's me...Dillon.'

'Yeah, I got that from the caller ID. What's up, little brother?'

'I...erm...have to work tomorrow, but I was wondering if you wanted to go to the house...Mum and Dad's I mean. I thought maybe you could make a start on clearing things out for me? I know it's a lot to ask, but I don't know when I'm going to get the time to do it. But I think we at least need to make a start. On our rooms maybe. It needs doing. You know... so we can both just move on after the funeral. Oh and the funeral is next week... Thursday at noon. They couldn't do it any sooner. I hope that's okay with you.'

'Oh...right...yeah of course. I'll erm...I'll go and make a start.'

'Yeah, thanks. Leave my old room though, eh? I'll sort that. Just maybe start on your room. That way you take anything that you want to keep. It'll be a bit of a painful trip down memory lane for you, I guess. I might get a clearance company to do the rest. I just don't think there's anything I want from the rest of the house. It's all...it's all tainted.'

Jason exhaled. 'I know, Dillon. It's going to be difficult for both of us I think. I'm...I'm sorry, mate.'

'No need to be. I'll maybe see you tomorrow night if you fancy going for a drink, eh?'

'Sure thing. That'd be good. I'll give you a call.'

'Yeah...bye Jace.'

'Bye, little bro.'

Jason climbed off the bike and headed for her front door. He suddenly couldn't stand the idea of going back to the hotel alone. He knocked hard, and she flung it open immediately as if she had been waiting for him.

'Couldn't stay away, eh?'

'Not for long, no. Look, Dillon called and asked me if I'll go and sort my old room tomorrow. Pack up any shit I want to keep. Although I doubt that there'll be much. I wondered...'

A smile spread across her face. 'If I'd go with you and hold your hand?'

He turned his mouth up at one side. 'Yeah...would you?'

'Well, it's my summer holidays you know, and I have lots of things I could be doing.'

285

His smile faded and he shook his head. 'Oh, shit of course. Sorry, I—'

'But none of them are as important as helping my dear friend Jace clear his childhood bedroom.'

He huffed out a sigh of relief. 'Awww, thanks, Stevie. I really do appreciate it. I just couldn't bear the thought of going there alone.'

'No, I'm sure it'll be difficult for you.'

'Yeah, I can't say I'm looking forward to being there again.' He stepped back, but inside he was praying she'd stop him. 'Anyway...I'll see you tomorrow.' He turned away.

'Look...I've ordered pizza. Why don't you just come in and eat with me. Stay over if you like. You may as well.'

Yes! Thank you God.

Turning back to face her, he nodded. 'Thank you...thank you so much.' He stepped inside the door checking around for Rowdy, the hound from hell, but he seemed to elsewhere. 'I didn't want to be alone in that hotel, but at the same time, I don't want you to think that I'm taking advantage. We seem to keep...you know...ending up in bed. But we don't have to do that. Your friendship is more important.'

She nudged his shoulder. 'Stop being such a girl and go grab us a beer from the fridge, will you?'

Jason chuckled at her lack of subtlety and did as she asked. He placed the beers on the table and went up to the guest room to strip out of his leathers.

Stevie followed Jason up the stairs after deciding that if she was slobbing out with pizza, beer, and Jason she needed to be wearing less clothing. The layers she had donned for the bike ride were now making her feel suffocated and far too warm.

She was about to pass the guest room door but stopped when she glanced through the opening. Jason was removing his leathers. She had a mighty fine view of his sculpted derrière as he bent to pull the tight pants from his legs. He stood again and stretched his arms over his head revealing his tattooed back and fading bruises from his run in with Dillon. She swallowed as her mouth began to water, and the muscles south of her waistline clenched needily.

Frustration that he affected her this way took over and she sighed. *Why couldn't he have gone patchily bald, lost his teeth, and acquired a flabby beer gut? It would be so much easier than seeing his sculpted muscles, smooth skin, and...oh my word, those tattoos.*

'Like what you see, pervy?' he asked without turning around.

She inhaled sharply and widened her eyes. 'I wasn't...I didn't...I mean, I...erm...sorry.' She cringed just as he turned around to face her, his fitted boxers leaving nothing to the imagination. 'Don't you wear jeans under your leathers?'

'Nah...Not enough room.' He smirked.

She gulped as her eyes slid, involuntarily, to his crotch. 'No...I...can imagine.' Her mind wandered off somewhere entirely inappropriate and *very* smutty.

Laughter erupted from his chest. 'Oy! I didn't mean because of my package! You really are a perv, aren't you?'

She narrowed her eyes at him, annoyed that the blush in her cheeks had betrayed her. 'Food will be here in five. I suggest you let *me* go to the door. *I* will clearly be the one wearing clothes.'

Jason pouted, which didn't help matters. 'Really? That's a shame. I was hoping I'd get to ogle *your* ass all night in those skimpy knickers of yours.'

'Funny. My *ass* is going to be well and truly covered up,

thank you. And who's being the perv now, eh?' She walked away, hearing him laughing, and closed her own bedroom door behind her so that he couldn't peep in. She couldn't help the huge grin on her face.

She was well aware that she had filled out in the last ten years. She wasn't huge, but she was definitely a lot curvier than when he had last seen her. But he didn't seem to care and she *loved* that. His every glance told her that he desired her, and that instilled a confidence in her that she hadn't felt in so long. It almost made her feel like walking around in something skimpy just to wind him up. She toyed with the idea for a while, but then decided on yoga pants and a hoodie.

She was on her way downstairs when the doorbell rang, so she grabbed her purse and opened the door. Swiftly paying the spotty teenager—an ex-pupil no less—she took the large box through to the lounge.

'Hmmm, smells good. I hope there's enough here for you too.' Jason grinned.

She raised her eyebrows at him. 'Oh don't worry. I'll resort to *dirty* measures to ensure I get my fair share.' As soon as the unintentional double entendre had left her mouth, she knew what his response would be, and her cheeks heated.

Jason's voice dropped to a sultry whisper. 'Oh *really*? Do tell. I'm intrigued about these *dirty measures*.' He bit his bottom lip and she almost groaned.

Instead, she shook her head. 'Actually, I meant that I would just get Rowdy in here to watch you whilst I eat my share of the pizza.'

His face dropped. 'Oh...shit. Where is the mad hound anyway?'

She stuck out her bottom lip. 'He isn't mad. Don't be mean. My friend and neighbour Joe has him today. He goes hiking and Rowdy loves to chase birds. God only knows what he'd do if he was ever quick enough to catch one.'

Jason's eyes widened. 'Erm, I think it's pretty bloody *obvious* what he'd do if he caught one. I remember the way he was looking at my goods. He would've happily ripped them off if you'd left the room for long enough.'

'Seriously, Jason, he's a sweet little thing. He's just...misunderstood.'

He snorted, almost choking on his beer. 'Sweet? Little? Who are you trying to kid?'

Once their pizza was gone and they'd drunk several beers, she yawned and stretched. 'Well, I think that's me done for the day. All the excitement of the bike ride has worn me out.'

'Yeah, I'm pretty bushed myself... I'll...I'll sleep in the guest room.'

She bit her lip as disappointment washed over her. 'Oh... really? You don't have to.'

Jason's smile didn't quite reach his eyes. 'Yeah, I think I do. It's probably for the best.'

'Okay, goodnight then.' She bent to kiss the top of his head and made her way upstairs, feeling too tired to argue.

Once she was gone, Jason sat for a while in the silence of the living room. He drained the last drops of beer from his bottle, ran his free hand through his hair, and then rested his head back on the couch. His mind whirred with the events of the last few days. And still his heart ached at the thought of leaving her again. But there was no way around it. He decided that distancing himself was the best policy from now on. Not that it would help in the long run. But he figured he would at least try. He sat and contemplated this for a little longer until his resolve began to weaken. Just the thought of her softness beneath him. Her smell. Her eyes as she locked her gaze on him whilst she ascended skyward and pulsed around him.

He shook his head. He needed to eradicate the thoughts. He placed his empty beer bottle in the kitchen recycle bin and switched off the lamp in the lounge. On each step, he climbed he told himself *guest room, guest room, guest room*.

He turned the door handle and stepped inside, stripped himself of his clothing, and sat on the edge of the bed. It was no good. All he could think about was Stevie and her body and how being in the next room wasn't helping him. He stood again, not really sure why he had or where he was going, but what he did know was that he couldn't and wouldn't go to her. Could he? No, it would be going against his gut feeling. And a gut feeling was something to take notice of, wasn't it? He paced back and forth trying to talk himself out of doing something silly. Rubbing his hands roughly over his face, he was contemplating putting his clothes on and leaving when the door opened.

She stood there in her pale blue satin underwear. He watched her as she trailed her eyes up and down his naked form, her chest rising and falling rapidly. Her eyes were filled with a mixture of emotions. He opened his mouth to speak, but she interrupted his train of thought.

Twisting her hands in front of her, she spoke just above a whisper, 'I...I completely understood your reasons for sleeping in here. I really did...but...knowing that you're in here alone is killing me. I don't expect anything from you, but...I would really like it if I could stay with you tonight. I understand if you say no but—'

Jason crossed the room in two strides and scooped her up into his arms. He crushed his lips into hers as she wrapped her legs around him and thrust her tongue into his mouth. He staggered forward until he pressed her up against the wall beside the door, his lips never leaving hers. Holding her under her bottom with one arm, he reached around and unfastened her bra, roughly pulling it down her arms and throwing it to the floor. He devoured her nipple, circling it with his tongue and biting just hard enough to make her cry out and grab at his hair. His urgent kisses moved up her body until he reached her neck and sucked the silky skin into his mouth.

He pulled away and looked into her eyes, his erratic breathing and heartbeat almost in sync with hers. 'Is this what you want, Stevie? I know you said you wanted to be in here with me, but if this is not what you *really* meant, you need to tell me right now. Tell me and I'll place you down, and I'll leave...I'll go back to the hotel.'

'It is what I want... I want you, Jason.' Her breathing mirrored his own.

'I need to get...oh shit...I haven't brought any—'

'It's fine...it's fine...I'm covered,' she panted.

He frowned. 'Covered how?'

'Pill...now shut up and just take me, Jason.' Knowing he was clean, having never done this with anyone without protection before, he just stared at her. She covered his mouth once again with a luscious wet kiss, drawing the air from his lungs. He tugged at her panties, and she unravelled her legs from his torso long enough for them to be dragged away completely. Once there were no barriers left, she wrapped her legs around him again.

He entered her with a guttural growl, his movements desperate and filled with need. He covered her with kisses as she leaned her head back against the wall, taking him in with each ragged breath. Desire pulsed through his body, and she clenched around him. Nothing could ever replace this feeling. *No one* could ever drive him this crazy with such an intoxicating combination of lust and love. Only her. Only Stevie. There was nothing slow or gentle about how he took her. It felt too good. Pleasure radiated from where they were joined and spread like fire through ever nerve and every muscle.

They grasped each other with urgency and passion, tugging hair and biting flesh. Their slick bodies collided with each thrust of Jason's hips. Her climax hit and she gripped his shoulders, dropping her head forward and biting onto his shoulder. Knowing he had this effect on her both thrilled and saddened him. He took her face in one hand and looked deep into her eyes as her desperate cries sent him tumbling after her.

He collapsed to the floor, taking her with him and clutching her to his chest as they caught their breath.

CHAPTER THIRTY

*A*fter breakfast, Stevie cleared the pots away whilst Jason finished his coffee. There seemed to be a tense atmosphere surrounding him this morning. After their animalistic lovemaking, they had collapsed and fallen asleep in the guest room bed without talking about what had happened. Jason had been quiet and subdued this morning too. He had made no attempts to talk to her about last night, and she had been disappointed, but put it down to the trepidation of going to his parents' house again. Neither spoke as they finished up. She kept glancing over to him but he remained stoic.

Eventually, her emotions got the better of her. 'Jason, is everything okay? You're so quiet and I'm worrying about you.'

He snapped his eyes up to hers. 'What? Oh, sorry. Yes, I'm fine...just wondering what to expect this morning, I suppose.'

She sighed. 'I can understand that. Look, why don't we go in my car? That way if you have any things you want to bring away you can put them in there?'

'I was going to ask if we could go separately. I'll go over on my bike and you in your car. That way I can stick some stuff in your car, but I can get away if Dillon needs me at all. He's seeing the solicitor in his lunch break about the house. I'm not sure if I'll be needed.'

With a twinge of disappointment, she nodded. 'Sure... okay. Whatever you want. I'm ready when you are.'

Feeling a little uneasy about how things had gone the night before and about his impending visit to his family home, Jason grabbed his keys and made his way out to the bike. Stevie followed and they set off for the leafy suburb where his parents had lived their entire married life. The modest house stood in the bottom of a cul-de-sac surrounded by trees and backed onto fields. The grass out front was overgrown and the paintwork on the windows was peeling. Seeing it in this state gave Jason an aching sadness. It had fallen into such disrepair that it was hardly recognisable as the place he grew up. Not all of his memories of the place were bad. But now it resembled the relationship he had endured with his father. A complete shambles. A mess.

Using the key his brother had dropped in for him, he unlocked the front door and stepped over the mountain of junk mail and bills that had been pushed through the letterbox. A smell of damp and dirt filled his nostrils, making him wrinkle his nose. The house had clearly not been cleaned in a very long while.

When Stevie followed him in and glanced around at the house, which was formerly like a show home, she cringed. 'What do you want me to do, Jason?'

He turned to see a look of sadness in her eyes that mirrored his own. 'You don't have to do anything down here.

I'm touching nothing that belonged to *him*. Only my own stuff. If there's any still here. For all I know, it's long gone.' He made his way up the stairs towards his old room and she followed. The stair carpet that had been relatively new when he had left now looked threadbare and filthy.

They arrived outside his old bedroom door and Jason took a deep breath as he clung onto the handle. His heart thumped at his ribs and his jaw clenched.

She placed a reassuring hand on his arm and smiled. 'It'll be fine Jason. Don't worry. I'm here with you.'

With her words of encouragement, he turned the handle and stepped inside. The pair audibly gasped in unison at the sight before them.

'Bloody hell...it's like stepping back in time.' He gulped down a knot of emotion and suddenly felt a little light headed as he looked around the room where he once found solace from his unpleasant existence. His old stereo deck stood covered in a layer of thick dust along with piles of CD's. The notice board above his desk still had the same certificates and photos pinned in place. The striped duvet cover still lay atop his bed. The old guitar that he had learned to play on still stood in its stand. Dust motes danced in the beams of the hazy morning sunshine filtering in the through the curtains at the window, and she sneezed, making him jump. He swung his head around and looked at her.

'Sorry, but my nose is a bit tickly.' She walked over the bookshelf and pulled out a copy of Jason's favourite book. *The Catcher in The Rye* had been a book he had read several times. She used to poke fun at him, saying he had memorised the story and didn't need to read it anymore but that he was too scared to move onto anything else in case it didn't come up to scratch. She wasn't far from the truth. The book held a special place in his heart thanks to its portrayal of teen angst.

He had related to the story and to the main character, Holden Caulfield.

Jason slumped onto his bed, suddenly feeling a little over-whelmed. His eyes traversed each and every feature of the room that had been untouched for so many years. It seemed eerie, like someone had built a replica of his room for a film set. A kind of detached and uneasy sensation knotted his stomach as he took in the surroundings that had once been his safe haven.

She sat beside him and rested her hand on his thigh. 'It's okay to be a bit freaked out by this you know. It's like a time capsule. It's like you walked out only yesterday, not ten years ago.'

He pulled his brows into a frown. 'I don't get it. Why didn't he clear it out when Mum died? Why did he just leave it all here? He hated me, Stevie. I don't understand.'

'Honestly, who knew what went on in that man's mind, Jason? I doubt that he ever came in here though.'

'No, I reckon you're right about that.' He stood again and walked over to the stereo. 'Remember when we used to listen to music and just kiss for hours?' He smiled at the memory as it came back to him.

'I do. It's a wonder our mouths didn't seize up or some-thing.' She giggled.

'It's a wonder your mum didn't kill me. She must've thought we were doing more than kissing and watching DVD's over here in my room.'

'She trusted me, I suppose. And she *did* ask me in a roundabout way how far we'd gone. I was honest. She could see that I was. She could always tell when I was lying.'

Jason flicked a switch and looked through the CD's. He selected one and slid it into the drawer, searching until he found the track he wanted to hear. It was a song that had meant a lot to him but had always been painful to listen to. The lyrics called to mind things he wanted to forget but also conjured up images of her lying beside him in this very room, kissing him and caressing his wounds through his clothing without even realising it.

He knew that last night had been a mistake and that he should put an end to the way things had been progressing with her. Continuing in this way would only make things more difficult when he left to go home, but his resolve to stop was weakening more and more each day. Being in his old room overawed by melancholy didn't help that fact. At that moment, as he stood there with his back to her, he knew that distance was something he couldn't allow right then and there. The pain inside of him relating to what had gone before was too real, and he needed to experience the one thing that felt right in this place.

Being with Stevie was that one thing.

Pressing play, he turned back to face her. 'Want to recreate a memory with me?' He held out his hand to her as 'It's Been Awhile' by Staind filled the air around them. She gazed up at him and held out her hand, slipping it into his outstretched one. He pulled her to her feet and enveloped her in his arms. His mouth found hers as he overtook her in a deep, urgent kiss. He kissed her like she could unlock all the hurt within him and set it free. And maybe...just maybe that was because she could.

She pulled away and looked deeply into him with her bright blue eyes. Running her fingers through his shaggy hair, she breathed. 'Instead...do you want to make a *new* memory with me?' She brushed his hair back from his face. 'A memory that we *should* have had, here in this room but never got the chance to make.'

Understanding what she meant, he pulled at the hem of

her top and lifted until he could discard it on the floor. This time he would be gentler. This time he would savour the experience, savour her taste and the feminine softness of her curves. He caressed her breasts through the lace of her bra and she gasped. After unfastening her skirt, he let it pool around her feet. She pushed the leather jacket down his arms and it fell and landed in a heap beneath them. His leather biker pants were also relinquished.

With her arms around his neck, she pulled him towards her until their lips were almost touching. As his eyes locked on hers, he could feel her breath as it mingled with his own. His heart rate accelerated as it always did when they were this close, and he ran his fingers down her bare back. She shivered and closed her eyes, her breathing becoming less controlled and more rapid too. When she opened them again, she slipped her hands down his chest, lightly grazing his skin with her nails, making him inhale a shaking breath. All the time their lips remained so close but not touching.

'I'll never get enough of you, Stevie...*never*. I want you so much. I want to be inside you right now...to hear you call my name...to feel you wrapped around me.'

'I want that too.' She never broke eye contact as she breathed her reply.

'Last night was wrong. Everything was rushed and I was so rough...I regret that.'

'You regret it?' Sadness and hurt tinged her whispered voice.

'No, you misunderstand. I mean I regret how fast things went... I should have taken my time, but—'

She placed her fingers over his lips. 'Shhh, we have time now. Please don't have regrets about last night. It was passion-ate, and I wanted it that way too. But now I want to take things slower.'

He slipped his hands down inside her panties to her behind and pulled her closer still, pressing her into his prominent arousal and clenching his jaw. 'I need you. Now that I have you back, how am I supposed to just walk away? How can I let you go? You know I can't stay, but how do I leave?' He searched her eyes, trying to see deep into her soul, the other half of his own where it remained locked inside her.

'Just make love to me...let's make this memory... Let's not think about tomorrow or next week. It's just you and me right now, and I want to feel you inside of me too, Jason. Body and soul.'

Her words fuelled his desire, and they tumbled onto the bed, grabbing at each other's remaining clothing, tossing their underwear aside as if their joining couldn't happen quickly enough. Jason entered her with a long moan through clenched teeth and began to move slowly. Each movement made with purpose to show her how much he loved her. This was where he belonged. Wherever Stevie was. *Surely* he could make this his home too? He shook his head and rested his forehead on hers, and they moved together on the bed he slept in before he left all those years ago. The bed they had kissed on for hours as innocent teenagers. The bed they should have given themselves to each other in for their very first times. But instead, here they were ten years on making love intensely and passionately as if this was the last time.

And maybe it was.

She was the first to cry out. Her climax triggered Jason's as he clung to her like a lifeline. Feeling overcome with emotion, he clamped his eyes shut and rested his head in the crook of her neck, breathing heavily. Dampness appeared on the side of his face and he lifted his head. Her eyes were closed and tears spilled from them as she shuddered beneath him. He rolled to his side and pulled her into him, stroking her hair. She obviously felt the same despair he felt.

'Hey...shhh...it's okay, sweetheart. We'll figure this out. I know we will.' But he really didn't know that at all. Unless...

Once they were dressed again, Jason collected a garbage bag from the kitchen and began to go through the things on his desk. Everything had been left there. Cinema stubs, receipts, train tickets. Nothing had been thrown away for *ten years*.

Photographs of Jason and Stevie together adorned every available surface, and he collected them together. *Now* he would take them with him. They would be a painful reminder of the girl he had loved, but better to have a reminder than none at all. How does the saying go again? Something about it being better to have loved and lost, etc. What a shame it was that the words brought him no comfort.

He searched through the drawers and found old T-shirts he had once loved. All neatly ironed and folded by his mum. He smiled at the thought that they wouldn't fit him now he was so much broader.

'Hey, fancy taking some of my old T-shirts to sleep in? No point me taking them seeing as they won't fit...and well there's nothing sexier than a girl wearing a blokes T-shirt to sleep in.'

She smiled fondly. 'I'd love to take them...thanks... I have so many memories of you wearing them.' She took the pile he held out to her and placed them with her bag.

The room was like a shrine. Left perfectly as it would have been when he lived here. Before he left. He smiled to himself as she straightened the crumpled bedding as if his mum was expected home any minute and would be angry at their lurid behaviour.

He looked back to the certificates on the pin board, at his many achievements, none of them good enough for his dad. Schoolbooks and novels weighed down the shelf above the foot of his bed. And a keepsake box that he would take with him and look through in private. He knew the contents would embarrass him. Love notes he had penned to Stevie but never given her. Poems and song lyrics he had written about her. Things that would make him cringe, no doubt. He shook his head remembering how sappy he used to be about her.

As he stood there looking at the tiny slivers of his past a new realisation began to settle in. He *could* live here. There was no threat to him now. He *could* be with Stevie. He *could* have the best of both worlds. He could find someone to run the camp and he could maybe start something up down here. Something working with underprivileged kids maybe? His heart began to beat faster and a wide smile spread across his face. He just had to be brave. That's all. And hell if he hadn't been brave before. Surely he could do it again?

Behind him and unaware of his current train of thought, Steve gasped. 'Jason...Jason...you...you need to see this.' Her startled, stuttering voice made him spin around.

He frowned. 'Why, what is it?'

'I think...I think it's a letter.' She held out what looked like an envelope.

'You seem to have acquired a stutter.' He sniggered. 'It'll just be some love letter I wrote to you and never gave you or something.' His cheeks heated a little at his admission.

She shook her head slowly. 'No...this is...it's actually addressed *to* you.'

Jason grabbed the envelope from her hand. 'To me? Where did you find it?' He was a little confused as he glanced down at the object she had handed to him.

She pointed to the bed. 'It was just there...under your pillow.'

'It looks like...shit it *is*...it's Mum's handwriting.' His voice was a strangled sob as he eagerly tore at the envelope and pulled out several sheets of hand written paper. 'It *is* from my Mum.' He flopped to the bed and looked at her with tears in his eyes.

She sat beside him on the bed. 'Oh Jason, what does it say?'

'The date... It's dated two years ago...just before she died.'

He nervously looked back to the paper and began to read the letter to himself. His heart hammered in his chest.

She stayed silently before him, waiting.

Dear Jason

My darling boy. This isn't the first letter I've written to you since you left, but I have a feeling it may be the last. I've never had an address to post them to and so I just keep them in a box in my wardrobe. The most recent one I always place under your pillow, just in case you ever come home. But of course you never do.

The thing is now I'm sick and I'm not getting any better. I'm not sure how many more I can write. It's my heart. I've had lots of treatment and tests, but well, there isn't much to live for really, and so I'm giving up. I know that sounds so negative, and I don't want you to be angry with me. I deserve this, you see. I'm getting what I should. My just desserts. The things I left unsaid and undone have eaten away at me for all these years, Jason, and now at least, it won't be long until I can stop feeling like this.

I sit alone in your untouched room often. I wash and change your bedding in case you return. It's all I have ever wanted, your safe return. To see your beautiful face again.

As I think this may be the last letter I write, there are some things I need to tell you, and they will be painful to hear. But I want you to know that nothing you can think of me will be any worse than what I have thought of myself for the last twenty-six years. I've tortured myself enough for both of us.

Stevie looked on as Jason read, his face a confused mask. The line between his brows deepened. What the hell was in that letter? He looked down at the envelope and pulled out a photo. He stared at it for a long while. From where she was sitting, she leaned forward and could see that it was a photo of Jason with another girl. Judging by his fresh-faced appearance in the picture, it must have been taken just before he disappeared. Handsome eighteen-year-old Jason. The man she had loved so deeply.

She touched his leg. 'Jason? Are you okay?' No reply. 'Jason? Who's that girl in the photo with you?' Still nothing. Panic rose within her and she nudged him. 'Jason!' She raised her voice this time, causing him to look up.

'What?' he snapped. His face had paled, drained of all colour. But there was anger in his narrowed eyes. And maybe a little fear.

'What's in the letter?'

'Sorry? Oh...it's...' He shook his head. He looked back at the letter and the photograph again. His eyes widened, he was clearly horrified at the contents. He opened and closed his mouth as if searching for the right words. Then a look of disbelief washed over his features. He stood slowly as if in a trance like state. 'I've...I need...I need some air.' He almost staggered towards the door, clutching the papers and photograph in his grip.

She stood too and followed. Something was very wrong. 'Jason, are you all right? You're scaring me.' She followed him down the stairs and watched as he pulled on his leather jacket, shoved the scrunched up letter and photograph into the inside pocket, and walked out of the front door. 'Jason for goodness sake, will you *please* tell me what was in the letter? And who was that girl in the photo with you? Please!'

Jason stopped and turned to face her. 'Stevie...I...I can't do this now. I need to go. I need some time to think. I can't talk... not now. I just need to go. Please, just let me go.'

'What do you mean you *need to go*? Go where? What the hell's going on, Jason? Talk to me!' Her chest heaved and tears needled the back of her eyes.

Whatever was in that letter had changed him. It was like someone had flicked a switch. Loving, sweet, playful Jason had gone. The menacing mask descended once again. Jason from the first days in Scotland was back. He stalked towards her with an angry determination and leaned in until his face was only inches from hers.

His jaw was clenched. 'I. Need. To. Go.' Each word was uttered in a staccato rhythm.

She stepped back. 'B-but, you'll be back? I mean...when you say you need to go...you just mean for a drive...or for...for some air...don't you? And there's your dad's funeral...and Dillon.'

His nostrils flared and he stared angrily at her, running his hand through his hair. 'I already said I can't fucking *talk* about this now. Just leave it, Stevie, for fuck's sake. Why do you always have to push things?'

Tears welled in her eyes, and she bit back a sob. 'I'm not pushing things, Jason. You're scaring me. Just tell me the truth. Are you running again? After you said you wouldn't to Dillon...and to me for that matter...is that what's happening here? I know...I know we agreed that you and I were temporary, but I don't want you to just leave me now without explanation. Not again. I don't think that would be very fair of you.'

He snorted. 'Think whatever you like. At this moment in time, I don't really care. The world doesn't fucking revolve around you. All right? It's. Not. All. About. You!' he shouted pointing at her.

Her eyes overflowed with angry and confused tears. She watched helplessly as he pulled his helmet on, swung his leg over the bike, started the engine, and sped off up the street and out of sight without looking back once.

'Jason!'

TO BE CONTINUED...

ACKNOWLEDGMENTS

I'm going to keep this brief as I know you don't want to read reams and reams of waffle from me!

I just want to say a simple thank you to every single reader, blogger and reviewer I have come across in my writing journey. As always your support means the world to me.

And a special thank you to Tammy from The Graphics Shed who designed the stunning covers and who continually comes to my rescue. You're an absolute star.

ABOUT THE AUTHOR

Lisa is happily married to her soulmate and they have a daughter and two crazy dogs. She especially enjoys being creative and now writes almost full time.

In 2012 Lisa and her family relocated from England to their beloved Scotland; a place of happy holidays and memories for them. Her new location now features in all of her books. Writing has always been something Lisa has enjoyed, although in the past it has centered on poetry and song lyrics. Some of which appear in her stories.

Since she started writing in 2012 she has loved every minute of becoming a published author.